FIRST READING . . .

Aradia dreamed she was Reading her baby at last. Her mind took her inside her own body, and she saw the shape of her child. The child was a girl—not an infant, but an infant-sized, perfectly formed young woman, long golden hair drifting about her slender body. Her back was to Aradia, who approached slowly, wondering at the revelation.

As she came nearer, the girl's body turned over, very slowly, to face her. As she watched, Aradia saw the girl's lips begin to move. //Yes!// Aradia urged. //Speak to me. I'm your mother. Tell me that you're there, child!//

The child spoke. Very clearly, in a voice not of youth and innocence but of incredibly weary experience. "Aradia. Mother. You and Leonardo have given me life. You owe me that—and after I am born, I will give you what I owe you . . ."

Empress Unborn

A Tale of the Savage Empire

Jean Lorrah

A SIGNET BOOK

NEW AMERICAN LIBRARY

NAL BOOKS ARE AVAILABLE AT QUANTITY DISCOUNTS WHEN USED TO PROMOTE PRODUCTS OR SERVICES. FOR INFORMATION PLEASE WRITE TO PREMIUM MARKETING DIVISION, NEW AMERICAN LIBRARY, 1633 *BROADWAY, NEW YORK, NEW YORK* 10019.

SIGNET TRADEMARK REG. U.S. PAT. OFF. AND FOREIGN COUNTRIES
REGISTERED TRADEMARK—MARCA REGISTRADA
HECHO EN CHICAGO, U.S.A.

SIGNET, SIGNET CLASSIC, MENTOR, ONYX, PLUME, MERIDIAN and NAL BOOKS are published by NAL PENGUIN INC., 1633 Broadway, New York, New York 10019

First Printing, June, 1988

1 2 3 4 5 6 7 8 9

PRINTED IN THE UNITED STATES OF AMERICA

Foreword

The entire *Savage Empire* series is dedicated to the person who got me into professional sf writing and then encouraged me to start my own series:

Jacqueline Lichtenberg

Special thanks go to Winston A. Howlett, who read right behind me as I worked on this book, and helped me keep my facts straight. Winston might be called the official historian of the Savage Empire. Besides coauthoring two books with me, he is editor of *Wolf-Stone*, a fanzine dedicated to the series. Send a SASE to the address below if you are interested.

Thanks to Camille Bacon-Smith, Patricia Frazer Lamb, Candace Pulleine, and Mary S. Van Deusen, who provided just the inspiration I needed, when I needed it, to pull out of a writing slump.

I would also like to thank the many readers who have sent comments about previous books in this series; I hope you enjoy this one as well.

If this is your first experience of the *Savage Empire* series, welcome! Each book is designed to be read independently, so don't worry that there are currently six others. If you like this one, you can read the rest later. Please don't try to collect all seven before you start reading. Any series that goes on for this long always has some volumes out of print. As the ones out of print now are reprinted, different ones will go out—so there will always be readers starting a series somewhere in the middle.

We authors of series work very hard to make each and every book accessible to the new reader. Trust me!

If there are readers who would like to comment on this book, my publishers will forward letters to me. If you prefer, you may write to me at Box 625, Murray, KY 42071. If your letter requires an answer, please enclose a stamped, self-addressed envelope.

All comments are welcome. I came to professional writing through fan writing and publishing, where there is close and constant communication between writers and readers. Thus I shall always be grateful for the existence of sf fandom, which has provided me with many exciting experiences, and through which I have met so many wonderful people.

Jean Lorrah
Murray, Kentucky

Chapter One

Aradia, Lady Adept of the Savage Empire, paced the halls of Castle Blackwolf as she waited impatiently for her husband, Lenardo, to bring home her brother, Wulfston.

I'm already thoroughly tired of being pregnant, she thought, *and I still have six months to go!*

She wondered if Lenardo was humoring her, or if he, too, was concerned about Wulfston. Her brother had invited them to come for a celebration, but once they arrived he did not seem happy with their company.

In fact, today he had walked out in the middle of a family gathering.

And Lenardo had followed him, taking Julia—but not Aradia.

I shouldn't ride horseback at this stage of my pregnancy, she reminded herself. Nonetheless, it felt as if her husband had chosen his adopted daughter over his wife.

I will not have such irrational thoughts! Aradia told herself. *Lenardo loves me. He will help me through this pregnancy, and afterward I will regain all my powers.*

But it galled her to rely on others, when all her life she had depended on her own strong Adept powers.

Only six more months, she reminded herself, laying a hand on her abdomen. Alone, she could hardly tell there was a second life growing within her. With Lenardo, she had Read the tiny living creature that would become a little girl . . . but it did not seem real to her.

Sometimes Aradia worried that she had no feelings of maternity. Physically, she noticed nothing so far except a slight thickening of her body; she could still move freely, and of course her powers kept her from the sickness many women suffered in their early months.

But those powers were weakening. She was so strong an Adept that only she would notice, but there was a change from day to day in the effort it took to perform any but the most ordinary Adept functions.

And for what? To give Lenardo a child . . . when he was so obviously contented with the one he had adopted? Perhaps if the child were a son, rather than another daughter. But not even an Adept could govern that.

Where was Lenardo? Why hadn't he brought Wulfston back? Aradia strode to the tower stairs, and climbed up to where a Watcher stood waiting for signals. There were none. The day was calm, the land serene.

"Lord Wulfston is riding toward the sea, my lady," the Watcher told her.

Just then flashes of light flickered from a hilltop beyond which lay the ocean. "There is a ship putting people ashore," the Watcher translated, although Aradia knew the code. "My lord is riding to investigate."

But how could Wulfston have known? No message had been brought to him. Why had the ship not sailed into the harbor at Dragon's Mouth? Was it a prearranged meeting?

The Watchers' signals began again—fast and furious!

Aradia read them as they came in, her heart sinking. Her brother was under Adept attack!

Julia rode happily at her father's side. Lenardo was shielding his thoughts by bracing for the use of Adept power, but Julia could still Read his excitement.

She was certain he'd had one of his precognitive flashes, but he had learned to shield so that he did not catch up every Reader in the vicinity in his visions. Julia hoped this one meant action. She had eagerly looked forward to their visit to Castle Blackwolf, but it had turned out as boring as her days in Zendi.

At thirteen, Julia had already had more adventure than most people have in a lifetime. When Lenardo took her from the people who would have killed her for her Reading powers, she had become part of the small group of Readers and Adepts who defeated Drakonius, brought down the Aventine Empire, and created their own Savage Empire.

But then her father had married Aradia, and while they cleaned out the hill bandits and forestalled insurrections to establish a firm rule, Julia had spent most of her time studying, usually with old Master Clement, the Master of Masters among Readers.

Master Clement had been Lenardo's teacher, and she was fortunate indeed to have the tutelage of the Master of Masters. Nevertheless, Julia often ached for the action of her younger days. Today's ride after a petulant Lord Wulfston was the closest thing to an adventure she had had in months!

As Julia and Lenardo topped the crest of the hill over which Wulfston had disappeared, they saw a ship anchored not far off shore. It had put down boats, in which people were rowing toward land.

Wulfston was already down on the beach, riding to greet these strangers. He became blank to Julia's Reading as he braced Adept powers—

Thunderbolts exploded around the lone rider!

Wulfston leaped from his saddle and hit the ground rolling, bouncing to his feet in an Adept's fighting stance.

The Lord Adept used his power to deflect the thunderbolts. People began clambering out of the boats. He sent three of them sprawling on the sand in Adept sleep.

From their vantage point, urging their horses down the hill, Lenardo and Julia saw Wulfston's attackers fan out, dividing his attention. He needed a Reader at his side!

Julia kicked her horse.

//No!// her father warned her. //We can't help Wulfston if we fall down the cliff.// And he continued to guide his horse along the precarious path.

Julia did the same, but her attention was seized by the impact of a bolt of lightning on the beach.

She looked and Read: Wulfston was momentarily blinded, and his horse, Storm, screamed and fell, taking long seconds to die in an agony of burnt flesh.

Julia fought nausea, deliberately turning her attention to guiding her own mount down the steep trail.

When she dared to Read the beach again, she saw that Wulfston had identified the most powerful Adept among his attackers: a tall man standing in one of the boats. Under the full fury of a Lord Adept nearing the peak of his powers, the man gasped once, and fell unconscious into the surf.

With a glance, Wulfston dropped another man rushing at him from the right.

But not even a Lord Adept could keep up such steady use of his powers! If someone still on the ship were an Adept—

Apparently no one was. Wulfston walked into the waves to grasp the last boat and beach it. There were only two people now in it: a woman and a little boy, huddled together in fear.

At the bottom of the hill, Julia and Lenardo spurred their horses.

Wulfston whirled at their approach, braced again.

Julia expected the Lord Adept to make some joke about their belated rescue attempt. Instead he stared as if he hardly knew them, until Lenardo demanded, "Are you all right?"

Then the old Wulfston was back, releasing his Adept mental stance on a wave of inner amusement. "Yes, I'm all right," he said. "But—" He sobered as he glanced toward the smoldering corpse of his favorite horse.

Julia Read weariness overtaking him now that the danger was past. After such rapid and extensive use of his powers, a Lord Adept needed to rest. Wulfston, though, started toward the man he had knocked out of the boat, who floated facedown in the water.

Lenardo swung down off his horse and helped Wulfston

drag the man ashore. "Why did you come out to face these people alone?"

"I didn't," Wulfston replied shortly.

"Well, you must have had some reason to leave a celebration at your own castle and go riding this far south! I should have been Reading."

Julia could Read her father's guilt. He could easily have Read the ship from Castle Blackwolf if he had not been relaxed, his attention on family and friends.

But Wulfston could not Read, and was pursuing his own train of thought. "I was . . . restless. Something drew me to this place, to these people."

As she studied the people who had come ashore, Julia was not surprised that Wulfston had gone out to meet them. "But why did they attack you?" she asked.

"I don't know, Julia," Wulfston replied. "I don't even know who they are."

"You don't?" she asked, Reading only bafflement from him. "But Wulfston, they're all black—just like you!"

The Watchers reported Wulfston's defeat of his attackers, so Aradia had calmed herself by the time her family returned to the castle. It had cost all her patience to obey Lenardo's instructions to stay, after he finally bethought himself to contact her.

After all the excitement was over.

Aradia's Reading abilities were minimal, but Lenardo was the most powerful Reader yet known. He and Wulfston were rowing out to the ship before his mind touched hers, letting her look through his eyes, Read through his powers that her brother was unharmed.

Assigning Julia to escort their captives to the castle, the two lords boarded the ship and instructed the Nubian captain and crew to move the ship into Dragon's Mouth.

Their interrogation of the ship's crew provided little information. The ship had been hired by one Sukuru, the Adept who had attacked Wulfston. He and the others who had gone ashore were the only passengers, and the captain had asked no questions about their strange destination. They paid him, and he took them where they wanted to go. All the way from Africa.

The mystery plagued Aradia long after Lenardo broke contact, and she went down to see the captives being brought to the castle. Sukuru was carried in unconscious. The other men were obviously awed, and the woman with the little boy would say nothing. She was veiled, so that only her eyes showed, but mahogany skin was revealed around her eyes and on her hands. Every one of these people was as black as Wulfston.

More irrational thoughts flickered through Aradia's mind: in retaliation for her jealousy of Lenardo's adopted daughter, some god she didn't believe in had sent these people to take away her beloved adopted brother.

But Wulfston had not come from Africa.

His parents did, she reminded herself.

What if he were the long-lost heir to an African throne?

Then why did they attack him?

Besides, he had his own throne right here, his own lands, his own people.

And he is feeling restless, unhappy. . . .

The moon was riding high by the time Lenardo and Wulfston returned. Lenardo wanted Aradia to go right to bed, but she insisted on talking to Wulfston first.

She knew where to find him: an Adept had to replenish his strength, and his cook had prepared him a meal worthy of three ordinary men. He should have eaten hours ago, and long since been asleep, so it was little wonder Aradia found him uncooperative.

"But why did you go out there in the first place?" she wanted to know. She was really asking why he seemed so alien, and his response only heightened the impression.

"Aradia, why do you ask me when you know I don't have the answer? Don't give me that innocent look. I know that you were in contact with Lenardo the whole time."

You're wrong there, little brother, she thought, but Wulfston continued, "For the last time, I don't know why I left a celebration I'm supposed to be hosting and went riding along the cliffs. Now, will you please leave me alone?"

His harsh words wounded. Reader or no, Wulfston must have realized it, for he reached across the table to put his hand over hers. "I'm sorry. I—I guess I'm more upset than I want to admit . . . especially about losing Storm like that."

She nodded in sympathy. Wulfston had planned to use the beautiful stallion to improve his stock, but it was more than that. He had always had a strong affinity for animals.

"Do you think it's possible," she asked tentatively, "that you might have . . . *Read* that the ship was there?" To learn Read was his fondest dream—and Aradia, too, yearned to meet her brother mind to mind. There were times, such as now, when words were inadequate.

But Wulfston shook his head. "If I could sense a strange ship several miles away—which neither Lenardo nor Julia did until they started following me—then I should be able to pick up someone's thoughts nearby. But nothing has changed for me. I don't know what drew me into that confrontation, but it wasn't Reading. I'm still your mind-blind little brother," he said with a rueful chuckle.

Yet *something* had drawn him away from his family—something that frightened Aradia.

When she went upstairs to the room she shared with Lenardo, her husband was already in bed, although still awake. His mind met hers, Reading her conversation with Wulfston and the vague, unsettling fears this day had brought.

Without speaking, Lenardo got up and pulled on a soft woolen robe against the castle's chill. Aradia's maid was in the antechamber, waiting to help her mistress undress, but Lenardo went to the door and told her, "Go on to bed, Devasin. I will help the Lady Aradia tonight."

Devasin handed Lenardo Aradia's chamber garments, and Lenardo closed the door. Then he turned to his wife. "You are upset."

"My brother was attacked today."

"His attackers were fools. Aradia, their combined powers are nothing to Wulfston's. He didn't need my help, or Julia's. By the time we got there, the battle was over."

"I know. Yet . . . Lenardo, I have such a strange feeling about these people. Why have they come here, all the way from Africa?"

"We'll find out tomorrow," he reassured her, and reached to take off her outer robe of silver-bordered velvet. Then he unhooked the satin overgarment, and helped her out of the layers of silk undergarments and into her chamber robe.

She didn't really need the help, of course, but her husband's hands made every move a caress, soothing away her unexplained anxiety.

When she sat down and began to unbraid her hair, Lenardo's strong hands took over that function, too, untangling the pale blond strands, then brushing them smooth.

Such ministrations were not routine. Lenardo did not even have a valet, having grown up in an Academy of Readers. Once he had professed surprise that a Lady Adept should require a maid to dress her, but he accepted Devasin as custom, and usually left Aradia to her care.

Tonight, though, when Aradia needed the comfort of her husband's touch, he gave it, putting her to bed as tenderly as he might a child. Then he lay down beside her, taking her in his arms.

Lenardo was a tall man, with a body well formed by years of work and exercise. Aradia rested against him, feeling the lean hardness of his muscles irrationally reassuring. Even diminished by pregnancy, her powers far outweighed the physical strength of any man, even one as huge as Zanos the Gladiator. Nonetheless, she felt secure in her husband's arms.

Perhaps it was that Lenardo, with only Reading and no Adept powers, had proved his strength to her when they first met, defending her with his sword when she had exhausted her powers in their first battle with Drakonius. Later, Lenardo had learned to develop the Adept portion of his powers, but since exercising the abilities to affect the physical world with the mind impeded Reading, he had never become a Lord Adept. Master Reader satisfied him, and he satisfied her, in every possible way.

"Lenardo?" she murmured.

"Hush," he said. "Go to sleep. We'll talk in the morning."

"No—tell me. What did you see today?"

"What do you mean?"

"I thought you were just humoring me when you went after Wulfston—but now I wonder. You had one of your visions, didn't you?"

For a moment he didn't answer. Then, "Yes," he said reluctantly.

"What was it? Did you see him being attacked?"

Again the pause, and even though Lenardo was far too skilled to let someone of Aradia's meager ability Read what he didn't want her to, she knew with a wife's certain knowledge that he was considering lying to her. But he didn't. "I saw Wulfston on board ship, that Nubian woman and her child beside him, sailing away to the south."

Her skin prickling with cold sweat, Aradia whispered, "I was right! They *are* here to take him away!"

His arms tightened about her. "We don't know that. Aradia, you know how my flashes of precognition are. Yes, they always come true—but never in the way I expect. Wulfston may just sail a few miles south on that ship. Or he may decide to go and do some trading in our visitors' lands."

"After they attacked him the moment they saw him?"

"He was not a prisoner in my vision," Lenardo offered. "He was standing freely on deck, urging the captain to hurry southward. Aradia, he wasn't hurt, and he was clearly in charge. Wulfston is a grown man—you can't think of him as your little brother forever."

"Little, no. But Lenardo, he *is* my *brother* forever.

Remember what Torio said? 'Wulfston must seek his destiny far away, only to find where he began.' "

"Torio!" Lenardo snorted. "Don't start me thinking about Torio, Aradia. I should never have let him go off to Madura, just when he had developed a new talent. And of all the irresponsible acts after he learned Adept powers there, to go wandering off who knows where instead of coming home here, where you and Master Clement and I could train him!"

Aradia let him fume, knowing that having a second student he had trained go off to use his powers in unknown and possibly dangerous ways frightened Lenardo. He felt responsible for those he taught.

It was his search for Galen, the student who had gone over to his enemies, that had originally brought Lenardo into Aradia's path some five years ago.

There was nothing she could say, except that she knew Torio to be strong-willed and unlikely to be used as Drakonius had used Galen. But the boy was young, inexperienced. He had learned strange things in Madura, according to the reports he had sent with Zanos and Astra. Lenardo's fears that he might be tricked into using his developing powers for evil were certainly justified, and Aradia agreed wholeheartedly that Torio should have returned to his friends. But he hadn't. And there was nothing Lenardo could do about it except worry.

At last he came back to the original subject. "Anyway, prophecies are just like my visions: incomplete and misleading."

"Not always," said Aradia, running her hand over Lenardo's right forearm. She could feel the brand embedded into his flesh, a dragon's head that showed red against his skin, even years after the wound had healed. "In the days of the white wolf and the red dragon," she murmured.

He held her close. "Yes—we finally did bring peace to all our lands," he agreed, looking up at the room's ceiling. Wulfston had decorated this suite of rooms especially for Lenardo and Aradia. Even in the dim light their emblems, Aradia's white wolf's head and Lenardo's red dragon, could be made out, entwined in the painted relief.

"And if Wulfston has to find where he began," Aradia added, snuggling sleepily into a more comfortable position against Lenardo, "he was born in a village between Tiberium and Zendi. So even if he does go far away, he'll have to . . . come home again."

The next day, their uninvited African guests were brought before Wulfston, who sat on his throne, flanked by a formidable array of Readers and Adepts: Lenardo, Aradia, Julia, and Wulfston's Reader, Rolf.

Sukuru, revived and healthy, was shaking in his sandals as he apologized profusely, stumbling over his words in the language called Trader's Common.

The tall, gaunt black man seemed to have only minor Adept powers. He insisted they would never have attacked Wulfston had they known him to be the Lord Adept they sought, but when they saw another black man, wrapped in a plain woolen cloak, they had thought him one of their enemies, trying to thwart their expedition.

They had expected to find "the most excellent Lord of the Black Wolf," Sukuru explained in annoyingly obsequious terms, to be "as you are now, most gracious lord, crowned in gold and seated upon a throne."

Aradia listened, Reading fear, but a certain level of sincerity in the man. She didn't like him: he was here to ask a stranger to do what he feared to do himself.

Sukuru and his small band claimed to represent "many tribes and peoples who share a dream of freedom." He told of a powerful witch-queen, Z'Nelia, who held in thrall a large number of African lands. "Besides her own formidable powers, she has many followers with powers of their own, as well as a huge and powerful army."

Z'Nelia sounded like Drakonius—and Drakonius had been defeated.

"But why come so far to seek *my* help?" Wulfston asked.

Sure enough, the story of the defeat of Drakonius had traveled as far as Africa. But, it seemed, the version popular there was a distorted one in which Wulfston had defeated Drakonius in single combat.

Julia snickered, and Aradia could feel Wulfston smother laughter. "That's a song," he explained, "created by a bard seeking favor in my court. East of here, in the city of Zendi, you would hear a much different version, celebrating the exploits of my sister and her husband."

The puzzlement of the envoys was clear to Read when Wulfston identified Aradia as his sister. But they did not ask; they were too eager to press their case. Despite Wulfston's insistence that only an alliance of Adepts and Readers could defeat such a strong opponent, they wanted one single champion—someone the equal of their fabled Z'Nelia.

When Sukuru's words won no promises from Wulfston, he called forward the veiled woman, Chulaika. She spoke of oppression, slavery, and murder, begging, "Please, Lord Wulfston—come to our aid. Only a great Lord like yourself can help us now."

"You are a Son of Africa," Sukuru said suddenly. "Surely you will not refuse to help your own people?"

Aradia smothered a gasp of indignation, but Wulfston replied exactly as she would have hoped: "My own people are right here. I was not born in your land, but in the Aventine Empire, where my parents were proud to have earned citizenship. I will consult with my allies to determine what help we can offer you—but you must understand that I cannot leave my lands unattended to go adventuring in yours."

That afternoon, Aradia was examined by Astra, who was acting as healer for her on this expedition. Astra and her husband, Zanos, were direct allies of Lady Lilith, and represented her at this meeting; they were another couple brought together by the turmoil surrounding the fall of Tiberium. Astra would soon be taking her tests for the rank of Master Reader—even though she was a married woman—while Zanos was a former gladiator in the Aventine arena.

If Lenardo and Aradia were an unlikely team, the quiet, slender Reader and the huge, flame-haired gladiator seemed an incomprehensible match. Yet they were obviously quite happy together. Zanos had minor abilities as both Reader and Adept, while Astra, like Lenardo, had developed some Adept powers, but would rarely sacrifice her Reading skills to practice them.

"The baby is doing very well," Astra told Aradia, "but you are tired. You should take a nap this afternoon."

"I'm not tired."

"My lady, do not deny your condition to a Reader. Your husband will say the same."

"But it's such a lovely day," Aradia protested.

"There is no need to stay indoors," said Astra. "Come with me into the herb garden. The walls will protect you from the breeze."

So Aradia was installed on a chaise in the herb garden near the castle's kitchen. Astra remained with her for a while, gathering herbs which did not grow in Lilith's lands, and then left her alone, not protesting that Aradia was reading rather than sleeping.

Later that afternoon, Lenardo's mind touched Aradia's. //Come join me?// she suggested.

//Gladly. Wulfston is with me.//

Wulfston and Lenardo, it seemed, had been discussing their uninvited guests. "It doesn't make sense," explained Wulfston. "Why would they come to strangers for help? There's something Sukuru's not telling."

"And that I can't Read," added Lenardo. "We're going to try to draw them out at dinner tonight."

Aradia smiled wryly. "And then you and Astra will provoke the rest of us by Reading something important, but being bound by your Reader's Oaths not to reveal it!"

"You are bound by the same Oath, Aradia," her husband reminded her.

"Yes, but how likely am *I* to Read any secrets? I still

can't even Read our baby. I tried again today, but Astra had to Read with me."

"At least you *can* Read," Wulfston reminded her. "I won't get to meet my niece until after she's born!"

When Wulfston had gone, Lenardo said, "Our daughter is developing well. Read with me."

Through her husband's powers, Aradia Read the shape in her womb, the tiny being already equipped with arms and legs, eyes and mouth. But there was no consciousness yet. "Soon," Lenardo promised. "Soon she will become aware, and then I'm sure you'll be able to Read her, Aradia."

She wanted to. She wanted to love the baby, Lenardo's child, product of their love. But how could she love someone she didn't know? Automatically, she braced as if to use her powers so Lenardo would not Read her thought: *I don't feel like a mother—I just feel as if I have some nagging minor illness draining my powers.*

At dinner that night, Julia watched and Read with interest as Lenardo, Aradia, and Wulfston told their African guests how they had first met and joined their powers to defeat Drakonius. Part of her preparation to govern lands of her own one day was to learn Trader's Common, and she found that she had little trouble following the conversation.

Lenardo ended the story by emphasizing the strength of their relationships: "So Julia is my adopted daughter, though I don't think either of us often remembers that she's adopted. Aradia is my wife, and that makes her brother Wulfston my brother, too."

Sukuru asked, "How comes it, Lord Wulfston, that these pale folk claim you kin?"

"Ties of love may be as strong as ties of blood," Wulfston replied. Julia glanced at Lenardo, trying to take comfort in the thought. She often wondered if the baby Aradia carried would take her place in his affections.

Her eyes focused on the ring her father wore, matching the one on Aradia's hand. Wolf and dragon intertwined in gleaming gold. Their wedding rings, a gift from Wulfston. Julia knew he had meant them as a symbol of unity. To Julia, though, they seemed to mean that Lenardo was joined to Aradia, shutting his adopted daughter out. She knew that was an unfair thought, and tried to put it out of her mind.

Wulfston was telling how Aradia's father, Nerius, had spirited him out of the Aventine Empire when his Adept powers manifested at the age of three, and the folk of his village would have killed him. In those days, only Readers were accepted in the Empire, and any child who showed Adept talent was killed.

Aradia finished up, declaring that the child she carried "will not be only our daughter; she will be Julia's sister, and Wulfston's niece. That is the kind of family alliance you must have to fight a tyrant." Julia Read only sincerity from her stepmother. Why did she distrust her?

Sukuru expressed amazement, but seemed disappointed at Wulfston's advice to raise an alliance of people with powers in his own lands to fight the tyrant. Although he said, "We will heed your advice, most excellent lord," Julia Read that he did not really mean the words.

With her mind, she reached out to Lenardo, but he replied with an unverbalized warning to keep mentally silent. Were there Readers among the Africans that she had not recognized?

Her father was on his guard—if these people were hiding something, Lenardo would find it out.

Sukuru, meanwhile, was presenting Wulfston with a bottle of wine from his native land, insisting that they all drink a toast "to our success in gaining from you the means to save our land."

Now what did he mean by that? Julia wished she could get her hands on something of Sukuru's. She had one of the unusual Reading talents, the ability to Read the history of an object by touching it, including the stories of the people who had handled it. Perhaps before they left, she could touch something of this man's and find out his secrets.

Meanwhile, the wine was poured from a vessel like none Julia had ever seen before. It was pointed on the bottom, so it couldn't stand on a table, and painted in brilliant, jewel-like colors.

Julia reached for her goblet as soon as the wine was poured into it, but her father was right there with the water pitcher. When would he believe she was grown up enough to drink her wine like an adult, not watered down like a baby?

Sukuru raised his goblet. "To the defeat of Z'Nelia—and anything we must do to free our land from her evil!"

As she raised the goblet to her lips, smelling exotic spices in the wine, Julia suddenly Read Sukuru's only half-hidden thought: //Z'Nelia will be pleased with the way I have fooled them—they're completely unprepared for her attack!// And with it came a picture of an armada of heavily armed ships full of black warriors, waiting out of Reading range.

Aradia, having Read it through Lenardo, leaned over and whispered to Wulfston, but Lenardo just took a drink of the wine, giving no reaction to indicate that he had Read the man's secret thought.

Julia followed her father's example. Wulfston called for sweets and fruits and a drier wine, for even Julia found the one their guests had served them unbearably sweet and overloaded with spices. She took a long drink of plain water to wash the taste out of her mouth.

Why didn't Lenardo challenge Sukuru with what he had Read? Or ask Wulfston to end the dinner, so they could meet and make plans? Julia Read agitation from Aradia, who would want to alert all their allies, and prepare for invasion.

As the musicians played once more, Lenardo watched Sukuru through slitted eyes. Julia cautiously Read with him, careful not to let thoughts or feelings project, just as her father had taught her. Astra, sitting farther down the table, Read with them, while Aradia braced her Adept powers, for she could not possibly Read without being Read herself.

Sukuru could not be a very good Reader to make that slip—if he was a Reader at all. Lenardo was the only Reader known who could Read any Reader at all without being detected. Astra could do it with many Readers, but Julia was just learning. She felt warmly proud that her father trusted her now, and she fulfilled that trust, Reading only through him, making no attempt to reach Sukuru's mind on her own.

Lenardo found only Sukuru's feelings, however; he was now lightly braced for the use of Adept powers, his thoughts unReadable. When Lords Adept like Wulfston and Aradia braced for full use of powers, even their feelings became unReadable. But Sukuru was no Lord Adept. Although he kept them from Reading his thoughts, a definite smugness came through, and something more. . . .

When she recognized it, Julia dropped out of the rapport before she allowed herself to react. Closing her mind in upon itself as Master Clement had patiently taught her, she realized, *He was lying! There was no invasion fleet!*

Lenardo's hand touched her arm. When she looked up at him, he smiled at her and nodded, and she glowed with the knowledge that she had done well in her father's eyes—and under circumstances in which a childish slip might have proved fatal. Sukuru did not know they had discovered his deception.

"What do you think he thinks we'll do?" Julia asked once they were in their suite of apartments after Wulfston had dismissed the musicians.

"Gather our allies, perhaps," replied Lenardo. "Then I suppose he'll try to get us all to join in his fight."

"That's a . . ." Aradia paused to yawn. ". . . terribly foolish plan."

"What's keeping Wulfston?" Lenardo wondered.

"I told him to come here," Aradia replied, and yawned again. It was contagious; both Lenardo and Julia yawned.

"It's been a long day," said Lenardo. "I'll have Devasin

help you get ready for bed. You too, Julia. I'll go get Wulfston."

Julia didn't know why she was so sleepy, when she should be excited. In the next room, she could hear Devasin telling Aradia to lie down—something about being asleep on her feet. Julia put on her nightgown, and a robe over it, wondering why her father hadn't come back yet with Wulfston.

As she sat down on the edge of her bed to put on her slippers, a wave of dizziness swept over her. She tried to Read for Lenardo, but couldn't find him . . . and then couldn't remember why she wanted him as she sank onto the bed, sound asleep.

Aradia woke to a touch on her forehead. Her brother was bending over her.

"Wulfston, what—? Why have I slept so late?" she asked as she realized that strong morning sunshine was slanting between the curtains. She sat up, looking around, and remembered last night. Her husband had gone for Wulfston. "Where's Lenardo?" she demanded.

"Aradia, we were drugged," Wuflston explained. "The wine Sukuru served us—"

"Drugged?" A bolt of pure fear shot through her body, and she clasped her arms across her abdomen. "The baby! Oh, Wulfston—get Lenardo to Read whether the baby's been harmed!"

"I don't know where he's gone," Wulfston replied.

"Aradia? Wulfston?" It was Julia's voice at the door to the adjoining chamber.

"Julia—come in!" Aradia cried. "Can you Read where Lenardo is?"

"Not in the castle," the girl replied at once. "What's the matter?"

"Please," Aradia told her, "Read the baby—see if she's been poisoned."

"Poisoned!" Julia's eyes grew round with horror, but she laid a hand on Aradia's abdomen and concentrated. Aradia Read with her, finding the baby still there, its tiny heart beating as usual. "No," Julia said. "At least I can't Read anything but a healthy baby, Aradia. I'm sure Father will confirm that."

"You don't have a headache, Aradia," Wulfston said, thus telling her that he must have been so affected. "Your body instinctively protected your child—you probably went directly into healing sleep and purged the poison from your blood at once. The drug knocked me out so completely that I couldn't cleanse it away until I woke this morning."

She remembered how sleepy she had been—Devasin had had to support her. Yes, it had been the same weariness she knew when her body needed to heal an injury.

But when she asked again for Lenardo, Wulfston shook his head. "Our uninvited guests have gone. Perhaps he followed them."

Aradia saw that Julia didn't believe that any more than she did. She remembered the moment Sukuru had let slip the knowledge that a fleet was on the way to attack them: Lenardo had covered his surprise by taking a long swallow of the drugged wine.

As Aradia drew breath to say it, though, Julia suddenly spoke, her eyes focused on something not in the room with them. "I can Read as far as the harbor, and I can't find Father anywhere." Then she gasped. "The ship! Wulfston—the ship is gone!"

"Julia," Aradia demanded, "is there really a fleet of ships out there?"

"No," the girl replied, and Aradia heard the respect in her voice. "Father Read that it was a lie."

"Designed to fool Readers!" said Aradia. "And it did. In the excitement of thinking Sukuru was the point of an invasion, nobody Read the poison in the wine!"

Wulfston went to awaken Zanos and Astra, for a Magister Reader could go out of body to Read over great distances. Astra verified that there was no invasion fleet, but she found Sukuru's vessel, and with it Lenardo—still asleep, and locked in the hold.

Wulfston called for a ship.

Aradia heard the news from Astra, who came to verify her baby's health. Zanos and Astra were going with Wulfston, the Magister Reader explained. With their abilities and Wulfston's, they would quickly catch the fleeing vessel.

Aradia agreed. As soon as Astra had gone, she began preparing herself to join in the rescue of her husband. Dressed in serviceable garments for travel, she joined Wulfston in his room just as he was turning his private coffer out on the bed.

It was just a precaution—taking enough money for a long journey—but nonetheless it made Aradia uneasy. "Hurry, Wulfston," she said. "We don't want to miss the tide."

"Aradia—" he began.

"I'm going with you," she told him firmly.

"No, you're not."

"Wulfston, it's my husband they've taken!"

"And that's his child you're carrying," he reminded her. "You were fortunate that the drug did not harm the baby—for Sukuru still let you drink the wine after he knew you were pregnant. You don't know what these people are capable of if they have no care for the health of an unborn babe. Will you be as careless as they are? Will you take your child into the midst of Adept conflict?"

"I can take care of my baby and myself," Aradia insisted.

As if the matter were settled, Wulfston turned away and began putting coins into a leather pouch.

He thought she wasn't capable of helping! To prove her strength, she let her powers reach out to her brother, grasping control of his body, paralyzing his muscles.

As if her powers were nothing, he straightened and turned on her, moving as freely as if she had done nothing! "You see?" He spoke her own horrified thoughts. "Aradia, you just don't have your old powers right now."

It was true! She had always been stronger than

Wulfston. Now he was coming into the full strength of his powers, while hers . . . .

She tried to fight down tears. *I never cry*, she told herself, but even that weakness would not be denied. Wulfston saw, and gently put his arms around her. "Please . . . we both know it's best that you stay here. I know it won't help for me to tell you not to worry, but I promise you this: we will bring Lenardo back to you, safe and sound. I swear it."

It was just as difficult to persuade Julia that she could not go along. "If I'd only developed Adept powers instead of Reading!" the girl fumed as she and Aradia stood on the quay, watching Wulfston's ship sail out through the entrance to Dragon's Mouth.

"Julia, we need a good Reader here, to follow their progress," Aradia told her.

Julia did not dignify that offering with a response. She knew she was no more able than Wulfston's Reader, Rolf, to tell where Sukuru's ship was out on the ocean—and since it would be even father away by the time Wulfston caught up with it, they would have only the Watchers' reports from Readers closer to the action to let them follow Lenardo's rescue.

The ship dropped below the horizon, but Julia could still Read it, and Aradia Read through the girl. For a long while they stood there, but finally Julia put out her hand to Aradia—something the girl had never done before. "Let's go back to the castle," she said. "There's nothing more we can do."

"We can prepare for a homecoming party," Aradia suggested, and Julia managed a small smile.

Together, Lenardo's wife and his daughter walked up to the end of the quay, where servants waited to take them back to Castle Blackwolf.

All that day, Watchers sent Readers' reports on the progress of the two ships, but by morning there was nothing more. The last thing anyone Read was that they had disappeared into a storm.

A storm, Aradia wondered, or an Adept battle? If the latter, then surely they would be home soon, for Wulfston's powers were far superior to Sukuru's.

But the next day passed with no word, and then a third day. Aradia did not sleep well the first two nights; she kept waiting for Lenardo's mind to touch hers, and would not deliberately put herself into deep slumber lest she miss his first contact. She *knew* he would go out of body, to tell her as soon as he was safely on his way home!

And when he didn't, she knew that something was terribly wrong. Wulfston had not been able to catch Sukuru's ship. She refused to face the worst possibility—that Lenardo and Wulfston were dead, whether in Adept battle or natural disaster.

No—they were her husband and her brother. If either were dead, surely she would *know* it!

So she faced the fact that it might be weeks or months before the two men she loved best could get themselves out of whatever predicament they were in and return to her. She nearly cursed the child in her womb that had turned her into a passive female who could do nothing but wait while her men were in danger.

But it was Lenardo's child. Possibly the baby was all she would ever have of him. She lay down and folded her hands over her abdomen, trying once again to Read the child in her womb.

Frustrated, she realized that it was essential to keep herself healthy, and that meant sleeping. Deliberately, she used the mental exercises her father had taught her when she was a child, to put herself into a deep, restful sleep.

Aradia dreamed she was Reading her baby at last. Her mind took her inside her own body, and she saw the shape of her child, sleeping sweetly in its private ocean. It moved gently, drifting with its mother's breathing.

She moved. The child was a girl—not an infant, but an infant-sized perfectly formed young woman, long golden hair drifting about her slender body. Her back was to Aradia, who approached slowly, wondering at the revelation. This was what her child—Lenardo's child—would be.

As she came nearer, the girl's body turned over, very slowly, to face her. The face was utterly beautiful, although the eyes were closed.

Still sleeping, still unconscious—when would there be an awareness for her to touch as Lenardo had promised?

Nonetheless, it was wonderful to see her child, so perfect, so beautiful, rosy-cheeked with health. She could count her fingers and toes, see that her limbs were straight and strong. Lenardo would be so proud of such a daughter!

As she watched, Aradia saw the girl's soft pink lips begin to move—it was as if she were trying to speak.

//Yes!// Aradia urged. //Speak to me. I'm your mother. Tell me that you're there, child!//

The lips moved again, but still Aradia could Read no thought, no mental presence. She went closer, looking into the beautiful face with its still-closed eyes fringed with dark lashes. If she watched the lips move, perhaps she could make out what her daughter was saying.

No . . . not quite. Not . . .

The child spoke. Very clearly, in a voice not of youth and innocence but of incredibly weary experience.

"Aradia. Mother. You and Lenardo have given me life. You owe me that—and after I am born, I will give you what I owe you."

Bewildered, Aradia stared at the serene face, speaking such strange words. Then the girl's eyes began to open—

She woke up.

It was morning again, and she knew there had been no news of Wulfston and Lenardo, for she had left strict instructions that she was to be awakened if there were.

So she lay there for a moment, remembering her strange dream. *I probably dreamed of our daughter grown up because if she were, she'd be able to help us now*, she thought.

Again she tried to Read the child for herself—

—and touched something!

There was an awareness!

It was incoherent, no more than a vague sensing of life—but what did she expect of a babe in the womb, not to be born for six months yet?

Oh, Lenardo, she thought, *your child is conscious! Come home safely, my husband, as soon as you can. Meanwhile, I will care for our daughter, until you can see her for yourself!*

Chapter Two

Julia and Aradia remained at Castle Blackwolf, waiting and hoping for Wulfston and Lenardo to return. As weeks passed with no word, their fears grew; the Africans' plot was far more devious than it had seemed at first.

Sukuru and Chulaika wanted Wulfston, but he would not cooperate. They had had both Wulfston and Lenardo helplessly drugged—they could as easily have kidnapped the two men together. Instead, they took only Lenardo, knowing that with Aradia pregnant, it was Wulfston who would follow. They must be holding Lenardo hostage to force Wulfston to fight for them.

If they had taken the two men together . . .

"We were fools to tell them how well we work together," Aradia told Julia. "They know better than to take Lenardo and Wulfston on the same ship—they'd have taken over the crew the moment they woke up, and been back here the next day."

"The moment Wulfston finds Father," Julia said, "they'll escape."

"But Wulfston can't Read," Aradia reminded her. "Lenardo can't contact him except through Astra. If they can knock her out, or separate her from Wulfston . . . that could be why it's taking so long."

As the days dragged on, the two women often repeated the same conversation, encouraging each other not to think of all the possible reasons there was no word of the two men.

Although there was no invasion fleet from Africa,

Wulfston's lands could not be left unprotected. His network of minor Adepts gathered at the castle, along with several Magister Readers and a dozen from the Path of the Dark Moon, while reinforcements were sent from Tiberium to aid the Watchers along his coasts and borders.

Then one day, when Julia was helping a healer to direct his powers toward eradicating a tumor in a boy's knee, she felt the touch of Master Clement's mind. //Go to your room, Julia. We must discuss what you and Aradia should do now.//

//But we're healing—// she protested.

//Panatus can take over,// he told her.

Reluctantly, Julia turned her duties over to the young Magister Reader and went up to her room. She could, of course, have held the conversation with Master Clement anywhere, but it could be unnerving to nonReaders to have a Reader sitting apparently in a trance while she communicated with another Reader far away.

Aradia was also in the rapport, created by Master Clement all the way from Zendi. The Master of Masters was out of body for this communication, his mental voice firm and clear, similar to his normal speaking voice except that mentally he sounded younger than he really was.

//All precautions have now been taken to care for Lord Wulfston's lands in his absence,// Master Clement told them. //It is time for you to return to Zendi.//

//But Lenardo—// Aradia began.

//When Lenardo returns, he will contact you from wherever he lands,// Master Clement pointed out. //Aradia, the journey to Zendi is safe for you now. Later in your pregnancy it could be dangerous to your child. Also, I want you here, under observation of the best Readers we have.//

//Yes, Master Clement,// Aradia replied with uncharacteristic meekness. But she had an underlying reason. //With so many members of our alliance missing, our strongest Adepts should be centrally located in Zendi, prepared to moved in any direction from which an attack might come.//

//Until your child is born,// Master Clement agreed, //you should be sheltered here, protected by lands we hold on all sides.//

Julia wondered if Aradia could Read that Master Clement did not verbalize all his concerns. She had a lesson scheduled with him, so after Aradia had left the rapport to set their retainers to work preparing to leave Castle Blackwolf, she asked, //Do you fear an attack, Master?//

//An attack? Child, what would give you that idea?//

//Our situation might give *anybody* that idea,// she replied. //Since the Aventine Empire fell, we have more land than has ever been under one government before. But we have lost key members of our Alliance. Torio and Melissa are gone, and now Father and Wulfston. Lilith meant to leave her lands in the care of Zanos and Astra while she came to aid Aradia in her confinement. Her lands are bordered by enemies. If Zanos and Astra are not back by then, will she dare leave her lands with only her son to care for them? Ivorn's not much older than I am.//

She clearly felt the old man's surprise as he told her, //Julia, these are not problems for one so young.//

//But they *are* my problems,// she insisted. //Master Clement, the word will spread beyond our borders that Father and Wulfston are gone. Our best Reader, and one our strongest Lords Adept—and if the news of Aradia's pregnancy spreads as well, they'll know she can't function at full strength. Don't you think some of our neighbors might take this as the best time to attack?//

There was a pause. Then, //Yes, Julia, I do. However, they will mistake our vulnerability.//

//What?//

//Where do you think they will attack, child?//

//Along the northern borders—especially here, along Wulfston's northern coast, and Lilith's borders to the north and east.//

//Why do you think the attacks will come there?//

//Along those borders are lands which have refused

our offers of peaceful trade agreements,// she replied. //With Wulfston gone, they'll try for a foothold here. Lilith is a strong Adept, and her son is growing in power—they may attack now, knowing that once Ivorn comes into his full powers, they will face a much stronger adversary.//

//Yes, you are quite right. Now, Julia . . . if you wanted to attack our Savage Empire, knowing what you know, would you choose the same plan of attack?//

The way the question was worded, the answer was probably no. But then he would ask—

//Think of your father, when Aradia first gave him the city of Zendi,// Master Clement prompted.

Suddenly Julia knew. //Wulfston's lands and Lilith's, and Father and Aradia's lands—their people will defend them to the death! They've known tyrants like Drakonius—and it's worth fighting to remain part of the Savage Empire. We're most vulnerable in the old Aventine Empire, where most people had a pretty good life under the Emperor's rule. In only four years they haven't had time to develop any loyalty—and lots of them see us as worse than the Emperor because we caused the earthquake in Tiberium.//

//Child, you are too wise for your years,// said Master Clement. //Lenardo and Aradia are teaching you well. If Portia had treated the Readers she ruled as the members of our Alliance treat their people, they would not have turned against her. But we are wise if we can learn from the mistakes of others, and not make them all ourselves.

//Now,// he continued, //enough of government; Aradia and your father will teach you that. Show me what you have been practicing of Reading.//

Julia had been practicing her fine discernment, and earned praise from Master Clement when she showed him how she could Read something like the tumor in a boy's knee down to the level of individual cells.

//Not Torio, not even your father, could Read so well at your age. Now show me distance.//

Julia enjoyed these lessons, for her horizons were

constantly expanding. Reading was a joy—had been ever since Lenardo had first touched her mind and taken her out of her life as a misfit among the guttersnipes of Zendi. Once she understood the necessity for etiquette and protocol in someone who would rule her own lands one day, she had carefully developed her habits and her language until her teachers could find no fault.

She loved to learn—it was the one quarrel she had with her friend Galerio, for he found the fascinating knowledge she longed to share with him quite boring.

She demonstrated for Master Clement how far she could Read, and with what accuracy, then showed him her new skill at Reading other Readers without being detected. She Read Panatus, now helping the healer with one of many sessions to straighten the bones of a child who had suffered rickets before Lord Wulfston came to rule the land.

// Julia, that is not a skill for a Reader in training!// Master Clement chided. //Until you pass your exams to become a Magister Reader, you should not even try it.//

//Why not? I can do it—I learned it by Reading with Father when he does it.//

//Because, child, it takes a certain wisdom to use one's skills properly. I understand how difficult it is for you to see that some kinds of wisdom come only with age.//

//Or experience,// she protested. //Father says I've seen a great deal for someone my age.//

//And I agree. However, you are also at the time of life when your body is changing—you are becoming a woman, Julia. Until you have become accustomed to the changes, they will affect your feelings, your judgment. Your body will affect your mind.//

//Then teach me to leave my body!// she asked eagerly. //I'm ready—you've tested all my skills. Let me take the next step.//

//If it were only your Reading skills,// he told her, //I would agree that you are ready. But moving beyond your body must wait until you have passed completely through puberty. So practice your other skills, Julia, and learn other things. Let Aradia teach you more languages. Study music—//

//I have no talent for music,// Julia protested. //When I tried to play the lute, it sounded like a sick cow.//

//Then by all means practice upon the lute! I shall set Master Juna to teaching you as soon as you return.//

If there was anything Julia hated, it was being made to do something she was not good at, and never would be. Her only hope was that Master Clement might forget this part of their conversation, so she did not argue—that would certainly set the notion firmly in his mind.

Her ploy, however, did not work. Hardly were she and Aradia back in Zendi when Master Juna was there with her lute and a schedule of lessons. And when she protested to both Aradia and Master Clement, she got the same answer from both: "Learn to play well enough to accompany singing, and it will suffice. It is good discipline for everybody to learn to do some things he has no great talent for."

Aradia was glad to be back in Zendi, although her anxiety over Lenardo's safety grew as the weeks passed with no word from him. If he and Wulfston were detained in Africa, surely there were ways to send messages! Traders came from the Nubian lands. Was neither man free to write or send a letter?

The expected attack came upon Wulfston's northern border. Lilith and Ivorn rode to join Wulfston's army. Readers and minor Adepts flocked to their aid, and the attacking force was repelled as easily as swatting a fly.

Aradia was pleased that the attack was so easily routed, but frustrated to be left in Zendi, far out of the action.

It was Julia who pointed out, "If you were not pregnant, you would still not have gone so far for a battle that was over before you could've arrived."

Aradia had to smile. She had long ago accepted Lenardo's adopted daughter—but now she was learning to love her. The girl had been a bundle of mischief before Master Clement took over her training, but she was growing up into a fine young woman.

Zendi was a thriving city now, rebuilt after the series of battles that had raged over it during its years in disputed territory. The old wood and mud-and-wattle buildings were replaced with stone; fire was no longer the plague it had once been. The water and sewer systems were back in repair, and Lenardo's current project was to bring water and safe, comfortable heating into the homes of even the poorest of the citizens.

There was plenty for the Adepts and Readers to do: weather to be controlled so the crops would thrive, the sick and injured to be healed, the young people with their burgeoning talents to be trained.

The Academy system already existed to train young Readers, but there had never before been systematic training of those with minor Adept talents. Healers had apprenticed themselves to other healers, those with power over weather had been valued by the farmers, but the rest had generally used their powers sparingly, lest the local Lord Adept take too sharp a notice of potential rivals.

Then there was the ongoing research to bring out Adept talent in Readers, Reading in Adepts. Now that it was understood that the two talents were one, it was hard to see why so many who were skilled at one could not evoke the other. Wulfston longed to learn to Read, but had somehow never made the breakthrough. Master Clement only laughed when Aradia offered to teach him Adept tricks, saying, "I'm too old to start a new way of life. Teach Decius—he's eager to learn."

Decius was approaching his examinations for the rank of Magister Reader, a source of irritation to Julia. "I'm a better Reader than he is," she fumed, "but he gets to learn to go out of body and I don't!"

"Decius is eighteen," Aradia reminded her. "When you are his age, you'll learn those techniques."

She wished Decius and Julia were a little closer in age; she'd have much preferred Julia to focus her growing interest in the opposite sex on the young Reader than on her friend Galerio, a sixteen-year-old minor Adept who led a gang of youngsters with similar small talents. Aradia was hard put to explain why she didn't like the boy. He had no family, and lived by his wits and talents. Normally she admired such spirit.

But neither Galerio nor any of the young people he led would attend the classes designed to help them make the best use of their abilities. "He doesn't want you to tell him what to do with his life," Julia explained.

"Julia, you know that's not the purpose of the classes," Aradia protested. "You'd be doing him a great favor if you could persuade him to attend."

"He doesn't listen to girls' advice!" Julia exclaimed, and Aradia suddenly saw one reason Julia was fascinated by Galerio: he was one of the few people her age who did not treat her with the deference due Lenardo's heir.

Decius might have been a similar challenge, if he had paid attention to Julia at all. Aradia decided to throw them together. She had a valid reason: both were powerful Readers, but neither had mastered a single Adept talent.

So she told Julia she wanted to work with her and Decius together, apart from her other pupils. Julia agreed eagerly—she longed to add Adept powers to her talents.

Decius arrived right on time, striding confidently despite the peg leg he wore. When he was only thirteen, he had lost his left leg in a battle Drakonius had taken into the very Academy at Adigia, where Decius had then been a student. Those wars were over now, but they had scarred an entire generation.

Decius' scars were only physical. Emotionally, he was as sound as any young man Aradia knew—and today he was flushed with triumph as he joined Julia and Aradia in the private chamber where they would have their lesson. "It's my day for learning!" he told them. "This morning I moved to another plane of existence—it's even more exciting than going out of body!"

Aradia had never done either, but she knew that

Readers on the advanced levels could go into other dimensions, other . . . places, she supposed, where not even the best Readers could spy on them. Not physical places, though. For her, it was a strange concept—but she did not let it concern her, because she would have no occasion to try it. Let Lenardo worry about other planes of existence.

But she congratulated Decius, and then got down to the business at hand.

Before them on the table she placed a fireproof bowl, in which were shavings and tinder. "Fire is the easiest power to manifest," she said for the thousandth time, "although one of the most difficult to master. Never practice without an Adept skilled in fire control present."

Julia said, "I've tried this a hundred times, Aradia. It won't work."

"It won't work if you think it won't," said Decius. "I think it will."

"Do you, Decius?" Aradia asked.

"Yes," he said firmly.

"Then try. Concentrate. Envision the flames. Feel the heat. Put your mind to just that bowl, just the kindling—Decius, you're Reading!"

He blinked, and looked at her. "Sorry," he muttered, and returned to staring at the kindling. He was still Reading it, his disciplined mind probing the air passages beneath it, imagining how the draft would come up through—

//Decius—//

//Wait,// he forestalled her. //Let me—//

Suddenly he was blank to Reading—and the kindling burst into flame!

Decius sagged, catching himself by hanging on to the table. He stared at the bowl in astonishment, and a sudden grin seized his features. "I did it!" He looked at the two women. "I *did* it!"

"Show me how!" demanded Julia.

Decius smiled at her. "You just have to know you can. Really, Julia—Master Clement's been trying to teach you that. All I did was take the feeling I had this morning, when I *knew* I could move to the plane of privacy, and apply it here—I made myself *know* I could do this in just the same way!"

"But *I* know I can do it," said Julia, "and I still can't!"

"Julia," said Aradia, "you are getting upset. In that condition you won't learn anything at all. Use your relaxation technique—"

"I don't want to relax," the girl fretted."I want to start a fire." She fished more kindling from a container by the empty fireplace and piled it into the bowl, where the original fire had quickly burned itself out.

"Julia, don't," said Aradia. "Not being able to do it when you are agitated will contribute to your belief that you can't do it later, when you've calmed down."

"Why don't you want me to do it?" Julia demanded. "I'm as good as Decius! Master Clement teaches him to leave his body, but he won't teach me. Now you teach him to start fires, and you won't even let me try it. It's not *fair*!" And the girl got up and stomped out of the room.

Decius rose, but Aradia put a hand on his arm. "Let her go. She'll calm down. If we keep her here now, she'll just go on arguing."

"Girls sure are different from boys," he observed.

"You're an expert?" Aradia asked.

"I'm in charge of one of the boys' dormitories at the Academy," Decius explained. "It's all right, except when I'm also on sleep duty."

"Sleep duty?" she asked.

"Young Readers have to learn not to Read in their sleep—one boy with a nightmare would set off the whole group. Besides, you don't want other Readers knowing your dreams. So we older students have to take turns staying awake, and waking up any of the little boys who start projecting dreams." He shook his head. "It's hard on them—I remember. But we've all got to learn, or we'd be afraid to go to sleep. Dreams can be very embarrassing!"

"I know," said Aradia, thinking of the strange dream she kept having about her unborn child. Any number of times she had started to tell Master Clement, but decided it was unimportant. Why shouldn't she dream about what her daughter would look like as a young woman?

Fortunately, she had not had to go through the regimen Decius described when she learned to Read. Lenardo said that when she dreamed, she seemed to brace her Adept powers automatically, which of course kept her from being Read.

"Now," she said to Decius, "let's see if you can light the fire again—and don't work so hard at it!"

This time she had him smother the fire before it burned itself out, then rekindle it and direct the flames to consume specific bits of wood. Accustomed to the disciplines of a lifetime in the Academy, Decius learned quickly. Still, by the time she was satisfied he was panting with exertion, although he had not left his chair.

He leaned back, pleased with the day's work.

"Now don't be worried," Aradia warned him, "if you can't Read as well as usual until you get a night's sleep. And eat plenty of supper tonight—meat if there is any, but at least some fish. No arguments."

"I'm not arguing," he replied. "Lady Aradia, next lesson, would you teach me healing techniques?"

He gestured toward his left thigh, where the stump of his leg was hidden beneath his white tunic. Aradia understood. Decius refused to live at a slower pace than any other eighteen-year-old boy. As a result, the healers often had to heal bruises or blisters to his stump, no matter how they adjusted and padded the wooden leg.

"Of course," she said, knowing what a relief it would be for him to heal it himself. "You will probably learn quickly. I'm proud of you, Decius—what a day you've had!"

"Master Clement was right," he told her. "The whole secret is in believing you can do it."

"Then why can't he learn Adept powers?" Aradia wondered.

"He could," Decius replied. "But I can understand why he won't. Right now my Reading is . . . hazy. It's frightening to have my powers diminished, and I'm not even a Magister Reader yet." He smiled at her. "I guess it's funny to you when I say I'm too old to adapt really well to having both powers."

"You may never get to be any better at Adept powers than I am at Reading," Aradia agreed.

"Perhaps not. But I wonder what the little children will be like—the ones growing up with both powers. Will they be like the sorcerers Torio met in Madura?"

"I hope not! Those stories Zanos and Astra told, about cold fire that almost destroyed their land . . ." Aradia shuddered. "Decius . . . you're not still thinking of going to Madura to see if they can restore your leg?"

"Maybe, one day," he said. "Not now. Whatever Torio found there, he was afraid to bring it back. Melissa stayed to keep it confined to Madura. But Lady Aradia, if power exists, there are those who will seek to use it. I'm going to try to become as good an Adept as I am a Reader, because someday I may have to confront power such as we have never seen in all our Savage Empire."

Julia stormed out of the villa and walked northward, zigzagging through side streets until she came to the main north-south road, north of the forum.

Hordes of people crowded the wide street, buying and selling at the shops and stands. They were prosperous, not a single person in the rags or bedraggled finery that had been common in her childhood. Stout farmers bought furbelows for their apple-cheeked wives, and sturdy children chased one another between the wagons or munched on sweets while staring wide-eyed at the passing throng.

Julia was often recognized. People gave her bows and curtsies as she passed, and she quickly cheered up. This prosperity was partly her doing, and she felt rightfully proud. When she opened to Reading, she felt the love of the people—they were happy, beginning to trust in the security Lenardo and his family had brought them. They were no longer forced to work, as under Drakonius, but found that working now made them prosperous despite the taxes levied on their goods.

Theft was uncommon; Readers could be anywhere in the crowds, making it simply too dangerous a trade to ply in Zendi. It was still being eradicated in Tiberium, she had heard.

Under Master Clement, the corruption had been cleaned out of the Readers' system—bribes and threats no longer compelled certain Readers to Read in another direction while a crime was being committed. But Tiberium was larger than Zendi, and even more crowded. And the people felt they had been conquered, unlike these on the winning side in the most recent conflict.

Julia passed jugglers and musicians entertaining the crowds, and turned out of the North Road into a side street near Northgate. Here were the shops of wine merchants, where wagons were being loaded with barrels for the village inns, and for the homes of a few prosperous farmers.

A few streets along, though, the buildings became residential. These were new blocks of flats for working families. Their landlords were carefully supervised lest they permit them to turn back into the kinds of slums that had burned in the battle for Zendi.

Every few streets there was an open area planted with grass and young trees. Eventually these would become carefully gardened parks, but building homes for Zendi's growing population was a higher priority just now, so the little parks were left with their natural grass and wildflowers. In one of them, a group of young people were wiling away the time.

Dilys and Piccolo lay in the shade of some bushes, kissing and pawing at one another, oblivious to the rest of the group. Giorgio was eating bread and cheese—he was always eating, resulting in a physique that caused the others to call him Fat Giorgio. Antonius and Mosca were wrestling, their muscles standing out with the exertion, while Blanche and Diana cheered them on.

Atop a small mound that would one day become terraced flower beds sat Galerio, leader of this loosely associated group of minor Adepts.

Young, talented folk like these, ranging in age from twelve to twenty, were one of the problems Lenardo and Aradia had yet to solve. They had no education, and no formal training in using their talents. Many of them, like this group, refused the offer of training, and so except for occasional odd jobs, their talents were wasted.

"Ho, Julia!" called Galerio. "Come sit by me and help judge this contest. You can Read if anybody cheats."

She climbed the mound, with no care for grass stains on her white dress. Except for special occasions, the white of a Reader in training was her usual wear.

Galerio was sixteen, and to Julia's thinking, the handsomest boy she had ever seen. He had wavy dark hair, and deep brown eyes fringed with thick black lashes. His skin still had the rosy fairness of youth, while his body was sculpted by exercise.

Of course Galerio never told his cohorts that he exercised other than swimming at the baths, but Julia had Read his private exertions, supplemented with Adept direction. He had some healing potential, but would not admit it. He kept the public use of his powers to moving small objects.

Julia Read the wrestlers. They were evenly matched in size and weight. Antonius was fourteen, Mosca fifteen, both still clumsy with adolescence. They fought like street urchins, kicking and kneeing, trying to bang one another's heads against the ground. Julia understood the rules: "wrestling" for these boys meant simply no punching, eye-gouging, pinching, or biting, and no surreptitious use of Adept power.

Suddenly Mosca went blank to her Reading, and Julia Read a sharp cramp in Antonius' side. "Cheat!" she cried. "Mosca, you gave Antonius that cramp!"

Mosca rose with a threatening growl, but Galerio said, "You know the rules, Mosca. Antonius wins."

The younger boy got up, dusting himself off. "Thanks,

Julia," he said shyly. Antonius was dark, like Julia and Galerio. Mosca had hair of the shade between dark blond and light brown, and light blue eyes that looked at Julia coldly.

Galerio said warningly, "You know Julia's right, Mosca." Then he grinned. "If you can learn to fool her, you're gonna get past most Readers."

"Yeah," said Mosca, only partially placated, "I'll have to learn that."

"So," said Galerio, "what're you doing here, Julia? You usually have your stupid lessons in the afternoons."

"They're not stupid when I'm learning to catch people cheating," she replied. "But Aradia's in one of her pregnant moods today—I can't do anything right."

"No wonder. She'll want her own brat to have the throne, and you're in the way."

"No," said Julia, "there are plenty of lands for all of us. Tomorrow Aradia will think I'm wonderful. Father warned me that pregnant women act a little crazy at times. That's all it is."

"Yeah? Well, your father's not here to stand up for you now, is he?"

Julia changed the subject. "Let's go out Northgate and into the woods."

"What's in the woods? We're not allowed to hunt the deer."

"Well, we can . . ."

Julia was open to Reading, although not concentrating on it. As she spoke, something impinged on her consciousness. Outside Northgate, in the area she was thinking about, people along the road shuddered uneasily.

"What's the matter?" Galerio asked.

"Something's happening," she replied. "I can't tell what it is exactly, but people are frightened."

Then it touched them: a cold wind out of the warm air. It swept through the little park, tearing at their clothes, pulling the girls' hair out of its fastenings.

"Brrr!" said Fat Giorgio. "It's gonna rain."

But there were no clouds. The sky was hazy blue above them.

The wind continued, churning up the city's dust, making their eyes smart.

"What is it?" cried Dilys.

"A whirlwind!" Galerio shouted. "Get down!"

He scrambled down off the mound, and the nine of them huddled at its base as icy wind pelted them with debris.

But there was little there to hurt them. They were merely getting dirty.

Out on the crowded market street, Julia Read the wind wreaking havoc.

Wagons overturned. Animals screamed in panic.

Signs fell.

Canopies whipped about, slapping people down.

Screaming children, unable to find their parents, were crushed beneath tumbling cartons or run over by wagon wheels.

Parents seeking their children saw them whipped out of reach by the howling gale.

A foodseller's stall collapsed, dousing his customers with boiling oil. Agonizing pain burned into Julia's own flesh—a Reader caught in the deluge of oil—but even as she screamed the pain cut off, and she was left gasping in reaction.

As quickly as it had come, the wind died—but the panic in the market continued.

Julia jumped to her feet, wiping away tears caused by dust and shared pain. "Come on!" she shouted. "People need our help!"

Galerio cried, "Follow Julia!" and they dashed toward the madhouse in the North Road.

To get there, they had to wade through wine, spilled from the barrels outside the wine merchants' shops. But Julia Read that the damage there was only to merchandise, not people, and hurried on.

Cries of pain greeted them.

The market street was a shambles of food, wine, goods, and blood.

They almost fell over a man with a broken leg. Julia Read his pain, and directed, "Blanche, put him to sleep. Galerio, you and Antonius set the bone, and start him healing till a healer gets here."

There were a few other Readers in the market street. Everywhere there was someone in a white dress or tunic, people turned for help. Others approached the Readers, saying, "I can heal," or "I can move things," and together they sought to save those in danger of dying, and ease the pain of those whose injuries were not so severe.

Hands clutched at Julia. "Reader, please! My little boy!" The woman pointed to a mound of broken crates. "It all fell on him! I couldn't reach him!"

Mosca and Piccolo started at once to toss the crates aside, but Julia Read—

"I'm so sorry," she said as gently as she could. "The child is dead. Dilys, please help this woman," she added, for Dilys had the talent to affect people's feelings. "The rest of you come with me. We must help the living."

A little farther on they came to a group of people heaving a smashed wagon off a woman's chest.

"Lady Julia!" cried a merchant who recognized her. "Is she alive?"

Yes, there was a fluttering heartbeat, but broken ribs had penetrated the woman's right lung and severed arteries. She could not live much longer.

//I need a healer here!// Julia projected to all the Readers, showing them the extent of the woman's injuries.

//I'm bringing one,// came a mental voice she recognized as Master Juna, her music teacher. But the woman was blocked by people and debris—it would take several minutes for her and the man following her to reach them.

In the meantime, the injured woman's heartbeat grew weaker as her lung filled with her own blood.

"Can anyone heal this woman?" Julia shouted aloud. No one responded. "Mosca!" she suddenly remembered.

"Pull those ribs out to their normal position, and then pinch off the arteries. She'll die if she bleeds any more!"

The boy stared at her. "How can I—?"

"Use your talent! If you can pinch a nerve to make a cramp, you can pinch off a blood vessel."

He swallowed hard, then nodded. "Show me where."

Julia directed, and Mosca concentrated—but he was a very minor Adept, and soon was shaking and sweating with the exertion. He couldn't hold on. Where was that healer?

//We're coming,// Master Juna assured her. //You're doing fine.//

But Mosca wasn't. He gave everything he had—and keeled over in a dead faint.

The woman's bright blood spurted once more.

"Oh—*why* can't I learn Adept skills?" Julia demanded of no one in particular.

Then Galerio was kneeling by her side. "Show me."

At once he stopped the leakage he could see, then under her direction pinched off the other artery deep inside. Somehow, the woman's heart still beat, although her chest heaved in her struggles for air.

Finally the crowd parted for Master Juna and the Adept healer. Galerio rocked back on his heels and let go on a wave of relief.

"Good work," said Master Juna. "Son, you must come to the Academy and learn to work with Readers. We always need healers."

Unlike Mosca, who was sound asleep on the cobblestones, Galerio was not even breathing hard.

Julia said, "I'm so proud of you! Come on—let's see if anyone else needs us."

"Sure," he replied, getting to his feet, "but don't think I'm gonna spend my life obeying Readers just 'cause I helped out in an emergency!"

Decius was just leaving Aradia when he suddenly stopped, his eyes taking on the look of a Reader concentrating on something at a distance. "My lady—" he began, but Aradia was already Reading with him, his stronger powers revealing the sudden destruction occurring in the market street.

Without another word, they both ran from the villa and strode rapidly toward the main north-south road. By the time they reached it, other Readers were converging, a parade of men and women in white, the gowns and tunics of the Masters and Magisters edged in black. Among them were Adepts who could Read, Adepts who happened to be working with Readers when the storm occurred, and some Dark Moon Readers, pools of color in the white tide.

Aradia was slower on her feet these days, and Decius was hampered by his wooden leg, so they were in the back of the pack by the time they reached the area of destruction.

The storm was over, but the market was devastated. Every hand was needed to dig out the injured, and every Adept was quickly put to work, those on the scene quickly teaming with Readers to save as many lives as possible.

Aradia and Decius started into the melee, only to be accosted by Master Clement. "Lady Aradia!" the old man exclaimed. "We need you to direct things here. People will listen to your orders."

That was true, although she knew his underlying motivation was to keep her from exhausting herself—and thereby threatening her baby—with the use of Adept powers.

So she sent out the word: healers to the forum, all injured to be sent there as soon as life-preserving measures had been taken. There was now a hospital in Zendi, but it did not have room for so many. Only those requiring much further healing would eventually be taken there. Once it was organized, the healing talent in Zendi would easily suffice to help everyone who had been injured in the freak whirlwind.

Decius helped broadcast the directions to the Readers, most of whom had not been in Zendi during the battles when this plan had first been developed. Soon the evacuation of the ruined area was proceeding apace.

Aradia resisted employing her own powers, until a man pushed his way through the crowd to fall on his knees at her feet. "Lady," he begged. "Oh, Lady—please. My friend—"

He spoke the savage language with a strong Aventine accent, and his appearance was Aventine: clean-shaven, hair cut short. But the former Aventine Empire was now part of the Savage Empire, so he and his friend were her people now.

Aradia asked, "Where is your friend?" intending to see how badly he was injured and get help for him—but when the small Aventine man led her to his friend she gasped in horror.

The man lay writhing on the cobblestones, his face twisted in agony. He was burned hideously, having been caught when a food vendor's vat of boiling oil overturned.

One side of his neck and face were swollen, blistered, and puckered, and where his chest and shoulder were soaked with oil she knew even without Reading that he was just as badly burned beneath his clothing. How could he have been overlooked?

But as she tried to Read him, Aradia realized how: he was as blank to Reading as an Adept exercising his powers.

But he was no Adept; his burns were reddening and raising further blisters even as she watched. No healing was going on here.

A woman knelt beside him, pale with shock, trying to wipe the oil from his face with her kerchief. A child clung to her skirts.

The woman looked up as the crowd cleared a path for Aradia. "Oh, my lady! Please help him! He saved my baby!"

"That's right!" the man's friend exclaimed excitedly. "When the vat overturned, Pyrrhus grabbed the kid out of the way, threw him to me—but the oil hit *him*! Help him, Lady—please!"

Aradia laid her hand against the uninjured side of Pyrrhus' face and willed his pain to stop.

At once the ghastly twisting of the man's face abated, and Aradia smiled at his relief. But then his eyes opened, and he stared up at her in utter shocked astonishment.

The eyes were brown, shadowed under heavy brows. They studied her, and then he asked in a tense, hoarse voice, "Who are you?"

"I am Aradia, Lady Adept," she replied. "Do not fear—you will be completely healed. I will put you to sleep now."

"No!"

"It is necessary," she said gently, understanding that these Aventines did not yet fully trust the people they had always called savages, especially Adepts. But Pyrrhus would when he woke to find his pain gone, his body unscarred.

He fought her, but his injury had taken his physical strength; his body was weak with shock. His strength of will was astonishing, though—she had to force him into unconsciousness as if he were an enemy Adept resisting her attempts to put him out of commission.

But Aradia had conserved her strength. She eased Pyrrhus into healing sleep, setting his own body to repairing the damage the boiling oil had done.

Then she turned to the woman, asking, "Are you hurt? Or your child?"

"No, my lady—thanks to these men." The woman was not Aventine; she spoke the savage language with a peasant's accent.

So their Adventine visitors had risked their lives to save the child of someone they still regarded as a potential enemy. A moment's unconsidered reflex, but one of many small incidents that would eventually build a bridge between conquered and conquerors, and help them to forget their relationship had begun under those conditions.

"I will see that they are rewarded," Aradia assured the woman.

The injured man's friend was kneeling beside him, his hands clenched into fists, as if he wanted to help, but didn't know how. "What is your name?" Aradia asked him.

"Wicket," he replied. "Look!" he gasped excitedly. "The blisters are going down already!"

"Yes," Aradia told him. "Pyrrhus will be perfectly well in a day or two. I will have him taken to the hospital as soon as I finish here."

And Aradia vowed that no matter what Master Clement said, she would visit Pyrrhus there and aid his healing until he recovered.

Decius joined her again, ostenisibly Reading what she was doing in order to learn to heal, but she knew that he was carefully monitoring her condition, ready to stop her if she showed signs of exhaustion.

But the one healing effort was well within her limits. By the time she was satisfied, the last of the injured were in the forum, and reports of deaths and property damage were ready for her attention.

Five people had died, killed instantly in the storm, no one able to help them in the midst of the whirlwind. All those alive after the storm had been saved, and she heard Julia and her band of reprobate friends being praised on every side. They had come in from the north end of the market—the part least accessible to the Readers and Adepts who had run to help—and were credited with saving at least a dozen lives.

Now what am I doing with that scamp? Aradia wondered. *She walks out like a spoiled brat, and comes back a heroine.*

Julia had Read that the reports were in, and was wending her way across the forum to take her place beside Aradia. Only when she saw the child's condition, hair a rat's nest, face smeared with grime, clothes torn, did she realize that Julia had actually been caught in the storm.

Aradia could not scold her before their retainers, so she said nothing to Julia as she received the reports. The well-built new structures in that area of town had stood firm; if the wind had not struck the market, few people would have been harmed.

But as the last man turned to leave, Master Clement came up to them. "Don't Read," he told the two women. "The news will reach the other Readers soon enough, but you should know it first, Aradia."

"What has happened?" Aradia asked, bracing Adept powers.

"I have just received news from Tiberium, from Adigia, from numerous villages throughout our lands. There was not only this one freak whirlwind today. There were almost twenty, each one occurring where it would create the greatest damage and loss of life. It cannot be coincidence, my lady. Although no Reader anywhere in our lands Read anyone behind it, such a series of storms can only be the product of Adept attack."

Chapter Three

The next day, Julia stood proudly before the people of Zendi as Aradia gave out awards to those who had helped to save lives after yesterday's storm. The older Readers were embarrassed by the ceremony—they were not accustomed to being rewarded individually for their services.

Master Clement had set up an Academy here. Almost all of the Academy-trained Readers lived there, continuing the life-style they had always known. The only difference now was that men and women worked there together, something that still made some older Readers uneasy.

Money in an Academy was communal property; if the Readers earned some, it went into the community coffer; if a Reader had to travel, he was given funds for the journey out of that coffer. Master Clement had instructed that the gold Aradia handed out today was to be kept by the individual Readers, not placed in the Academy treasury. Many of the Readers receiving it had no idea what to do with the money.

Not so the minor Adepts and other citizens! They burgeoned with pride and plans. Many were merchants who had lost property in the storm; they, of course, would rebuild. Others thought of presents for their families, dowries, necessities or luxuries.

Galerio's cohorts would probably drink and gamble their reward away, Julia knew. Galerio himself, though, wanted a horse, and she wholeheartedly approved. They'd be able to ride out into the country—alone, without his pack of followers. She carefully shielded her thoughts from Master Clement, who would surely feel compelled to relay them to Aradia. Rules of privacy didn't apply to children when adults thought they violated them "for the good of the child." How she wished her teacher would stop thinking of her as a child!

Toward the end of the ceremony, Aradia called forth a man who looked less like a hero than anyone Julia had ever seen before. It wasn't exactly his appearance, although he was perhaps the most "medium" person Julia had ever seen: medium size, medium build, medium age, medium-brown hair slightly receding. It was his demeanor, as if he wasn't sure why he was there, his glance darting about as if he expected someone to chase him away.

But Aradia announced, "Wicket, and his friend Pyrrhus who is still in the hospital, are Aventines, but they risked their lives—and Pyrrhus was badly injured—saving the child of one of Zendi's citizens. It is especially important to remind ourselves that the Aventines are no longer our enemies, but citizens of our empire. Pyrrhus and Wicket proved yesterday that they are brothers to us all. Wicket." She handed the man two gold coins. "One measure for you, and one for Pyrrhus, in token of the gratitude of your fellow countrymen."

Wicket stared at the gold, which Julia guessed was more money than he had ever had at one time in his life. She tried to Read his surface feelings—not exactly a forbidden invasion of the privacy of a nonReader if she did not search his thoughts, although she knew she would get a stern lecture from Master Clement if he caught her at it.

But Wicket's feelings were hidden behind a strange barrier—a wall of nonsense: snatches of songs, jokes, stories swarmed on the surface of his mind, masking not only what he was thinking, but what he felt as well.

Smothering the urge to giggle, Julia stood in silent amusement as Aradia bestowed the Empire's honor on a common criminal.

Some sort of confidence man, she assumed, pickpocket maybe, or cheat at gambling. NonReader, he had been trained by somebody who knew the Readers' Code to set up a mental screen lest he be caught at his unlawful activities before he could even perform them. Julia had Read such criminals in Tiberium, where they had operated boldly during the brief time of chaos after the city's fall.

Later, she had helped her father recognize such people and discourage them from plying their trade in Zendi. Wicket must be new here; there were Readers in the town now who would recognize that barrier. All he had to do was trigger any citizen's suspicions, and he'd be caught.

Meanwhile, though, Julia found it amusing that no one else yet knew what Wicket was—and since he had not broken the law, she was not about to tell. Such people who lived by their wits had been her friends in childhood, often willing to amuse a little girl with jokes and stories when no one else had time for her. Of course in the Savage Lands, with no Readers to pry into their heads, they had not needed such mental barriers then.

Flustered at being the object of attention from those in authority, Wicket was saying, "Uh—thank you, Lady Aradia."

Julia wondered if Aradia noticed that he did not say "*my* lady." She knew many Aventine Readers who, while they acknowledged the titles which indicated the status of the Lords Adept, refused to accept their right to rule them. A single instance, of course, told her little about Wicket's attitude. It was obvious that he had never met a Lady Adept before.

Neither Aradia nor Master Clement ever referred to Julia as "Lady," although the people did. It was an issue Julia remained silent on; if she asked for the term of respect from her guardians, they would tell her she was too young. Master Clement, she was certain, would say she should not have the title until she had passed the tests for Magister Reader—and that event was five years away!

So she said nothing, but also never corrected her people.

Galerio never used the title, though. When the ceremony broke up, he joined her, saying, "How about putting your talent to some use for me, Julia?"

"What do you want me to do?" she asked eagerly, pleased at the chance to have Galerio owe her a favor.

"The horse market's tomorrow. Come Read the animals for me, and what the dealers are thinking about them. Help me get the best I can for my money."

"Of course," she replied. Actually, Galerio did not need her help to keep from being cheated; Readers who knew horses much better than she did patrolled the market to be certain that hidden problems were not palmed off on unwary customers. But their job was not to influence the dealing; Galerio would get a better bargain with a Reader to determine what the dealers really considered their animals worth.

"Julia," Aradia called.

Knowing she would see him tomorrow, Julia did not linger with Galerio. She had a momentary advantage with her stepmother, since the friend Aradia disapproved of had become a hero, so she could afford to be cheerfully obedient.

In fact, Julia was cheerfully obedient most of the time; she had to admit that Aradia was always just with her, and encouraged her to grow and extend her powers. If pressed, she would also have to admit that Aradia treated her better than her real mother, who had neglected her, often hit her when she was an inconvenience, and eagerly sold her to Lenardo when Julia was revealed as a Reader.

Julia had never known her father—her mother wasn't even sure which of several possibilities he was—so Lenardo had felt "real" to her from the moment his mind first touched hers. It was harder to accept the stepmother who took his attention from her, but Lenardo had trained her always to seek the truth, the facts.

And the fact was that Aradia went out of her way not to come between Lenardo and Julia.

With Lenardo away, Julia found herself becoming closer to Aradia. Something Aradia had said last night haunted her with its truth.

Julia had been waiting to be scolded for running away in frustration when she had not been able to manifest Adept talent. She had been braced with arguments in her own defense, ready to point out how she had recognized the worth of Galerio and his followers, who had proved themselves heroes in the aftermath of the whirlwind.

Instead, after supper, when Julia was bathed and already in her sleeping garments, Aradia called the girl to her study.

Julia loved that room. It was Aradia's study, but both Julia and Lenardo often went there in search of books and scrolls, for Aradia was determinedly rebuilding the library she had lost in the destruction of Castle Nerius.

Aradia sat quietly by the window that opened onto the courtyard, on one of the two comfortable lounges. She was also in her sleeping garments and robe, her pale hair loosened from its intricate daytime style.

On her way in, Julia picked up a wax tablet and stylus from one of the tables—a tablet Lenardo had written on many times. Then she sat down on the lounge where Lenardo usually sat, and swung her feet up.

With her ability to Read the history of an object, she was thus able to feel surrounded by her father, protected by his love and caring.

Aradia watched her in silence for a moment, and then said, "I wish I could feel him as you do, Julia."

The simple statement brought sudden, unexpected tears to the girl's eyes. "Read with me," she offered, and Aradia's mind touched hers, sharing the memories of Lenardo sitting on that lounge, writing on that tablet.

But if she could share the sweet with Aradia, Julia also shared the bitter: each time she touched something of her father's, the most recent memories were farther away. The days were passing. No message came from either Wulfston or Lenardo, and none of Aradia's inquiries brought an answer.

Mind to mind, neither woman knew whose throat tightened first with unshed tears. They looked into each other's glistening eyes, and broke the rapport.

"We both miss him," said Aradia.

"Yes," Julia agreed.

"Julia—you know that I am trying to care for you as Lenardo would."

"I know," she had to admit.

"Never mind the events which followed—would Lenardo have approved of your running away from your lesson today?"

Julia looked into Aradia's violet eyes, but her stepmother had become deliberately unReadable. So she had to focus on the question—nothing about Galerio, but about leaving an unfinished lesson.

A sad smile came to Julia's lips. "You're right. Father would scold me for giving up a lesson I need to learn. I'm sorry, Aradia. I won't do it again."

"At least you will try not to," the other woman acknowledged. Then she also smiled. "Julia, you and I have more in common than our concern for Lenardo."

"Our concern for the Savage Empire," Julia responded immediately.

"True," Aradia said with a nod, "but I meant personal concerns. At the moment, we are both having great difficulty working with nature, because nature is toying with us."

Julia frowned. "What do you mean?"

"You are undergoing puberty. Your body is changing—and as a Reader you certainly know the body affects the mind. Your feelings are often confusing. Sometimes you don't know what you think about something. Then on some other idea you will feel completely convinced one way one day, and the opposite way the next."

Julia said, "Yes, I know you were my age once."

"That's not what I mean," Aradia replied. "You think it doesn't matter that I've been through what you are going through, because I'm not feeling it now. But you're wrong, Julia. Being pregnant does very much the same things to my body that puberty is doing to yours."

"Father asked me to be careful about your feelings while you're pregnant," said Julia.

Aradia smiled. "Your father may be the greatest Reader the world has ever known—but although he may delve into women's minds, he will never live inside a woman's body. You do, Julia, and so do I. There are some things you and I have in common that Lenardo will never, ever understand."

And Julia suddenly knew why Aradia would not say a word about Galerio. She smiled back at her stepmother with a new understanding. "May I Read the baby?" she asked.

"Of course," said Aradia. "I was going to ask you to."

And the two women shared sensing the small life Aradia carried that was a part of Lenardo.

On the following day, Julia was in a benevolent mood toward her stepmother. When Aradia called her away from Galerio, she went at once, and found that Aradia and Master Clement were going to the hospital. She was not being arbitrarily called away from her friends; she was being called to work with the healers.

It was an adult responsibility Julia had been performing for years—and one area of her powers where not even Master Clement questioned her judgment or her competence. Eager to help her people, Julia followed the others from the forum.

At the hospital, Aradia moved from one ward to another, greeting the recovering patients who were awake. Most needed only rest and nourishment now, and would be ready to go home within the day.

The healers had been able to care for all the injuries, but today most of them were themselves in recovery sleep. Minor Adepts now joined Readers in nursing the patients.

Julia and Master Clement went to help Read the patients still in healing sleep, to be certain all was going as intended. Aradia made sure they were well involved in their work before she sought out Pyrrhus.

Pyrrhus was awake, Wicket already at his side. As Aradia approached, she saw that his friend had given Pyrrhus the gold coins, and Pyrrhus was holding them on the open palm of his left hand, staring at them.

He was in one of the small wards where severely ill or injured patients were cared for, with only three other beds. One of those beds was now empty, and the other two men were still deep in healing sleep.

As Pyrrhus should have been.

The entire right side of his face and neck were vividly red and sore: regenerated flesh that in another day under Adept care would heal unscarred to its normal condition, but today must be as painful and sensitive as if flayed.

Pyrrhus seemed to be hiding his pain successfully from Wicket, but without Reading Aradia could see it in his eyes, dilated so they appeared black rather than their natural dark brown. Although it was pleasantly cool within the stone building, his brow showed a faint sheen of perspiration. Yet even with Reading, she still could not detect his pain.

It made no sense. She might be a very weak Reader, but pain such as Pyrrhus was experiencing should have had her sending him to sleep in self-defense. She had never heard of anyone masking such strong feelings except Lords Adept, but a Lord Adept in Pyrrhus' condition would not have the strength for such effort.

Was Pyrrhus a secret Adept grown up in the Aventine Empire, where until four years ago such powers had been anathema? No, even the greatest Lord Adept would be at the mercy of his own body's defenses, which would put him back into healing sleep whether he willed it or not. Besides, a Lord Adept would block the pain, not suffer it while blocking transmission to Readers. There had to be some other explanation.

However he was doing it, *why* was he masking his pain? It meant only that no Reader called an Adept healer's attention to him, and he suffered for no reason.

Aradia crossed the room to Pyrrhus' side, and waited for him to look up at her. Although it was discolored, his face was back to its normal contours now, thin with sharp planes, high cheekbones, pointed chin, eyes set deep under a heavy browbone. A large, straight nose saved it from appearing pinched, but it would have been a severe, even frightening face were it not for a sensuous, beautifully sculpted mouth, now tense with suspicion as his eyes met hers.

"You remember Lady Aradia," Wicket said brightly, too eagerly cheerful. "She's the one healed you, Pyrrhus—and gave us the gold!"

"Why give us money?" Pyrrhus asked, his eyes like twin weapons trained on Aradia.

"Because," she replied gently, "although there is no adequate repayment for saving a life, such a deed cannot go unrecognized and unrewarded."

"I assure you," Pyrrhus said acidly, "my action was unpremediatated. Simple animal reflex."

"The reflex of a good man," Aradia told him. "Witnesses told us what happened: when you saw the vat of oil toppling, about to spill onto a little boy, you ran in and snatched the child up. And when you could not move fast enough to escape the burning liquid, you tossed the child to Wicket, who carried him to safety."

"At least it was a child," Pyrrhus said, closing his hand over the coins with an audible snap. "Although of course he will grow up, won't he?" He made it sound like a curse.

By now it was clear to Aradia that Pyrrhus was wounded far more in mind than in body. Such cynicism could only cover deep scars of betrayal. It was not an uncommon symptom among the people their Savage Alliance had conquered, and the only cure was to prove their benevolence over time.

The sole medicine she could offer Pyrrhus at the moment was to continue his healing. "Have you eaten?" she asked.

He frowned slightly at the abrupt change of subject. "No."

There was fruit and bread on the bedside table, along with a pitcher of water. "You must be hungry," Aradia said.

"Yes," Pyrrhus replied. "Wicket, have you a knife? I don't know what has happened to my clothes and belongings."

Of course—he would be ravenous with the hunger that came from depleting the body's reserves in Adept healing, but the pain in his face would not allow him to bite into the fruit. Aradia opened to Reading, sending an order to the hospital kitchen for the revitalizing soup that was kept ready for awakening patients.

Wicket handed Pyrrhus a knife with a thin blade, in trade for the coins. But when the man in the bed tried to move, simply to reach for the fruit, the pain escaped his control, and he gasped as his body twisted. Wicket deftly caught the falling knife.

"Let me help," said Aradia, laying a hand against the back of Pyrrus' neck, where the nerve centers led to his cheek and down into his injured shoulder. Deliberately, she stopped the pain.

At the sudden relief, Pyrrhus collapsed back onto his pillow, eyes closed. Then he reopened them, and lifted his right arm with an effort, staring at his hand. "It's gone numb," he said, unable to control the slight hint of fear in his voice.

"Just temporarily," Aradia quickly assured him. "It's the only way to take away the pain so you can replenish the strength healing has taken from your body."

Wicket had already sliced up an apple. "Here," he said, putting it in reach of Pyrrhus' left hand.

Once the man began to eat, his body's needs took over. It was a common experience to Aradia, but obviously neither Pyrrhus nor Wicket had ever seen anyone eat after Adept healing. Bread and fruit disappeared as fast as Wicket could slice them, and when an attendant brought the soup Aradia had called for, it vanished with equal speed.

Wicket was staring at his friend in utter astonishment. "You won't stay so skinny if you eat like that, Pyrrhus!"

Aradia guessed that Pyrrhus was hardly satisfied, although his stomach was full. He lay back, looking embarrassed, but did not answer.

"Your friend is behaving normally, Wicket," Aradia assured him. "Adept healing takes the strength from his own body to repair the damage, and he has to replenish it. Even after he is healed, he'll need to eat far more than normal for several days."

"Well," said Wicket, "I can see where our money's going to go, then!"

"Don't worry, Wicket," said Pyrrhus, "I won't ask for any of yours."

Pyrrhus was not looking at Wicket; he did not see his friend's face fall. Then Wicket's look became determined. "We agreed we were in this together, didn't we? So it's *our* money, not yours or mine, and if you need it to get your strength back—well, where'd I be without you?"

Pyrrhus turned his head to look at Wicket. "Probably much better off," he answered.

"I'd be dead!" Wicket said.

Pyrrhus nodded. "Precisely."

Aradia knew that physical weakness was exacerbating Pyrrhus' attitude, so she said, "Pyrrhus will feel much better tomorrow, Wicket. You mustn't take anything he says now seriously."

"Why not? It's the way he always talks. Good thing he doesn't act the way he talks, innit?"

It sounded like a long and enduring friendship, and the way Pyrrhus raised his eyes to study the ceiling without attempting to answer confirmed it. Aradia upgraded her estimate of the chances that Pyrrhus would modify his cynical attitude with further experience of life in the Savage Empire.

She smiled at Wicket. "I'm going to put Pyrrhus back into healing sleep now, so—"

"Oh, no," Pyrrhus snapped. "No more of *that*, thank you!"

"If I don't," said Aradia, "you'll be in pain for several more days, and it will be weeks before you're healed enough to be active. Aggravate those half-healed burns in the meantime, and you could get scar tissue that would hamper the use of your right arm. Your sword arm," she added, remembering that when she first saw him, Pyrrhus had been wearing such a weapon, sheathed at his left.

"Do the healing," he said, "but don't try to knock me out again."

"It's the only—"

"Aradia."

She turned, to find Master Clement and Julia entering the room.

"What are you doing, Aradia?" the Master Reader asked. "There are plenty of competent healers. You must not exhaust yourself."

"I'm not," she replied. "It's only this one man."

"What is—?"

Master Clement approached the bed, and stopped in his tracks when he saw its occupant. "Pyrrhus!"

Aradia opened to Reading, and was engulfed in the old man's astonishment and concern, followed by sorrow. "What has happened to you?"

Pyrrhus looked back expressionlessly. "I had a brief encounter with a vat of boiling oil," he said flatly.

"You?" asked Master Clement. "I heard the name, but I never thought— Pyrrhus, what's wrong? Why aren't you Reading?"

Now Pyrrhus' voice was heavy with sarcasm. "Oh—hadn't you heard? I was sent on a short journey along the Path of the Dark Moon."

Aradia saw Wicket's eyes, wide with astonishment, go back and forth between his friend on the bed and the imposing figure of Master Clement in his scarlet cloak. It was clear that he'd had no idea his friend was a Reader.

"But—that's impossible!" Master Clement was saying. "I tested you for the rank of Magister myself. You should have been a Master Reader by now." Then he fell silent for a moment, gathering his emotions. "Yes," he said grimly, "I understand what must have happened. Portia."

"Indeed," Pyrrhus replied with a smile that would form ice crystals on a volcano. "Portia."

Aradia felt something then from Master Clement that she had known only once before in the wise, courageous, and benevolent man who had been her husband's mentor: guilt. "I sent you into her power," he said, "when I sent you to Tiberium."

Pyrrhus said in a voice of total insincerity, "It doesn't matter. It happened nearly five years ago. I've adapted."

"Portia is dead," said Master Clement.

Pyrrhus raised an eyebrow. "Oh, I know," he replied in a voice of savage satisfaction. "I was in the rapport. I helped you kill her."

Master Clement strode to the bed. "Then your powers are not severely diminished. Pyrrhus—we know how to heal the Readers Portia and her cohorts forced onto the Path of the Dark Moon. As soon as you're well, you will come to the Academy, and—"

"No!" That barked word seemed to drain the last of Pyrrhus' energies. He lay back against the pillow, pale and sweating again, and closed his eyes. Then, in a voice devoid of emotion, he said, "What Portia did to me was not her usual method of taking an uncooperative Reader out of her way. Oh, she had originally planned to marry me off, drug me with white lotus, drain my will so she and the other corrupt Masters could implant the belief that my powers were reduced."

The man's mouth twisted in a parody of a smile. "I found out what they were doing," he said. "You were right, Clement. I *was* one of the best Readers you ever trained. So I Read too much, found out what Portia was doing—and stupidly refused to join her inner circle. I still had the ideals you taught me. Much good they did me!"

"Pyrrhus," Master Clement pleaded, but the man continued inexorably.

"Then *she* stupidly tried to set me on the Path of the Dark Moon. But I told you, it was a short journey."

"You ran away," said Master Clement.

"The morning of my supposed wedding day. Never did meet my intended bride." He gave a snort of humorless laughter, and opened his eyes. "Have you ever tried to hide when Readers are searching for you, Clement?"

"As a matter of fact," said the old man, "I have. You have to Read, to discover whether they are tracking you, but every time you do you risk giving yourself away to them."

"Yes. Well, I escaped—and learned a skill that has since served me very well."

"Your ability to block sending out thoughts," said Aradia, "even pain. The reason none of the Readers noticed how badly you were hurt yesterday."

"Yes," said Pyrrhus. "I established an identity as an ordinary Aventine citizen, and began to contact some of my old friends from the Academy who had become Dark Moon Readers. Of course, most of them deserved to be, but even they resented the Masters' crippling some of the best Readers if they were dangerous to Portia's schemes.

"We made plans, tried to determine if any among the Master Readers were uncorrupted. We contacted a few Magisters we could trust, but we needed a Master Reader to persuade other Masters. We settled on Master Julius, head of the hospital at Termoli. I went to him, with three Magister Readers, healers from his staff. He . . . listened."

"And then," said Master Clement, "he went to the Council of Masters. Yes, Pyrrhus—I learned the full story later, after the fall of Tiberium. Your name was not mentioned, though."

"No—there was no need to record what happened to me," Pyrrhus said bitterly. "I was just another failed Reader on their books. But they had to account for the healers: Magisters Samantha, Tyrus, and Cylene, and Master Julius." He winced. "The man was a fool. He had immersed himself in healing, never been involved in politics. The very innocence that made us confide in him caused him to betray us."

Master Clement said, "Master Julius thought you were mistaken. He was concerned, though, that the tactics of the Council of Masters were causing misunderstandings among both Dark Moon Readers and Readers in training. He honestly thought he was helping your cause by reporting to the Council of Masters everything you had told him."

Pyrrhus gave another of his perfectly insincere smiles. "I learned an important lesson from that experience: never trust an honest man."

Aradia saw Wicket lean forward at that, and take Pyrrhus' uninjured left hand in both of his. Pyrrhus took no notice, but neither did he withdraw the hand.

"You were an honest man," Master Clement pointed out, "and Master Julius should have trusted you. As it was, Portia turned the Council against him, insisted he was incompetent, and had him retested. I don't know how he was made to fail the testing—I wasn't there."

"They drugged him," said Pyrrhus. "I *was* there. In spirit, anyway. One of the last things I ever Read: Did you know that when they told him he'd failed, and they were going to marry him off, he took poison?"

"Yes . . . I heard," said Master Clement. "But you, Pyrrhus. Why have you shut yourself off to Reading? How can you live that way?"

"I live that way because I have to," Pyrrhus replied.

"What do you mean? It's safe to make yourself known as a Reader now—it has been ever since the fall of Tiberium."

Pyrrhus looked directly up at Master Clement, and suddenly his smile was genuine, if brief. "You really are that innocent, aren't you?

"But then," he added, his face returning to its expressionless mode, "that means you are just like Master Julius. Clement—I *can't* Read." The voice was flat again, devoid of feeling. "Portia caught me spying on the testing of Master Julius. You see, I was stupid enough to care what happened to him, and when I Read them cheating him out of his life's work by testing him under drugs, I slipped. My anger showed. I learned another lesson too late: forget the rest of the world, and look out for yourself.

"The next day Portia and her cohorts went to work on me. I'll wager you didn't even know the techniques exist, Clement my innocent. But they do. They used drugs, and then they used their minds against mine—the combined power of thirteen corrupt Master Readers who didn't care how much pain they inflicted as long as they were sure I'd never be able to spy on them again."

Aradia felt sheet horror prickle her skin, Read the same reaction from Julia and Master Clement, but none of them could close themselves off from the rapport with fellow Readers as Pyrrhus stated in that cold, empty voice, "What it felt like was that they burned out pieces of my mind. After that . . . oh, I can project thoughts with the strength of a Reader, although I've learned not to. But I can't receive thoughts anymore.

"I cannot Read."

Julia felt sick, a terrible grim sickness such as she had never known before. To lose the ability to Read? Never to touch another mind again? Unthinkable!

Both Master Clement and Aradia were as deep in shock as she was.

Wicket was still leaning forward, holding Pyrrhus' hand, unnoticed. Julia saw him tilt his head back, fighting tears. "Why didn't you tell me?" he asked.

"There was no reason," Pyrrhus answered. "There was nothing you could do." He removed his hand from Wicket's grasp, no longer making the effort to keep his voice flat and steady. It betrayed his exhaustion by trailing off almost into a whisper on the last words. His perfect control was slipping; Julia could Read the throbbing sting of his incompletely healed burns.

Master Clement said, "You are tired, Pyrrhus, and

still in pain. The Lady Aradia will put you back into healing sleep, and tomorrow—"

"No!" His pain disappeared again as he regained control, eyes flashing. "I will not allow anyone to manipulate my mind!"

Aradia said, "I understand now why you fought me when I tried to help you yesterday. Pyrrhus, all I want to do is finish healing your wounds."

"Do it without putting me to sleep," he said.

"I can't. Conscious, your body cannot tolerate the stress of such extensive healing."

It was stalemate. After what they had just learned, Aradia could not use her powers to force Pyrrhus to sleep.

Then Master Clement said, "You know how to put yourself into trance sleep, Pyrrhus. Do so, and then Lady Aradia will start the healing process again. By tomorrow your body will be back to normal."

"But not my mind," Pyrrhus said flatly, defenses at full alert again.

"Pyrrhus, please," said Wicket. "Let them heal you. You can't leave here in that condition."

With a sigh, Pyrrhus closed his eyes. "There are times, Wicket, when even you are right." And he slipped off into the meditative sleep that Julia had only recently mastered, his body in total relaxation. He would not move or dream, as in normal sleep. His mind could not interfere with the healing of his body.

Master Clement said to Aradia, "Shall I get a healer to help you?"

"No, I have done no other healing today," she replied. "I have more than adequate strength for this."

Then Aradia went to stand beside Pyrrhus, her hand on his injured shoulder. She became blank to Reading, and Adept healing fire coursed through Pyrrhus' burned flesh—this fire renewing rather than destroying.

When Aradia stepped back, Wicket looked up at her. "Will he be all right now?"

"When he wakens tomorrow he will be completely healed, just ravenously hungry again."

The tears he had forced back while Pyrrhus was awake escaped Wicket's control as he looked at the sleeping man. "He never told me! Four years we been together, and he never told me who he really was. My best friend."

"Wicket," said Master Clement gently, "I do not believe Pyrrhus withheld the information from you to hurt you. I don't think he ever meant to tell anyone. But today he found good reason to tell it. To hurt me."

"But why?" the man asked.

"Because I sent him to Tiberium, where he came to Portia's notice. And because as one of the Council of Masters I should have known what Portia was doing. I do blame myself. Pyrrhus is right. I was sinfully naive. It is difficult for a Master Reader to comprehend that anyone—even the Master of Masters—could be so corrupt without other Readers noticing."

"Pyrrhus noticed," Wicket said bitterly, sniffing and wiping tears from his chin with his sleeve. Then suddenly he got to his feet and turned to Aradia. "Can you cure what Portia did to him? Can you fix his head so he can Read again?"

Aradia looked at Master Clement. "I don't know," she replied. "Will you Read him for me, Master?"

The old man nodded. "We certainly owe him to try," he replied. "Come sit down, Aradia," he said, leading her to the empty bed, and sitting beside her. "Julia—"

"Don't send me away," she said. "I won't go."

He smiled. "I wasn't going to send you away, child. I want you to Read with us. Sit down. This will take concentration."

So Julia sat in the chair beside Aradia and Master Clement, and let her mind open to the fullest, most perceptive Reading.

Julia well understood muscle and bone and blood vessels, for she had been working with Adept healers for years. The brain, though, and delicate fine nerves were areas in which she had little experience. It was easy to follow Master Clement's perceptions into Pyrrhus' head. What they found, though, brought on her sick feeling again.

When the three stopped Reading Pyrrhus and lifted their heads, they found Wicket's anxious eyes on them. "Tell me!" he demanded. "Did you fix it?"

"No," Julia told him.

"Why not? *Can* you fix it?" he insisted.

"I'm sorry," said Aradia. "To repair such nerve damage is beyond the ability of any Adept I know."

Master Clement spoke, not so much to Wicket as to himself, as if trying to convince himself that what they had Read was true. "It is actual physical damage—nerves literally burnt out in the area of Pyrrhus' brain that . . . translates what a Reader Reads into coherent images."

Wicket obviously understood only one word of that. "Burnt? But you can cure burns!"

"We cannot restore destroyed nerves," Aradia said patiently. "I am sorry, Wicket."

Master Clement, though, was still preoccupied. "Physical damage," he mused. "Aradia, there is no way that Readers could—"

"Remember what Zanos and Astra discovered?" Aradia reminded him. "Portia was giving her protection to at least one secret Adept in Tiberium, in return for his . . . favors."

Wicket got up from his chair and stalked toward them, all trace of the cheerful little nondescript gone. "Portia!" he exclaimed in fury. "Damn—I wish Pyrrhus hadn't told me she's dead. I want to kill her with my own hands!"

"You're too late," said Julia. "We already did."

"Julia!" exclaimed Aradia.

"Well, with our minds, then. It's the same thing."

"But it's as if she won't stay dead," said Master Clement. "Just as she wouldn't stay—"

"You, of all people, know she is dead," Aradia said firmly, and Julia remembered how the old Master Reader had lain for days, his mind trapped outside his body, lost on the planes of existence, for when Portia's body died her spirit had refused to depart peacefully to the plane of the dead. Master Clement had tried to escort her there—and only a circle of Adepts and Readers had been able to call him back to his body before he, too, died.

But later they had found out, to Master Clement's dismay, that Portia's angry spirit had not stayed on the plane of the dead. Torio had gone there to bring back the woman he loved. He had met Portia's spirit, still seeking revenge, on what he described as the plane of lost souls. He had made certain Portia could not follow, knowing she would trace him back to the physical plane if she could. So Portia's spirit was left trapped in a hell of her own making.

Master Clement said, "She is dead, but not at peace. I should not have let you call me back. I should have escorted her through the portal. If she escaped from where Torio met her, she could—"

"No," Aradia said. "Torio made certain she could not follow him back to the physical plane. Don't you trust Torio, Master Clement?"

Master Clement stood. "Yes, I trust Torio. Portia may be what prevents his return. He left her trapped, and feels the same guilt I do.

"Oh, yes, Portia is dead, but her evil lives on. Indirectly, she drove Torio from us. Directly . . . ." The old man shook his head. "The damage she did lives on. Pyrrhus—how could one Reader *do* such a thing to another? By the gods, it would have been kinder to kill him!"

When Aradia returned home that evening, she found it difficult to eat supper despite having used her Adept powers. Julia also picked at her food, and Aradia did not have to Read her to know the girl was as depressed as she was by what they had learned from Pyrrhus.

Feeling excessively tired, Aradia decided to be sensible and go to bed early. She didn't even hear Devasin's chatting, and dismissed the woman as soon as she was in her nightgown, her hair let down.

Then she sat for a while, brushing the tangles out of

her hair, thinking of Lenardo. She remembered how she had first come to respect him when he helped her and Wulfston cure their father of a brain tumor.

Healing such a condition had been impossible for either Adepts or Readers alone, and they had always been alone in those days, trapped on either side of the border in societies where the appropriate power meant respect and position, but exhibiting the wrong power meant that a child would be summarily executed. But when Lenardo and Aradia overcame their arbitrary division, together they had brought Nerius back to full health.

Only to have him die in the battle with Drakonius.

He died as he would have preferred—fighting like a man, she reminded herself. *He saved my life, and Lenardo, Wulfston, and I went on to defeat our enemies.*

For a time, it had seemed that Adepts and Readers working together could accomplish anything. Only now was it coming home to them how little they could really do.

What kind of ideal society were they building, where nothing could be done for someone as devastatingly wounded, physically and mentally, as Pyrrhus?

Small and recent as Aradia's Reading talent was, she shuddered at the idea of losing it, never to know again the touch of another mind . . . Lenardo's mind.

I may never know his touch again, on my body or in my mind.

Aradia stared into her small round mirror and shook herself. "No more maudlin thoughts!" she said aloud, getting up and taking off her robe. "I'm just being . . . pregnant!"

Still, as she lay down and tried to fall asleep, she was acutely aware that the other side of the bed was empty. No warm chest to curl up against. No strong arms to make her feel absurdly protected even though both she and Lenardo knew that she was the one with the Adept powers to throw thunderbolts or—using proper leverage—move mountains.

She would never fall asleep if she lay there missing Lenardo.

But when she tried to put her husband out of her mind, the confrontation with Pyrrhus replayed itself, unbidden. No wonder the man was so brittle, bitter.

Aradia sat up in bed, her arms about her knees. If all she could do was think negative thoughts, perhaps she should go into her study and read. But she was very tired. She had not slept well recently.

Then she remembered something Nerius had taught her when she was a little girl and couldn't sleep because she was upset over something she had no control over. "Make plans," her father had told her. "Make positive plans to correct something that is wrong. Remember, daughter, there are far more things in this world outside your control than in it—so worry about what you can *do* something about."

It had always worked in childhood.

She had no control over Lenardo's absence. She had no control over Pyrrhus' burnt-out nerves.

But if she could not restore Pyrrhus' Reading, perhaps she could do *something* for the ex-Reader and his loyal Wicket. "We're in this together," Wicket had said. What was "this"?

If they had a purpose, Aradia would try to help them achieve it.

If, as so many people did, they had come to Zendi seeking work, a better life, possibly she could hire them. She smiled. Tomorrow she would have to find out what, exactly, the two men could do.

On that positive note, she fell asleep.

And dreamed.

It began as a pleasant dream, one that was becoming familiar now. She saw her baby floating in the womb, as before not an infant but a fully formed young woman. Again the girl spoke serenely without opening her eyes, the same words: "After I am born, I will give you what I owe you."

Aradia felt warm love for her child, and watched as the girl's eyes began to open.

But as they did so, Aradia suddenly felt a sense of recognition. She knew this woman, but from long, long ago.

A childhood memory.

It was . . . her mother!

Fully open now, the eyes glowed with fury. The face was no longer the serene, doll-like face of Aradia's daughter, but the mad face of her mother, screaming as she had screamed the last time Aradia ever saw her.

"You're not my child! You're evil! You stole my powers!"

The face twisted, and the woman suddenly held an upraised dagger, grasping Aradia by the throat with the other hand as she howled, "You stole my powers, witch! But you can't control them yet—and I will have them back! Die, you sorceress! Die!"

Chapter Four

Julia did not sleep well that night. She had restless dreams, but could remember only one, and that only in snatches. She was in a strange country, lost in a tangled woodland where unfamiliar animals snorted and howled.

Somewhere nearby, her father was held captive, but she could not find him. Every time she tried to Read in the direction she was certain he had been taken, her head would fill with pain, and—

—she couldn't Read!

Julia sat up in bed, sweating and shaking.

She had been carefully taught not to Read in her sleep, and that stricture held her powers inactive just long enough for icy panic to seize her gut as she realized she was awake and not Reading.

Then the cobwebs cleared, her powers returned, and in relief she Read outward from her room to the early-morning streets of Zendi, where a steady rain was falling.

It was cooler than yesterday morning, autumn asserting itself. Julia pulled a long-sleeved dress from her chest. She had grown since the last time she had worn it; it fell well above her ankles when she wrapped a belt around her waist and bloused the top. But then, she had also grown a bosom since it had last been cool in Zendi—well, at least the beginning of a female figure—so it was not unflattering to let the dress hang unbloused, the belt knotted loosely.

Quickly, she braided her hair and wound it neatly at the back of her head, observing without her usual pleasure that the damp air curled the wisps about her face, so that she looked good even when Dilys and Blanche appeared bedraggled.

Julia's mind was not on vanity this morning, with the single exception of annoyance that the hem of her white dress would get dirty in the wet streets. Once she achieved the rank of Magister, her dress would be edged in black, no longer subject to every hint of grime.

Or if she had Adept power, she could keep her dress spotless, the way Aradia did—but today she could not even maintain that train of thought. She was still feeling sick at the notion of the powers she did have being taken away.

It was earlier than she usually got up, but in Lenardo and Aradia's household there was always someone in the kitchen, always food ready. Today hot porridge was cooking, and baskets of fruit and wheels of cheese lined the center of the long table.

The household staff had already eaten breakfast. Julia sat down, and Cook served her a bowl of porridge worthy of an Adept. "You didn't eat much supper last night, lass. That'll warm you up," she said, pouring milk over the cereal. "You want some fruit cut up on it?"

"No, thank you, Cook," Julia replied. "I don't think I can eat all of this. Could I please have some tea?"

"Of course, lass," said the motherly woman who had run Lenardo's kitchen since he had first come to Zendi. When she set the steaming mug in front of Julia, she paused to feel the girl's forehead, asking, "Still not feeling up to the mark this morning, young mistress?"

Julia couldn't help but smile at Cook's assuming she could discover the state of Julia's health by touching her brow, when the girl's environment swarmed with Readers capable of studying her down to her individual cells.

But she understood that the woman was truly concerned, so she reassured her, "I am not ill, Cook. There are just . . . things on my mind."

She sipped her tea, knowing Cook was bound to ask what those things were—anything that prevented her charges from appreciating her cooking was something she felt impelled to investigate.

Julia was saved from trying to explain by the appearance of Aradia. "My Lady!" Cook exclaimed. "Why are you up so early? You need rest, for the health of the babe you carry."

Aradia shook her head. "The baby is fine, and so am I. There are simply things I must do today. Julia, I will need your help."

Aradia did not ask why Julia was up before her; she obviously knew what was preying on both their minds. "I'll warrant Master Clement didn't sleep much either," Julia commented, drawing a wan smile from Aradia.

Aradia looked pregnant this morning. It was not just that her figure had reached the stage at which even loose, flowing robes could not conceal her condition. Today she was paler than usual, and lack of sleep had put circles under her eyes and given a puffy look to her face.

"Julia," Aradia began, "I can see that you are also disturbed by what we learned yesterday—what Portia did to Pyrrhus."

"Yes," Julia replied. "It gave me nightmares," she admitted.

"I don't wonder," Aradia agreed. "I had some, too. But it does Pyrrhus no good for us to suffer bad dreams. And I am certain he would not welcome our pity."

"That's why he never told Wicket," Julia realized.

"Or anyone else, until he decided to use his condition as a weapon to hurt Master Clement."

Julia nodded. "That was mean. But I can see why Pyrrhus blames Master Clement, too—if he can't Read, how can he know that Master Clement really didn't know what Portia was doing?"

Aradia nodded. "We have established that we cannot restore Pyrrhus' Reading," she said. "It does no one any good to feel guilty—especially you and I, who had no hand in what happened to him."

"Guilty?" Julia asked. Then she realized, "Yes. We feel guilty for being able to Read when Pyrrhus can't—and that doesn't make sense, does it?"

"No. It just allows us to sit here and do nothing."

"But what *can* we do?" Julia asked.

"I need your help to find out. Pyrrhus must have skills—he has survived for the past five years. Wicket said Pyrrhus saved his life, and that they had some plan in mind—something they are doing together. I would like you to find Wicket this morning. I think he will talk to you more readily than to me. Find out their plan—perhaps we can help them achieve it. Find out their skills. Perhaps we can offer them work."

Julia considered telling Aradia what she had Read from Wicket at the award ceremony. His plan with Pyrrhus might have included picking pockets in the crowded marketplace. But since she had no proof of dishonest intentions, she decided not to reveal her own breach of a Reader's courtesy, if not the Code itself.

"Pyrrhus should not awaken until late this afternoon," Aradia continued. "I have the feeling that his first inclination will be to put on his clothes and his sword and leave Zendi as fast as he possibily can."

Wicket obviously suspected the same, for Julia found him at the hospital, still at Pyrrhus' bedside. The ex-Reader was the only patient left in the four-bed ward.

"Did you stay here all night?" Julia asked Wicket.

"Didn't have anyplace else to go, did I?"

It was obvious he had slept even less than she and Aradia, for his eyes were red and ringed with deep circles. He also needed a shave.

"If Pyrrhus wakes and finds you looking like that," said Julia, "he *will* leave without you."

Wicket's eyes widened. "You're not supposed to—"

"I didn't Read you," she assured him. "It's obvious Pyrrhus doesn't want pity, but the minute he sees you he'll know you cried for him all night."

"Couldn't help it," said Wicket. "I mean, I knew he'd been hurt—you don't get a spiky shell like his unless life's been pretty bad to you. But I never guessed—" He blinked back new tears, then looked over at Pyrrhus. "Can he hear us? I mean—can you tell when he's going to wake up?"

"Aradia says not until late this afternoon. It's safe for you to leave him, Wicket. He's not going to run away."

The man stood. "Yeah. Need a bath and a shave. Besides, he can't leave without me."

"Why not?" Julia asked.

"Got all our money, haven't I?" Wicket replied with a hint of his earlier cheerfulness. It increased, as if he were donning armor piece by piece, until he was as she had seen him yesterday: charming, friendly, forgettable. "You're right," he admitted. "I can't let Pyrrhus see how I really feel."

"Let's go out into the courtyard," said Julia. "The rain's stopped. If you'll tell me something about Pyrrhus and yourself, maybe we can help you."

"Dunno how," Wicket said skeptically, but he followed her out to the hospital courtyard, where they sat on a stone bench that had already dried in the morning sun.

It was turning into a pleasant day. Recalling that she had promised to go with Galerio to the horse market that afternoon, Julia was glad the weather had cleared. Or perhaps the weather controllers had cleared it.

She considered what to ask Wicket, and decided on the least suspicious of her questions: "What kind of work do you do?"

"Odd jobs, mostly. Farm work, you know."

Julia reached over and turned his right hand palm up. It was an agile hand, not soft, but certainly not the calloused hand of a workman. "Wicket, there's never any use lying to a Reader, even if to preserve your privacy she is not Reading your thoughts." She took his hand between both of hers, finding small calluses on several fingers and a place on the palm that he would use to apply pressure to the end of some tool, perhaps an awl.

"You work with your hands," she told him, "with tools or instruments. Harnessmaker, maybe, or jeweler. Weaponsmaker, possibly."

Wicket's bright brown eyes widened. "How old are you?" he asked.

"Thirteen."

"How could you know all that, with so little experience of life?"

"Wicket . . . didn't you know it at thirteen?"

"Well, yeah—but I didn't grow up in an Academy, did I?"

"Neither did I," Julia told him.

"Oh, right," he said. "You're a savage. You'd've grown up hiding the fact that you could Read—or you wouldn't've grown up at all." He shrugged. "I'm a locksmith. Lost me trade when all the Adepts flooded into the Aventine lands—a lock's not much use, is it, when there's all these folk around can open it with one twist of their minds."

"And what have you been doing since?" Julia asked, quelling the suspicion that Wicket had picked far more locks than he had ever installed.

"Bit o' this, bit o' that. Pyrrhus and I do mostly bodyguarding."

"Bodyguarding?" she asked increduously.

"You haven't seen Pyrrhus in action," Wicket explained. "Best swordsman I've ever seen, and he can shoot an arrow, throw a knife, a spear—a rock, if that's all that's handy—and never miss. An' I guess I just come along as part of the package," he added with a shrug.

Julia guessed that Wicket had other talents he wasn't mentioning. "How did you two meet?" she asked.

"He saved my life."

"How?" Julia asked when she realized he intended to stop there.

He peered at her again, those guileless brown eyes suddenly shrewd. "How come you get to ask all the questions?"

"What do you want to know?" Julia replied.

"Did you know Portia?"

"Yes, I knew her—and yes, she is really dead. There can be no mistake about it. I was in the rapport that killed her, too, Wicket—and my Reading powers were unimpaired."

"I want to know about her anyway," said Wicket. "Will you tell me, if I tell you about Pyrrhus and me?"

"I'll tell you what I know," Julia agreed. "But first tell me how Pyrrhus came to save your life."

"It was after the fall of the Empire," said Wicket. "As I said, I'd pretty much lost me trade, so I took whatever work I could get. There was this rich lady, a senator's widow, who wanted a cask of jewels transported to her country villa. She thought it'd be safer than in the city. I took on the task."

"A senator's widow trusted you with her jewels?"

"Why not?" Wicket asked with a look of insulted innocence. "I'd worked for her husband, installed the locks in their homes. I warned her, with all the Adepts spillin' down into Tiberium, those locks weren't safe anymore."

"I see," said Julia. *You frightened her into letting you take her jewels.* "But why hire you instead of armed guards?"

Wicket might not be a Reader, but Julia was sure he knew she was interpreting what he said through her experiences as a child in the streets of Zendi.

"A coupla minor Adepts could take out armed guards, and what were they armed for if they weren't carryin' somethin' valuable? So it was safer for one person, lookin' not worth robbin', t'smuggle the jewels over the roads.

"Only an hour outside the city gates, I was set upon by brigands," Wicket continued. "Dunno how they guessed I was carryin' a treasure—'nless one of 'em was a Reader. Disguised as city guardsmen, they were, chargin' me with theft. They took and tied me to a tree, and broke open the casket. And then they started torturin' me."

"Torturing you?" Julia asked. "Why?"

" 'Cause when they smashed it open, the casket had just a layer of gold an' jewels across the top, y'see. The rest was filled with rocks. The minute I saw that, I realized the lady was testing me, as it were—an' after all, I couldn't blame her, now could I?"

"Oh, no," Julia agreed, "you couldn't blame her."

"But the thieves insisted I'd stolen the rest of the jewels and hid 'em, and they were gonna make me tell 'em where. I kept askin' 'em to take me back to the city to ask the lady 'erself— that's how I knew they weren't really city guards.

"Finally," Wicket continued, "the head torturer took 'is dagger, and threatened to put my eyes out if I didn't tell. But I *couldn't* tell, because I hadn't stolen any jewels. He didn't believe me—but I believed him."

Wicket was sweating at the memory. "I thought his ugly face was the last thing I'd ever see. But then all of a sudden he fell—with an arrow stickin' out of his back!"

"Pyrrhus," said Julia.

"Pyrrhus," Wicket agreed with a nod. Then, a look of shocked awareness crossed his face. "By the gods, now I know why he saved me. It was that they were going to put my eyes out."

Wicket covered his face with his hands for a moment, then drew a shuddering breath and let them fall again, gathering control. "Afore they could run, four more arrows took the rest of 'em, and then Pyrrhus came out of the forest.

"Y'understand, I still didn't know if I was gonna be killed. It was only one man, but he'd taken out five. He pocketed the jewels that *were* there, and then came over to me. You've seen how cold his eyes can be. I thought sure I was in for more torture—but he just asked me, 'Will you go back to the lady with me, and the surviving treasure? Or were you lying?'

"I told him I wasn't lying. We went back to the lady, told her what had happened—and almost got arrested.

"Turned out her maid had—uh, tried to protect her, she claimed. 'Twas Pyrrhus figured that out, too—saved me again, from prison or worse.

"The lady apologized all over the place for accusing me, gave me a reward for my trouble, gave Pyrrhus a reward for saving my life and the jewels I *had* been carrying, and then she hired the two of us to take the treasure to her estate."

"And you did it?"

Again the look of offended innocence. "Of course we did! D'you think we'd rob a widow?"

No—widows and orphans were considered out of bounds by the thieves and cheats I grew up among, too, Julia conceded. But what she said aloud was, "You and Pyrrhus have been together ever since."

"Yes."

"And you never found out anything about his background?"

"He was never very communicative on the subject." Wicket sighed. "Obviously he was used to schedules and discipline, and he talks educated. I figured younger son of a wealthy family, sent into the military. I always assumed he was a deserter from the army—lot of those, you know, after the Battle of the Bog."

"Battle of the—?" Julia giggled. "Oh, it *was* funny," she said, "when we created that quicksand to trap the Aventine army."

"Yeah, but not to them," said Wicket. "You defeat people in battle, outnumber them, outfight them—what's left will hang together, ready to fight again to the last breath. But you make fools of 'em, you get a whole army vowing vengeance. But there's no more unity, 'cause they don't trust officers that let them be made fools of."

"And Pyrrhus is obviously a man who will not be taken for a fool," Julia observed. "Your reasoning was sound; there was no way to guess he had been a Reader."

"Had been." Wicket shook his head. "No—won't think about that. It's your turn. Tell me about Portia."

"She was Master of Masters among Readers for many years," Julia said. "Master Clement says that for a long time she did her job well and honestly, but in the last years of her life she became corrupt. Perhaps we'll never know why—we're still finding out *what* she did."

"What she did to Pyrrhus," said Wicket. "Did she do that to any other Readers who found out about her?"

"Not that I've ever heard of—and I think I would have, Wicket. I've been pretty much in the center of everything here in Zendi, and I was in Tiberium when it fell. Portia usually arranged to have her enemies killed, but it didn't always work. She exiled my father to the Savage Lands, figuring he couldn't help revealing himself as a Reader, and he'd get killed."

"Your father?"

"Lenardo—Lord Reader of the Savage Empire. Aradia is his wife."

"But she's not your mother."

"She's getting to feel like my mother a lot of the time," Julia admitted.

"Go on about Portia."

"From her position as Master of Masters, she used Readers to spy on people, influence political decisions, business transactions. At the peak of her power, she had far more influence over what happened in the Aventine Empire than the Emperor.

"You probably know that a few Adepts survived inside the Aventine Empire, even when it was death to be discovered. Portia had at least one under her control, and there may have been more. As she grew older she acquired more and more power. But the Master of Masters isn't supposed to have that kind of power, so she had to cover up even more. That meant getting rid of Readers who found out.

"Her favorite method for putting such Readers where they could not harm her was what she originally planned for Pyrrhus: rig tests so that they failed, and then put them on the Path of the Dark Moon. That meant marrying them off to other failed Readers—but the ceremonial wine was drugged with a derivative of white lotus."

"The dream drug?" Wicket shuddered. "Yes—Pyrrhus said they were going to use it on him. No wonder he ran away. That stuff is worse than poison."

"Yes—but they didn't use the addictive part. It was an extract that destroyed the will and allowed the Readers present at the marriage to mold the minds of the bride and groom. Back when they failed only real Dark Moon Readers, who honestly didn't have the ability to reach the upper ranks, the drug was intended as a kindness, to make them fall in love with one another. But when Portia and the Council of Masters were failing Magisters and even Masters, they also used the drug to reduce their powers."

"Then why—?"

"What was done to Pyrrhus? Even with reduced powers, a Reader is a Reader. Wicket, I'm telling you what facts we know, but all the people who can explain *why* are dead."

"I'm glad Pyrrhus had a hand in killing Portia," said Wicket.

"I'm glad I did, too," Julia agreed.

They parted then, Wicket to the bathhouse, Julia to tell Aradia what she had learned, and then take her daily lesson with Master Clement. She found him in his study, reading scrolls brought from Portia's Academy in Tiberium.

"Read with me, Julia," he instructed. He meant the way he was reading—by Reading.

The scrolls remained in their racks, while Master Clement scanned through the writing on them in search of any reference to Pyrrhus. It was much faster than lifting each one down, unrolling it, and scanning the pages by eye.

But Master Clement had been at it all morning, and had not found what he was looking for.

"Would Portia write down such a terrible thing?" Julia asked.

"Perhaps not," Master Clement agreed. "But I have to search. I have to know—"

—if there are others," Julia completed the thought. "If there are, I doubt that they're alive. I think I would kill myself if it happened to me."

"Julia!" exclaimed the Master of Masters. "You must not think such a thing. Pyrrhus was right to salvage what he could of his life. Child, I have seen Readers lose their powers before."

"What?" She was horrified.

"It is rare, but it can happen from a head injury, a

disease, or an apoplexy, if it damages that area of the brain. Thus Portia knew exactly which nerves she could destroy, and leave Pyrrhus otherwise undamaged. With the help of Adept Healers," he added, "we can now heal such injuries when they come from natural causes. Nature does not burn out an entire section of nervous tissue."

They returned to Portia's many years of records, which had never been placed in proper order after transport to Zendi. After the earthquake that had literally toppled the Aventine Empire, the scrolls had been plucked from the shambles, brought here, and left until the day someone would have the time to catalogue them. So far, no one had. They found records from forty years ago next to records from the last days of Portia's tenure, her personal commentaries on her students beside technical studies of Reading techniques.

Suddenly Master Clement plucked an old, yellowed scroll from the rack and handed it to Julia. "Read that."

She held it, feeling in its faded, dusty contours the keen excitement of a young woman, enthusiastic, idealistic, proud of her accomplishments, and eager to use her newly acquired power for good.

"Portia?" Julia asked incredulously. It was unrecognizable as the evil old woman Julia had known.

"Portia as I first knew her, when I was just testing for the rank of Magister. Take that one with you, Julia; Read it at your leisure. Perhaps we can trace how the fine young woman who became the youngest Master of Masters in all our history turned into a manipulative, power-mad woman capable of crippling Readers to cover her corruption."

When Julia met Galerio and his friends at noon, she did not really have the horse market on her mind. She kept her promise, however, and the group of young people left Zendi by Southgate, walking toward the large open area set aside for fairs and celebrations, and the horse market once each month.

It had turned into a lovely sunny day, the ground just

damp enough to keep the dust down, the air just cool enough to be pleasant. Dilys and Piccolo never got as far as the market; holding hands, they wandered off the road toward a small woodland.

When they reached the market, Giorgio headed straight for the food vendors, while Blanche and Diana went off toward the booths where trinkets were sold to bored wives, daughters, and children with no interest in the horses. That left Mosca and Antonius with Julia and Galerio, drifting through the crowds to examine the horses in the various roped-off areas.

They passed straight by the young colts and heavy draft animals, and went on to where riding horses were being shown.

Galerio gravitated toward a large ring displaying five magnificent animals, sleek and slender, so built for speed that they almost appeared to be running when they were standing still.

Julia also admired them, but when Galerio asked, "What would a horse like that cost?" she was amazed to Read that he truly wanted one.

"Those are racing horses," she said. "Galerio, you can't afford one of those, and if you could it's not the kind of horse you need."

"What makes you an expert on what I need?" he demanded.

"You need a reliable riding horse," Julia replied. "One that can carry you for many miles at a reasonable pace. A horse with enough spirit to be fun to ride, but not too much for an inexperienced rider."

"Inexperienced—!"

"Galerio, you're a city boy. Have you ever been on a horse?" she suddenly asked.

"Of course I have!" he replied indignantly. "If this is the way you're going to help, I'm sorry I brought you along!"

Julia bit back a retort that she didn't need anyone to "bring" her, and had come as a favor to him. "All right," she said. "What would you do with a horse like one of those?"

"Um—race it, I guess. Win money."

"But you'd have to do more than just stable a racehorse. It has to be run every day. And the rider—"

"All right," said Galerio with a sigh, "I can't afford the horse, or a trainer, and I don't have the experience to race it myself. So a horse like that will have to wait till I get rich."

"You'll not get rich associating with friends like these!"

Julia and Galerio turned, Julia automatically Reading. "Wicket! What are you doing at the horse market?"

"I might ask you the same question," said Wicket, who was holding Mosca and Antonius by the arms, one with each hand. Surprisingly, despite squirming and kicking, neither boy seemed able to escape Wicket's grip. "Associating with pickpockets is not what I'd expect from the daughter of the Lord of the Land."

"Mosca! Antonius!" Galerio flashed. "Is it true?"

"No, of course not," Mosca said sullenly, but his light eyes shifted, showing anyone who was watching that he lied.

"But you received money enough yesterday to live well for half a year!" Julia exclaimed. "Why—?"

"Gambling," said Galerio angrily. "I told you Capero's gang would cheat you, didn't I?"

"Yeah, well—gotta pay what I owe them," said Mosca.

"You got into *debt*?" Julia asked. "And you too, Antonius?"

The younger boy mutely hung his head.

"I get it," said Wicket. "The gamblers cheated these kids out of their reward and then gave them a chance to get it back—only they lost twice the sum. Right, boys?"

Mosca refused to reply, but Antonius nodded glumly.

"Fools!" said Galerio. "When are you going to learn not to gamble with Capero and his thugs?"

"I'll have him run out of town," said Julia.

"Oh, good lesson," said Wicket. "Teach these kids that if they have friends in high places they can be as foolish as they please, 'cause you'll bail 'em out!"

Stung, Julia demanded, "Then what would *you* suggest?"

"If you can't teach 'em to be sensible—a lesson I've always had trouble with meself—teach 'em to solve their own problems, not expect someone else to," Wicket told her.

"That's what we *were* doing!" Mosca protested.

"And how long do you think it would have been before a Reader caught you?" Julia asked. "Wicket's *not* a Reader, and he caught you before you'd been at it long enough to— How much *did* you steal?"

"Nothing," Mosca said tartly. "Your friend here grabbed us before we got anything."

Although Mosca was braced for use of his small Adept talent, Julia was sure he was lying.

Wicket confirmed her suspicion by shoving Mosca forward as he let go of him. While the boy was off-balance, Wicket's hand moved so rapidly that Julia did not see how it happened, but Wicket was dangling a small leather money pouch from his outstretched fingers.

Wicket set Antonius on his feet more gently, and held out his hand, palm up. With a shrug, Antonius produced a ruby pendant and a lace-trimmed silk kerchief.

"Give them to me," said Julia. "The auction pavilion has a place where lost articles may be turned in."

"Except for the kerchief," Wicket said, "these are not items usually lost. You would be questioned, Julia. I saw where these came from. Let me just put them back."

"Now who's suggesting that someone else solve the problem?" Julia asked.

"Ah, but it's clear you've already learned that lesson, and who am I to lose a chance to do a favor for the daughter of the Lord of the Land?"

Still in possession of the stolen items, Wicket disappeared into the milling crowd.

"Interesting friends you have, Julia," said Galerio.

"Extremely interesting," Julia agreed, Reading after Wicket. His head was full of that nonsense he used to mask his thoughts from Readers as he slipped through the crowd, brushing against a woman watching her husband bargain for a pair of carriage horses. Wicket tucked the lace kerchief through her sash as he jostled her, murmuring an apology as he stumbled away.

A young, very pretty woman was buying an orange from a vendor when Wicket came up behind her, jogged her elbow, and caused her to drop the coin she was holding out.

"Oh, sorry!" Wicket said, stooping as the girl did, managing to kick the coin aside, stumble in front of her as she reached for it, push her enough off-balance that in her bent-over position she had to fling her arms out to keep from falling over, and at that moment fling the pendant over her shoulder from behind, so it fell right in front of her as if the chain had broken just then instead of when Antonius had pulled it loose.

"My ruby!" the girl gasped. "You fool—you almost made me lose my ruby!" But by the time she gained her feet and turned to vent her anger on Wicket, he was nowhere in sight.

Odd. At the moment Wicket had slipped the pendant over the girl's shoulder, his mental litany of nonsense had halted until he slipped away. Julia paid closer attention as he stalked the man from whom Mosca had filched the pouch of coins.

The still-unwitting victim was a tall man with curly brown hair, dressed to be admired by the women at the horse market. He wore tight britches that showed the hard muscles of his legs, fine polished leather riding boots, a green silk shirt open in front down to where his deep-veed tabard covered it, and a wide leather belt.

At the moment he was pretending to consider a fine chestnut mare parading in one of the rings, but his attention was actually on two women who were bored with horses and having a much better time considering him. Julia was amused to see him turn his handsome profile to them, and then shift his weight so the muscles in his legs rippled—all in a pretense of getting a better look at the horses.

Wicket slipped up behind the man, and Julia turned her attention to Reading the reverse-pickpocket. Wicket noted where his attention lay, came up on the other side of the man from the women, and waited. It wasn't long before the women decided to try to attract the attention of the man they thought had not noticed them. They giggled.

The tall man turned, lazily, as if it were the first time he had realized they were there. When he saw them, he gave an appreciative smile—and while his attention was thus distracted, Wicket slipped his hand over the man's shoulder and dropped the money pouch.

It slid inside his shirt collar, down his bare skin, and lodged inside his shirt, where the belt held the tabard against it—a most unlikely trajectory.

Feeling the movement, the man grasped for the pouch, thinking he was being robbed. Relief flooded his mind as he found his money where he expected it to be.

Julia's mind, however, was flooded with surprise.

For not only had Wicket's litany of mental oddments cut off when he dropped the money pouch—in that moment he had become blank to Julia's deliberate attempt to Read him!

Aradia's morning was filled with her usual duties. Since she had learned to Read, most of her reports came over the Path of the Dark Moon. Huge as the Savage Empire now was, it was possible with Readers to relay a message from one end to the other within half an hour.

In the lands Aradia was responsible for, little was happening except for cleanup of the chaos created by the mysterious whirlwinds, and healing of those who had been injured. Readers and Watchers were spending days and nights trying to trace the source of Adept power necessary to cause such winds, but to no avail.

To add insult to injury, this morning just after sunrise a freak hailstorm had destroyed acres of apples just ripe for picking, in the lands between here and Lilith's. No Reader had noticed the storm coming, and no weather controllers had been on the scene. By the time they reached the orchards, the storm was over, the damage done.

Was the hailstorm a part of a pattern which included the whirlwinds? Or was it an independent freak of nature? Aradia sent a message to Lilith, who had no Reading powers, wishing she could talk to her friend.

The reply came back, relayed by Readers, but although Aradia was pleased to hear that everything was well with Lilith and her son, it was not the same as being together. It was the first time in her life that she did not have another strong Adept at her side in time of trouble: her father, Wulfston, or Lilith had always been there when enemies threatened.

Now her father was dead, and Wulfston was far away.

In a few weeks, Lilith would come to be with Aradia for the final days of her pregnancy and her confinement. Each day Aradia looked forward more to that event. Readers could be good friends—she felt great joy at her deepening rapport with Julia—and they had their own strengths and skills. But Reading skills were not what Aradia had relied on all her life. When the world was pulling mysterious tricks, she longed for the strength of a fellow Lord Adept.

Especially as her own powers waned.

At midmorning Julia came to report what she had found out about Pyrrhus and Wicket. They worked as hired bodyguards, of all things.

Lords Adept didn't need bodyguards. The standing army in the Savage Empire was very small, and neither man, Wicket especially, seemed the type to be happy in the military.

What, then, could she offer them? Posts in her household? Household guards led boring lives most of the time, completely unsuited to either man's quick mind. She didn't really need more retainers, and both would recognize immediately that such an offer came from sympathy, not need.

Had Wicket told Julia the whole truth? Aradia doubted it. She decided to send out an inquiry to Tiberium via the Path of the Dark Moon.

A reply came back before noon: Pyrrhus and Wicket were indeed bodyguards and mercenaries, of excellent repute. They had even hired out several times to the new government of the city, helping to clean out gamblers and drug dealers who continued to prey on their citizens despite all that the combination of Readers and Adepts could do.

Before four years ago, Pyrrhus had been unheard of; he had seemingly appeared out of nowhere. His knowledge of the underworld suggested that he probably had criminal connections (Aradia laughed to herself, and had to break the connection for a moment before she let slip where Pyrrhus had really learned about corruption), but since he had teamed with Wicket there was no indication that he had been anything but scrupulously faithful to contracts he had made.

Wicket had at one time been a petty thief, pickpocket, breaker of locks—not very secure occupations in a city full of Readers. Some years before the fall of Tiberium he had apparently decided to turn his skill at picking locks to designing them, and had developed a modest business that might have expanded into a success, as his locks were impervious to the skills of common thieves.

But, as he had told Julia, the fall of Tiberium had ended his value as a locksmith. He had started hiring out as a protector of valuables, but with little success until he had teamed with Pyrrhus.

If they were doing so well, I wonder why Pyrrhus and Wicket left Tiberium?

But Aradia decided not to question Zendi's good fortune. Although the city was smaller than the Aventine capital, it had its share of criminals, most of whom had enough Adept power to manipulate ordinary citizens.

Unable to root out all of the criminal element even with Adepts and Readers combining their talents, Lenardo and Aradia had discussed putting together a full-time force of minor Adepts and Dark Moon Readers to police the city.

The problem was finding people who understood the criminal mind but could also be trusted. Their attempts using honest citizens had failed abysmally; it required a certain devious way of thinking to outsmart experienced criminals, a mind-set completely foreign to an Academy-trained Reader or the average healer, fire talent, or weather controller.

But now Pyrrhus and Wicket had practically fallen into their laps! From the reports she had received, they would be the perfect nucleus for the police force she envisioned. If she could only persuade them to accept the challenge.

Her morning duties finished, Aradia ate her midday meal and, having lost sleep the previous night, decided to lie down for an hour before going back to the hospital. Were Pyrrhus any ordinary patient, she would expect him to sleep almost until sunset. But he had wakened prematurely yesterday, and she expected that he would fight off sleep again today at the first moment his body was strong enough to do so.

Aradia was in no mood to fight off sleep, however. Content that she had something good to offer Pyrrhus and Wicket, she fell asleep the moment she lay down.

All the time Julia was following Wicket with her Reading, Galerio was scolding Mosca and Antonius. When he finally let up, Mosa said with a scowl, "It's all very well for you to be high and mighty, with Lady Julia as your friend—but Capero's gonna be after Antonius an' me tonight. We don't pay him, he's gonna slit our throats."

"Not if we all stick together," said Galerio. "Capero cheated you—you know that."

"How?" asked Antonius. "We won at first."

"I thought you were smarter than that!" said Galerio. "Of *course* you won at first, so you'd think it was a fair game and you *could* win. Then he started taking your money, and counted on you being stupid enough to think you could win it back. You know what he wants, don't you?"

"Yeah," Mosca said reluctantly. "He wants us to work for him."

"Do you want to?" Galerio asked shrewdly.

"Well . . . he's got money, connections," Mosca admitted. "People that work for him live well."

"Some do," Galerio agreed. "But for how long? Ever notice it's the kids the guards pick up for stealing, or cheating at gambling? You want to spend months in jail?"

"Better'n gettin' killed," Mosca muttered.

"Capero won't kill you if you pay the money you owe," Galerio said.

"But how?" Antonius demanded. "We gotta steal it. There's no other way to get that much by tonight."

"And then Capero will have a hold on you," said Galerio. "Once you steal for him, he'll find other ways to make you do the work, while he takes the money." He sighed. "We have to show Capero that Galerio's people won't fall into his trap."

By this time Wicket had returned the stolen items to their owners, and was on his way back toward the young people. Julia let her full attention return to Galerio, proud of the way he assumed responsibility for Mosca and Antonius because they were his followers.

"But how?" Mosca demanded again.

"By cheating Capero right back," Galerio replied smugly.

"What?" Antonious asked. "How? He's got a Reader at the game, Galerio; she'd know if we were cheating."

Galerio looked at Julia, his dark eyes questioning.

Looking into his handsome face, Julia could deny him nothing. "You can have a Reader on *your* side," she said.

"You?" Antonius' adolescent voice squeaked in astonishment. "But everybody knows you, Julia. You'd be recognized, and then they wouldn't play with us."

"I'll go in disguise," she said, charmed with the idea of an adventure to break up the routine of her life. "And don't worry—I can fool any Dark Moon Reader."

"What's this now?" asked Wicket's voice—and Julia realized the man had sneaked up on her a second time. "Who're you playing, and why do you need a Reader?"

Silence fell.

"Mm-hmm," said Wicket. He turned to Galerio. "I know you want to help your friends, but this Capero sounds like a real mean 'un. Even if he can't figure out how you're cheatin', he'll know you have to be if you win, right?"

"Right," Galerio was forced to agree.

"And then what will happen?" Wicket asked.

Galerio grimaced. "He'll want revenge—and there are only eight of us, when he probably has thirty people in his operation and another hundred who owe him favors. So what do I do about Mosca and Antonius? I can give them my share of money, but that's only half what they need—and I can't ask the others to give up their reward money because these two got themselves cheated."

"No, no," said Wicket. "You can't give in. Capero would snatch you up and make you worse'n his slave. No, what you gotta do is cheat him without him ever knowin' you've cheated him."

"Huh? How?" asked Galerio.

"You go with Mosca and Antonius to Capero tonight. Tell him you want to dice with him for the money they owe."

"I'm not that stupid, and Capero knows it," said Galerio.

"You underestimate the professional gambler," said Wicket. "Capero assumes everyone can be tempted. Trust me, he won't question your motives, and you, Galerio, are too fine a bait for Capero to resist. But just to make sure he bites—Lady Julia, will you help Galerio bait the trap?"

"I've already said I'd go," she replied.

"Not in disguise—or at least Capero must know who you are. That way he can't cry foul, because you can bet that he knows your face, Julia, and that his Reader constantly checks strangers to make sure no one's sneaking in a Reader of 'is own. Galerio, you make it a condition: you will provide your own Reader to make sure the game remains honest."

Julia frowned. "In an honest game Galerio might

win, true, but everything is reduced to chance. What if he loses?"

"He won't lose. *I'm* going to lose," said Wicket.

"You?" asked Galerio.

"I'm a rich merchant from Tiberium, likely to drop twenty times what these boys owe Capero."

"I don't understand," said Julia.

"Galerio, you have to make Capero agree that you'll play *tomorrow* night, to give me time to connect."

"I can say I need a day to get my stake together," said Galerio.

"You young men," Wicket continued, "tell me where in Zendi to let it be known that I'd like to do some gaming tomorrow evening. Then leave it to me to get into the game."

"But what good will it do for you to lose the award money Aradia gave you?" asked Julia.

"Were you planning to help these young men?"

"Yes."

"Then help by staking me to seed money. You'll get it back. Capero's to think I'm in Zendi because I've made a big deal, and I'll get paid day after tomorrow. He'll want me to win the first night, figuring to take it all back and much more the next. Now, the law would be on to this Capero if he had his Adepts obviously influencing the games, right?"

"Right?" said Julia. "Readers haven't been able to catch them at it."

"Well," said Wicket, "I can manipulate dice with my hands as well as one of your minor Adepts with his mind—and I've got the easy part. First I let them let me win, just as they plan. But just when they want to sink the hook by letting me win really big, I start to lose. To Galerio."

Julia studied Wicket. *He really doesn't know how he does it.*

Galerio was grinning. "I like it."

"Then," Wicket continued, "I start to complain that they've set me up. Lots of noise, threats to call the guards—and a nice fight to break up the game and get us all out of there, winnings intact."

"He'll connect you with us," said Galerio.

"How? I arrived in town two days ago. Any of Capero's people here?"

Although as they talked the minor Adepts braced their powers and Julia carefully kept from broadcasting what they were saying to other Readers, she was Reading Wicket, who had his usual camouflage running through his mind. Nonetheless, she could catch his feelings—and what she did not catch was any hint that he was either lying or trying to deceive them.

"There's just one thing," Wicket warned. "Don't get greedy. We're there to break Capero's hold on Mosca and Antonius, not to make any of us rich."

"I like your plan," said Galerio, "but why should you help us?"

Wicket grinned. "You're friends of the Lady Julia. Always good to have connections in high places."

"Wicket," said Julia, "there's something you ought—"

Screams erupted!

Human shouting was drowned by the snorts of frightened horses.

"Fire!" someone cried nearby.

Julia saw smoke coming from the other side of the market—the biggest pavilion was on fire!

Galerio, Mosca, Antonius—every Adept in the marketplace turned toward the blaze, uniting their efforts to put it out.

But it didn't go out!

Fanned by a sudden brisk wind, the fire engulfed the main pavilion. Julia's mind was assaulted by the fear of fleeing people, the terror of the horses.

Flames flashed upward, leaped from one pavilion to another, but no people were burned, although some were pushed or stepped on in the panic.

There was only one way fire could spread when dozens of minor Adepts were concentrating their efforts to stop it: one or more Lords Adept were deliberately feeding the blaze!

Julia Read, finding no one anywhere nearby who could possibly be the culprit.

Still the flames leaped from one tent to another, while the horses screamed in panic, pulling loose from their tethers.

Stallions, mares, geldings, racers and plowhorses, colts and fillies—all fled the flames, stampeding toward Julia, Wicket, Galerio. Mosca and Antonius took to their heels.

"Run!" Wicket shouted, following his own order.

But even with Adept strength, no human could outrun a horse!

The animals were mindlessly driven by fire. Inexorably, they bore down on the five fleeing people.

Heart pounding, Julia heard and Read the lead horses bearing down on her, felt the ground shaken by their hoofs.

The horses' panic filled her mind, mingling with her own.

In moments, they would all be trampled to death!

Chapter Five

Aradia was deep in the dream of her unborn daughter. The girl opened her eyes.

"You stole my powers, witch!" Aradia's mother accused. "Die, sorceress. Burn!"

Aradia was consumed in flames!

Searing pain! Her clothes burned, her hair—

Her flesh charred as she screamed—

Screamed—

"Lady Aradia! Wake up, my lady!"

"Help me!" Aradia begged, grasping at the person who had come to her aid. "She's burning me! My child is trying to kill me!"

Slowly, she realized that she was clinging to Devasin, seeing fright in the woman's eyes.

Gasping for breath, Aradia shook off the dream and loosened her painful grip on Devasin. "I'm sorry," she whispered. "It seemed so real."

"It was only a dream, my lady," Devasin soothed. "Lie back down now, and rest."

"Oh, no," said Aradia. "I have too much to do. Bring me my dress, Devasin."

"Yes, my lady," the other woman said primly, rising from where she had sat on the edge of the bed to comfort her mistress.

"Devasin," Aradia said.

"Yes, my lady?"

"I am sorry to inflict the foolish fantasies of pregnancy on you."

"It is quite all right, my lady," Devasin replied. "I'm glad I was there to help."

By the time she had dressed and smoothed her hair, Aradia could relegate the dream to the world of fantasy. But why had it seemed so real? Perhaps Master Clement would know a way to forestall it, let it remain the pleasant dream of her child, or at least let her wake up before it turned to nightmare. Determined to tell him about it, she left for the hospital, to see if Pyrrhus was awake yet.

Julia could not run as fast as the boys or even Wicket.

Her breath burned in her lungs. Her legs ached.

The horses' panic tore through her mind. Dust choked her lungs.

Galerio dropped back, gasping, "Run!" He grabbed her hand. She felt him trying to pour strength into her, but he hadn't enough power.

For a few steps they went faster, nearly catching Mosca, Antonius, Wicket—but in moments the horses would run over them all.

Clutching Galerio's hand, Julia was able to think again.

If only Wulfston were here!

He could make animals obey his will; he would calm those horses, or at least turn them aside.

Other Readers had found their Adept powers in moments of desperation—her father had, in order to save his people and Aradia.

Desperately she reached out to the lead horse, urged him to one side as the herd reached the fleeing people.

Galerio pushed her to the ground, flung himself on top of her, protecting her with his own body.

But Julia had it now! She sent images to the horses, directing their course.

The herd split, thundering on either side of the trembling, gasping people. Wicket fell, huddled into a ball. Mosca and Antonius leaned on one another, breathless, as the horses galloped by.

And Julia sobbed against Galerio's arm beneath her face as she realized.

"It's not an Adept trick!" she gasped as, the horses safely past, Galerio drew her to sit up against him. "Oh, Galerio—it's *Reading*, and he never knew it! He wanted so much to learn to Read, and now maybe he'll never know!"

Mosca and Antonius moved slowly, but Wicket jumped up and ran to where Julia and Galerio still sat on the ground. "Are you all right?" he asked anxiously.

Julia nodded.

"Then why are you crying? Who'll never know about Reading?"

"Wulfston," she replied. "My uncle. He—he went to rescue my father, weeks ago, and we haven't heard from them since." Julia got hold of herself, her tears abating as she continued, "Wulfston is a great Lord Adept, but he's always wanted to learn to Read, ever since we found out they're the same power. He never could—and yet he's always had this power over animals."

"Ah," said Galerio, "*you* made the horses go around us."

She looked up into his eyes, her lips trembling into a smile as she asked, "Are *you* Reading now?"

"No—but how else would you make such a discovery in the middle of a stampede? Thank you, Julia."

"Thanks, indeed!" Wicket added, squatting down beside them. "Now, what's all this about your uncle going to rescue your father? From what?"

"Nobody knows!" Julia replied. "People from Africa kidnapped my father—and Aradia couldn't go because she's pregnant, so Wulfston went, and now they're both gone!"

Galerio, who knew the story well, said, "They'll come back. After all they've been through together, how much trouble could a few Africans be? A Reader and an Adept working together—why, they'll be here any day now, with wonderful stories to tell."

But Wicket was puzzled. "Brothers? One a Reader and the other an Adept?"

"No—Wulfston is Aradia's brother," Julia told him. "But we don't worry whether kinship is by blood or marriage or adoption. We're family."

"Mm-hmm," said Wicket. "Well, then—you say your uncle can Read, but doesn't know it? That hardly seems likely."

Julia couldn't help laughing, although painfully. "No? Then why are you not aware of your own Adept powers?"

Wicket was squatting beside them, balanced precariously on his toes, but at Julia's words he paled, lost his balance, and sat down, hard. "What?"

"I Read you restoring the items Mosca and Antonius stole. You think you're just a skilled cutpurse, but you're using Adept power when you make something land exactly where you want it. The pendant, and the man's money pouch. You blanked to my Reading when you did those things."

Wicket put up a casually denying hand. "Oh—that's just a trick Pyrrhus taught me, to fool Readers." He winced. "Never thought to ask him how he knew what'd fool 'em. But it's just a bunch of nonsense to distract attention."

"No, Wicket, I don't mean your songs and rhymes and riddles," Julia told him. "I mean the moment when you want that necklace to fall exactly in the girl's line of vision. Then the nonsense stops. To a Reader, you become invisible. A Dark Moon Reader would miss it, unless he were focused specifically on you, and until four years ago few Readers in the Aventine Empire would've known what that moment's blankness meant."

Wicket was staring at his hands. "No. I can't."

"You can and you do," Julia assured him. "We'll test your talents now, and teach you to use them most effectively."

Wicket's eyes fixed on hers, wariness in their depths. "No!" he said. "Lady Julia, you must be wrong—but even if you're right, it doesn't matter. I'm not an Adept!"

"Wicket," said Galerio, "don't act as if it's something bad. You're not in the old Aventine Empire—nobody will kill you for it. You don't have to go to their training sessions and get lectured about using your talents for the public good. But—"

"I said *no*!" Wicket interrupted him. "You shut up about it, all of you. It's not so! And if any of you says anything to Pyrrhus—well, you can just forget me helping you get out of your problems with Capero!"

With that, Wicket got up, made a futile attempt to brush the dust from his clothes, and started toward the road back to Zendi.

The four young people stared after him. "Never saw anyone act like *that* when he found out he had a talent," said Antonius.

"I think I understand," said Julia, aware of people from the horse market running to see if they were hurt. She climbed to her feet saying, "Let him go. And do as he says. Don't tell anyone, not even your closest friends."

At the hospital, Aradia was not surprised to find Pyrrhus awake, although she had not expected him to be up and dressed. The door was open, and she could see him standing by the bed, his attention on items laid out on it.

The plate on the bedside table was empty except for apple cores and the skeleton of a bunch of grapes. Pyrrhus wore the same clothes in which he had been injured, which Aradia had paid no attention to at the time. Now she noticed that although his accent, short hair, and beardlessness showed his Aventine origins, Pyrrhus chose to dress in the savage style.

Wicket had called his friend "skinny." Actually he was thin and wiry, and his dark gray clothing did nothing to make him appear larger. It was plain in cut, linen and wool of the highest quality, with fine black leather boots suited for riding but looking soft and comfortable enough for walking.

His tabard was wool, its only decoration a single line of discreet silver embroidery across the top.

Wondering if Pyrrhus should be on his feet, Aradia started to Read his physical condition as she neared the doorway—and Pyrrhus snatched his sword from the scabbard on the bed, whirled, and faced her with weapon at ready!

Aradia's throat constricted at the idea of a Reader at the mercy of his physical senses; how painful it must be to have someone sneak up on him. She had not meant to; with her advancing pregnancy she was simply most comfortable in soft slippers that made no sound on the marble floors.

When he saw who it was, Pyrrhus saluted her with the weapon. "Lady Aradia. Come to see that I do not escape?"

"Not without a proper meal," she replied, sending a mental call to the hospital kitchen. "Actually, I did not expect to find you awake."

"Obviously neither did Wicket," he said, replacing his sword in its scabbard. "Or has he gone?"

"Gone?"

"He does have all our money," said Pyrrhus.

"Don't you trust him?" Aradia asked.

"More than I ought to, I expect." Leaving the sword on the bed, Pyrrhus put on a black leather belt with a square silver buckle and plain silver decoration along its length. Aradia noted that he had to buckle it two notches tighter than where the worn place in the leather indicated it was usually fastened.

"You need a few good meals under that belt," said Aradia.

"Why should you be concerned about my health?" he challenged. "I'm a stranger to you."

"The child you saved was a stranger to *you*," she countered.

Instead of answering, he turned and began plucking items off the bed and stowing them about his person.

Aradia sat down in a chair, bemused, to watch a dagger disappear into his left boot, a larger knife that she suspected was weighted for throwing into his right. What appeared to be a plain white linen kerchief did not move with normal lightness; it was obviously weighted with lead. Pyrrhus folded it to look quite ordinary, and tucked it into his tabard.

He put on leather bracelets, the kind gladiators wore to protect and support the vulnerable wristbones, but when he bent his hands forward as far as they would go, sharp blades sprang from them, across the backs of his hands. With a tight-lipped smile of satisfaction, he touched hidden catches, and the blades slid out of sight again.

But that was not all. Aradia's amusement grew as she wondered whether the razor he tucked into his tabard, where there must be hidden pockets, was the same one he used on his face, or whether this one was merely another weapon. The man was a walking arsenal!

Several bodkins, of varying sizes, also went inside the tabard, along with braided leather thongs, a sling, a burning glass, a lodestone, and some objects whose purpose Aradia could not guess. Finally, Pyrrhus clipped another dagger, quite visibly, to his belt. All that was left on the bed was a bow, a quiver of arrows, and his sword.

For all the paraphernalia, no bulges showed in his outfit, nor did Pyrrhus move as if weighted down. He looked over at Aradia, tilting his head to one side as if waiting for her to comment, and sat down on the bed.

She grinned at him. "Just what army do you expect to face single-handed?"

"Yours, possibly," he retorted.

The attendant arrived with Pyrrhus' meal. He glanced at Aradia, but accepted the tray and began to eat. She noticed that, like Lenardo, despite his hunger he ate little meat.

Readers kept to a vegetarian diet, saying meat dulled their powers. Aradia often argued with Lenardo, insisting that he could improve his Adept powers if only he would eat more meat. He would counter that if she ate less, she would be a better Reader.

But no diet would enable Pyrrhus to Read again. Probably, like most people, he simply preferred foods he had grown up on. Aradia took the opportunity while Pyrrhus was eating to study him without enduring that piercing gaze.

Now that his burns had healed, his coloring was back to normal. Aradia noted that his eyes seemed darker than they actually were because his skin was very fair. Even sun-darkened, it was lighter than Lenardo's olive tones, and the brown of his hair was in the medium range, not the dark brown to black more usual among Aventines. His eyelashes were long and thick, but lighter than his hair, the contrast with the brown eyes increasing the impression that they were mysteriously dark and deep.

Pyrrhus finished eating, set the tray on the bedside table, and took the wool of his tabard between thumb and forefinger. "How did you get the oil out of my clothing without ruining it?"

"Adept talents are useful for many purposes," she replied.

He pondered that, then shrugged. "Why not? But you are not here to discuss laundry. Perhaps you haven't noticed: I still can't Read."

"I beg your pardon?" she asked at the abrupt turn of subject.

"Isn't it a little late for that?"

"What do you mean?"

"Come now," he said coldly, his eyes pinning her, "you won't claim you resisted poking around in my head while you had me at your mercy?"

"No, I won't," she said flatly, and saw a flicker of surprise on his face. "We will *not* lie to you, Pyrrhus."

"Perhaps. But you won't respect my privacy, either."

"It was not a breach of healer's ethics," she said. "But then you must know that—it is the same for Readers as for Adepts. You were my patient. If, in treating your burns, I had discovered some other problem, such as a tumorous growth, you would have expected me to remove it. Didn't you learn the same thing when you studied at Gaeta?"

Gaeta was the huge hospital where all Readers of the upper ranks in the Aventine Empire were once sent to learn the rough medical techniques which were all they could practice without Adept powers. Herbs and potions, bonesetting by force, amputating limbs as had been done to Decius, actually cutting into people's bodies.

But even with those primitive methods they had healed many people. And now that Readers and Adepts were working together, there was almost no condition that could not be cured at Gaeta.

Except Pyrrhus' condition.

The man's composure slipped enough to allow a brief puzzled frown. "I did not know that *you* had studied there."

"I didn't, but my husband did," she replied. "He is a Master Reader."

"Oh, yes—Lenardo the Traitor."

"So Portia and her cohorts called him," Aradia struck back.

She hit her target. "Very well," said Pyrrhus. "Tell me what you found inside my head."

There was no way to put it gently. "We cannot restore your Reading powers. Nervous tissue has been destroyed, something even a Lord Adept cannot heal."

He did not blink, although she knew that she must have crushed the last hope, however denied, buried in his heart. "Thank you for telling me the truth," he said finally.

"You do believe me?" she felt compelled to ask.

"Oh, yes," he replied, cynicism returning to his tone. "If you lied to me, Master Clement would contradict you. That is his greatest weakness: he is a completely honest man." He frowned again. "Physical damage? Done by Readers?"

"Portia had an Adept working with her."

At his suddenly feral expression she quickly added, "We know who he was, and he is dead."

"That," said Pyrrhus, "is unfortunate. Although it is fortunate for him."

Aradia was about to try to turn the discussion to similar criminals in Zendi when Master Clement arrived. "Aradia, Julia is unharmed," he began.

"Unharmed? What harm threatened her?" Aradia demanded, getting to her feet.

"No—there is no need for you to go," the Reader told her. "There are Readers and Adepts on the scene."

"*What* scene?" Aradia exclaimed in frustration.

"Julia was at the horse market."

"Yes. She had my permission." Aradia had decided that allowing Julia time with Galerio and his gang might lessen the appeal of something forbidden.

"A fire stampeded the horses," said Master Clement. "No one was killed, and all injuries were minor. Julia and her friends are helping to round up the horses." He allowed Aradia to Read the scene with him, to see that, indeed, all was under control.

But— "Fire? Stampede? Master Clement, is this another—?"

When the old Reader did not immediately answer, Pyrrhus asked, "Another what?" When he didn't get a reply, he suggested, "Another unexpected event like a whirlwind in the middle of a city on a perfectly calm day?"

That got their attention. "What do you know about it?" Aradia asked.

He shrugged. "It sounds like the Adept harassment we got when I was a boy at the Academy. Adigia was on the border, and sometimes the savages would try to drive people out of the area by sending storms to ruin crops, or starting fires to destroy villages."

Master Clement nodded. "These events appear similar. There were other whirlwinds at the same time as the one in Zendi. Yesterday a hailstorm destroyed some crops. Today the horse market was disrupted. Thus far, our Readers have been unable to trace the source."

"I'm afraid I won't be able to help you," Pyrrhus said with his well-practiced insincere smile.

Master Clement looked at Aradia. "You told him?"

"He asked."

"Yes, of course he would." He turned to the man on the bed. "Pyrrhus, it is best you know the truth. However, you should know the whole truth."

Pyrrhus was lounging in a deliberately casual pose, his legs stretched out and crossed at the ankles. If

Sistena saw his boots on her clean bedding, Aradia thought, she'd tongue-lash him out of such casualness.

But, head tilted curiously, Pyrrhus was asking, "What more is there to know? The nerves are burnt out. I will never be able to Read again."

"You have not lost all your powers."

"Oh, yes," Pyrrhus replied acidly, "I can still *send* thoughts with a Reader's power. I did so in the rapport that killed Portia. I suppose you could use me as a transmitter of messages to other Readers—but what good does that do *me*?!"

Master Clement gestured toward the weapons on the bed at Pyrrhus' feet. "Readers make the best swordsmen," he said. "Wicket says you are the best swordsman he's ever seen."

"Wicket is a fool," sneered Pyrrhus.

"You are still alive," Master Clement countered. "Pyrrhus. . . ."

At the tone of the old man's voice, Pyrrhus relented. "You're right," he said. "When I realized that I could not Read at all, I was afraid I could no longer fight—that I wouldn't survive to take revenge. But the first time I had to use my sword I was caught by surprise, and reacted instinctively. When it was over, I realized I had lost none of that skill."

Master Clement nodded. "That is consistent with what we found. Portia destroyed the nerve center for analyzing and interpretation what you Read. You *are* still Reading, Pyrrhus—but what you Read no longer reaches your conscious mind."

Pyrrhus shrugged. "It's all the same to me."

"No, it's not" said Master Clement. "You don't think and analyze when you're fighting. What you Read goes straight into action."

"What's that?" came Wicket's voice from the doorway. "There's actually something Pyrrhus doesn't analyze to death?" As he stepped forward, all of them stared, for Wicket was covered with dirt and grime.

At their looks, he gave a sheepish grin. "I was afraid

Pyrrhus might be awake already, so I hurried on over here. An' I was right, wasn't I?" he added brightly.

"Where've you been?" Pyrrhus demanded impatiently.

"The horse market. There was a fire, and then—"

"Oh, that," Pyrrhus said in bored tones. "We've heard all about it already." He gave one of his arctic smiles. "Isn't it convenient to have friends who are Readers?" Having effectively stopped the conversation, Pyrrhus savored the moment's silence before asking Wicket, "What were you doing at the horse market?"

"Thought we might need horses, didn't I? Thought you might want to leave."

"*Did* you?" Pyrrhus began dangerously, but Master Clement stepped in before he could continue.

"Pyrrhus, don't leave without discovering the extent of your remaining powers. Let us treat you at the Academy."

"My Academy days are long over, Clement," Pyrrhus replied.

"Then come and stay at my villa," said Aradia. "Both of you are welcome, and there is certainly plenty of room." In fact, more than half the rooms were empty, and would remain so until Lilith arrived with her entourage.

Wicket was watching Pyrrhus closely, and jumped in before Pyrrhus could refuse. "The royal residence! Think of it, Pyrrhus. When are we ever gonna live in the lap of luxury?"

Pyrrhus glanced at Wicket with tolerant amusement. "You didn't buy any horses?"

"Nah—they closed down the market on me."

"You realize you'll have to take a bath before you can set foot in Lady Aradia's home?" Pyrrhus teased him.

"What—two baths in the same day?" Wicket replied as if the thought pained him.

"That's the condition for sitting in the lap of luxury," Pyrrhus explained.

Because Wicket looked genuinely torn by the decision, Aradia laughed, and waved her hand toward him. The gesture was theatrical effect, of course—Adept power pulled the grime out of his clothes and off his skin and hair, leaving him cleaner than when he had left the baths earlier, since he was still wearing yesterday's clothes.

Wicket stared down at his sparkling clothing, and delicately stepped out of the circle of dirt that had fallen at his feet. Then he grinned at Pyrrhus. "Isn't it convenient," he asked conversationally, "to have friends who are Adepts?"

When Julia got home, she found she didn't have to Read for Wicket: Aradia had invited him and Pyrrhus to stay at the villa.

It was all she could do to get through the evening meal, worrying about Galerio. He had to face Capero with Mosca and Antonius tonight if their scheme was to work. If he didn't convince the gambler that it was worth his while to try to snare Galerio, all three young men would have their throats slit.

After dinner, Julia sat in the luxurious parlor, trying to follow the conversation between Aradia, Master Clement, Pyrrhus, and Wicket. Ordinarily, she would have been fascinated. Tonight she was only worried.

Finally, though, a servant brought her a message, scribbled in Galerio's almost indecipherable hand: "Tomorrow, one hour after sunset."

She saw Wicket notice, but his attention went immediately back to the conversation.

Aradia also noticed. "Julia, you are not going out tonight."

"No, Aradia, I had no intention to," she replied.

Aradia did not ask what the message was.

That trust made Julia want to tell Aradia. But she knew better. Her stepmother would feel compelled to stop it, but if she stopped Capero from harming Mosca and Antonius now, he would find another way to take revenge.

And Galerio would never forgive Julia if she brought Aradia into it.

No, it was best for Aradia never to find out at all.

When Julia got up to go to bed at her usual time, Wicket said, "I'm tired. I think I'll get some sleep, too. Good night, everyone."

Pyrrhus eyed his friend. "I've done nothing *but* sleep for the past two days. Will you leave me to the tender mercies of these two?" he asked, indicating Aradia and Master Clement.

"Aww, I don't think they're gonna cook you up for breakfast," Wicket replied. "Maybe *after* breakfast, though," he added, referring to Pyrrhus' reluctant agreement to let Master Clement test him in the morning. "But *I* gotta put up with you afterward. Better get my rest, Pyrrhus."

As Julia suspected, Wicket wanted to talk with her. He and Pyrrhus had been given rooms on the other side of the courtyard from the family suite. "Where is it safe to talk?" he asked. "Or is there anyplace? The old man—"

"You mean Master Clement? Wicket, he would not spy on us! And we're not being watched. Entryways, the treasury—those are guarded at all times by both Adepts and Readers. But don't fear being Read inside the villa, especially not in any private rooms."

"That's a relief!" he replied.

"You grew up in the Aventine Empire—you must know that the Reader's Oath protects the privacy of nonReaders."

"Never had much to do with Readers, did I?" he replied. "Least never knew I did."

Julia took him to her room, where she gave him her small supply of money. "That won't be enough to make you look like a rich merchant," she said.

"I'll claim I've been spending in anticipation of a large sum. This will do. But there's another problem: I need proper clothes for the part."

He was right. His plain tan shirt and hose and multicolored tabard were nothing like what a wealthy Aventine merchant would wear.

Fortunately, Aventine styles were loose, not like the

savage clothing that had to be fitted to the person wearing it to look right.

Julia said, "Aradia is still in the parlor, and Master Clement hasn't left yet. We have time. Come on."

"What happened to your Reader's Oath?" asked Wicket.

"All I did was check that they're still in a public room," said Julia. "Come *on*—and be quiet. Devasin will be in the anteroom leading to the corridor."

She took Wicket out the low-silled window into the courtyard, and into Lenardo and Aradia's room, where her father's clothes were kept ready in his chest. His red Master Reader's cloak lay on top, with several white, black-edged tunics beneath it. Once those were lifted out, though, there was a mixture of Aventine and savage-style clothing, all in the finest materials, much of it sumptuously embroidered.

Julia pulled out a yellow tunic with gold embroidery, a belt of gold velvet strands with bits of gold glittering in it, and a cloak of the same dark gold color as the belt.

Wicket nodded, but reached for another cloak, shiny green satin with gold embroidery on the edges. Julia shook her head; that cloak went over a plain green tunic, and even so Lenardo thought it too gaudy. Over the yellow tunic. . . .

But Wicket was nodding vigorously, so Julia shrugged, and carefully repacked everything else into the chest.

When they were back in her room, Julia protested, "There's too much glitter with both the tunic and cloak, and the different colors—"

"—are exactly what a man would wear who's got rich by his own wits," Wicket explained, holding the tunic up in front of him. "Hmm. Yer father's a tall 'un, isn't he?"

"Yes, he is. You'll have to belt it up, and let the cloak fall in long loops. Oh—what about shoes?"

"I've got some sandals with me. I'll shine 'em up tonight. Thanks, Julia. These will do just fine." He went to the door, opened it a crack, and peered out cautiously.

"Wicket," said Julia, "there is no one in the passageway."

He turned, flashed her a grin, and was gone.

A little after midnight, Julia was awakened by terrified screams from the next room.

Throwing on her robe, she dashed into the hall, Reading nothing to cause Aradia to scream so.

In fact, she could not remember ever hearing Aradia scream, could imagine only one thing that might bring on such a reaction: Lenardo's death.

Heart pounding, Julia tore through the anteroom. The door to Aradia's room was open, and Devasin knelt on the edge of Aradia's bed, trying to touch the sleeping woman's forehead to waken her. Aradia was tossing in agony.

"Wake up, my lady!" Devasin pleaded. "It's only a dream!"

"She's killing me!" Aradia shouted. "Help me! Lenardo, help me!"

Devasin grasped Aradia's shoulders, and Julia pressed her fingers firmly to Aradia's forehead, the only safe way to waken an Adept. The violet eyes opened, glazed. "She's killing me!" Aradia sobbed. "My baby is trying to kill me!"

Julia drew back in horror, but Devasin took Aradia into her arms like a mother comforting a child. " 'Twas only a dream, my lady. Your baby is well." She glanced over Aradia's shoulder at Julia, who took the cue to Read the fetus. Everything was normal; the child in Aradia's womb slept peacefully despite her mother's nightmare.

"The baby is fine, Aradia," Julia said.

"She's stealing my powers!" Aradia said.

"No, they're just weakened by pregnancy," Julia assured her, trying to hide her distress at seeing the strong, steady Aradia reduced to quivering terror. With Lenardo and Wulfston gone, who would protect Zendi?

But she joined her efforts to Devasin's, then encouraged Aradia to Read the baby with her, to see it developing normally and sleeping peacefully. Finally, between them, Julia and Devasin got Aradia calmed and back to sleep.

When they left Aradia's room, Julia asked Devasin, "Has this happened before?"

"Just once," Devasin replied. But Julia Read worry in Devasin that went beyond concern over a few nightmares.

"There's more to it than that," said Julia. "Tell me."

"I don't know if. . . ."

"Would you tell my father?"

"He already knows."

"But he isn't here, Devasin. So I have to help Aradia for him. If I don't have all the facts, how can I help her?"

"Oh, young mistress, I don't know if anyone can help her! It's happening all over again, just as it did with her mother—and nothing Nerius could do would save her!"

Nerius, Aradia's father. And the mother who was never mentioned.

"Tell me," said Julia.

"I was a child," said Devasin. "My mother was Tarina's maid."

"Tarina?"

"Aradia's mother. Afterward, Nerius would not allow her name to be spoken. He loved her very much—as your father loves Aradia. They risked their powers to have a child. Nerius recovered, but Tarina had a difficult pregnancy even with his help. As her powers waned, she became more and more demanding, more angry at the child.

"But then Aradia was born, such a beautiful little girl. Everyone thought Tarina would recover, and love the child.

"Only . . . Tarina's Adept powers did not return. Months passed, and she became more and more distraught. She imagined that Aradia showed Adept talent. A baby less than a year old! Tarina started saying Aradia had stolen her powers.

"Nerius tried to help Tarina, but she became more and more hysterical. My mother stayed with her constantly, because Tarina would fly into rages and threaten to . . . take back the powers Aradia had stolen, was the way she put it.

"Finally, Nerius would not allow Tarina to see Aradia unless he was there. And when Aradia was two, she really did start to show Adept powers."

"At two years old!"

"Yes. Nerius was delighted—but it set Tarina off worse than ever. I remember her rage, and my mother trying to calm her. Aradia was walking by then, but a closed door kept her in her nursery because she could not reach the latch. Then one day, when she had been left napping, she found that she could unlatch the door with Adept power, and went exploring . . . into Tarina's room. I was there, with my mother and Tarina. Mother was teaching me embroidery. The door opened.

"Tarina's chair faced the door. When she saw the child, she snatched up a heavy candlestick to set the girl on fire. The flame blew out, though, so she tried to crush Aradia's skull with the base.

"My mother grasped her arm to stop her—and Tarina hit my mother instead.

"I screamed. Tarina picked up the bloody candlestick and went for Aradia again, shouting that she would kill her and take her powers back.

"By this time Aradia was screaming and crying. I don't know how Mother remained conscious, but when I tried to help her, she said, 'Save the baby!' and I turned to try.

"Tarina lifted the candlestick to crush Aradia. When I tried to pick up the child, Tarina hit my shoulder, knocking me aside, and was about to swing at Aradia when the candle lit again. That was Aradia.

"Tarina screamed, swung—and the candlestick exploded in her hand.

"That was Nerius, running to see what all the noise was.

"Tarina shouted. 'You want her! You don't want me!' and ran out of the room.

"Nerius picked up Aradia, made sure she was all right, then came over and healed Mother. Then he healed my shoulder. And all that time, no one thought of Tarina. None of us will ever know whether Nerius knew what she was doing. She ran to the end of the hall, took a knife from the display, and plunged it into her heart. Tarina died by her own hand."

A tear trickled down Devasin's cheek. "And now Aradia dreams she is like her mother. May they be only dreams! She never says such things when she is awake. But the dreams frighten me, Julia—almost as much as they frighten Aradia."

The next day, Aradia seemed normal. Julia was back to her lessons, with Aradia and Decius in the morning, Master Clement in the afternoon. In the days between lessons, Decius had been practicing harmless Adept tricks, and had learned to move small objects. "The only trouble is," he explained with a laugh, "moving a stylus from one side of my writing table to the other sent me to sleep for an hour. It's much simpler just to pick it up by hand!"

"You'll learn not to expend extra energy," said Aradia. "That is excellent progress, Decius."

Knowing that she must go out tonight, at a time Aradia would not approve, Julia was on her best behavior. She tried to duplicate Decius' tricks, to no avail. However, she did not allow frustration to upset her today, although she was glad when Aradia took Decius off to the hospital to start teaching him to heal.

Wicket appeared at the noonday meal, and murmured to Julia, "Contact made. All set."

Pyrrhus raised an eyebrow to see his friend sharing a secret with Julia, but for once made no snide comment. He looked exhausted, and Julia wondered fleetingly what Master Clement had put him through.

Then it was Julia's problem to hide her excitement over the evening's plans from Master Clement when she joined him in the Academy library.

It was not difficult to hide her thoughts, however, when the Master of Masters said, "I have found the records we've been looking for," and held out a scroll to her. This one was new, still supple, but Julia Read without unrolling it. And without touching it. She did not want to feel the essence of Portia in those last days of power-madness. What the woman had written was poisonous enough.

The technique used on Pyrrhus was an experiment—one Portia deemed highly successful. The only reason it was not repeated was that the Adept she had used left Tiberium. If he had returned, or if she had been able to find another who could do the job, Portia would have crippled others.

When she had Read it, Julia asked, "Do you think Pyrrhus will feel any better knowing he is the only Reader they did that to?"

Master Clement replied, "I don't know. Possibly there are some acts that cannot be forgiven. I never believed that, but now I wonder. How could Pyrrhus possibly forgive Portia? Could I, if she had done that to me? But if Pyrrhus cannot forgive, he cannot heal."

There are some acts that cannot be forgiven. Julia understood why Aradia's father might have allowed his wife to die after she tried to kill their daughter.

Should she tell Master Clement about Aradia's dreams? No, she should urge Aradia to tell him. It was what Aradia would urge on Julia were their situations reversed.

Master Clement was piling scrolls on the desk. "Julia, take these home with you, and read them in the order in which they were written. Seeing how Portia changed over the years may help you understand her, as it has helped me."

Julia only nodded and gathered up the scrolls. Her thoughts were on how to get away to join Galerio an hour after sunset.

As it turned out, Aradia and Pyrrhus had an appointment with Master Clement after the evening meal. Julia could not help wondering whether Master Clement wanted Aradia there to discuss what purpose Pyrrhus might serve in the Savage Empire, or if he wanted an Adept for protection. Julia found Pyrrhus' habit of constantly shielding his thoughts eerie, and wondered if it also disturbed the Master of Masters.

She spent some time with the early scrolls her teacher had picked out of Portia's collection, Reading Portia's growing frustration at how little influence Readers had on Aventine politics. The Emperor at that time was Portia's brother, and it galled her that the very fact that she was family caused him to give her advice little credence.

Julia was far in the past when a sharp "Psst!" broke her concentration with a start. Wicket was at her window, dressed in the clothes she had borrowed for him. It was dark, "Aren't you ready?" he whispered.

"Yes," she replied, lighting a candle. She had changed into a cheap but gaudy orange dress belonging to one of the maids. Now she threw her plain blue mantle over it, and she and Wicket went out by the servants' entrance. There would undoubtedly be gossip tomorrow that Marilys had been Read slipping out with Wicket. Julia hoped that her skills were sufficient to make Torus, who guarded the door, accept the surface impression of Marilys.

Once outside, Julia went straight ahead to meet Galerio, Reading to make sure there were no spies on Wicket. He took one of the circular streets to the east, then turned and approached Capero's house as if coming from one of the elegant inns in that area.

Capero knew who Julia was, but the rest of the gamers were not supposed to. The gaming room was crowded, but the lighting was concentrated over the tables, leaving the players in subdued light. Gambling was legal; some people simply did not want to be identified—especially those responsible for other people's money. Julia was unsurprised to Read no Readers there other than Capero's Reader and herself. If his patrons found out Julia was there, they would never trust him again, and his business was built on their trust. Julia swallowed as she realized how important it must be to him to get Galerio into his power.

Capero was a minor Adept, of course, as Julia had to search for him visually. She was open to Reading, but not concentrating, lest Capero's Reader spot her. She wasn't sure if the woman knew that she was a Reader, or who she was.

Galerio put his arm around Julia as they threaded through the crowded room, Mosca and Antonius in their wake. They had agreed with Wicket to play the coin toss first, while he gambled at cards. All would then move on to the dice table. It would appear they were in the same game by chance.

Capero was a tall, balding man with a thick brown beard liberally sprinkled with white. He was dressed in understated elegance in brown velvet with satin embroidery that glowed softly, an occasional gold thread glinting here and there. The effect, though, was spoiled by his hands, where every finger carried at least one ring, solid gold or silver with huge, gaudy stones.

The owner moved through his establishment, quietly greeting patrons, occasionally glancing toward his Reader, a faded blond woman who sat at the back of the room. She was a Dark Moon Reader, ostensibly in the employ of the city, supposedly there to see that there was no cheating by either the house or the customers. Galerio said the house paid her far better than the city, though, so she quietly ignored subtle techniques that gave the house a higher percentage than allowed by law, at least as long as the extra percentage did not get so high that customers began to complain.

Capero watched Galerio play two tosses, both of which he won. "Good," said the big man. "But why play a boy's game? The stakes are too low here to make it worth your bother."

Julia stopped Reading for a moment to shed uneasiness. Wicket wasn't even here yet.

"I like this game," Galerio replied casually. "It takes a certain degree of skill. You didn't specify that I had to play any certain game, only that I had to win. I don't care if that takes all night."

Capero laughed cheerfully. "Be careful you don't die of boredom!" he warned.

Wicket came in, went to the card table without making any effort to locate Julia or Galerio—a real pro. He appeared just slightly inebriated, and cheerfully accepted a flagon of ale as he settled into the game. The barmaid whispered to the dealer as she passed, "That's the one. Let him win tonight."

They continued with their plan as Capero played into their hands. By the standards of this establishment, the sums Mosca and Antonius owed were small. Within an hour, Wicket had won almost half that much at the card table, while Galerio won more than he lost at the coin toss. Still, it was obvious he could not win enough at that game even if he did play all night, so he picked up his money and moved to the dice table.

Wicket remained where he was. It would be too obvious for him to move at the same time Galerio did. Besides, they had to give Capero time to cheat Galerio's stake and winnings away from him.

But as soon as the dice came around to Galerio for the first time, he threw a winning number. Julia was Reading; he had not used Adept power. Neither did Capero nor any of his men for the moment, letting chance have its way—perhaps until Galerio accepted the honesty of the game.

The surest way to fool a Reader was to have a number of minor Adepts about, posing as gamers, taking turns influencing the dice. It would be almost impossible for a Dark Moon Reader to detect, but Julia could Read the whole room at once. Perhaps Capero thought she was too young to do so.

Galerio threw another winning number before he lost control of the dice, then bet a small portion of his winnings on other players. Again, he won more than he lost, although his winnings did not pile up as Wicket's were doing.

Julia was beginning to worry about the time; the later she stayed away, the greater the chance that she would be missed. Capero should be making Galerio lose by now, but he wasn't losing, and Julia could detect no sign of Adept influence—no one going suddenly blank to Reading—anywhere in the room. She started to Read more carefully—

"Reader! Spy!"

The Dark Moon Reader leaped up. She climbed up on her chair, pointing over the heads of the gamblers, shrieking like a harpy. "Look! Lenardo's daughter! They've sent her in to spy on all of you, find out who's gambling, who's winning! Who's here, who's with them!"

Suddenly all eyes were on Julia. Some people gathered their money and began edging toward the doors.

"She's already Read you!" Capero shouted.

"If she escapes," said another man, whom Julia recognized as Tinius, money-changer and userer, "Aradia and Clement will know all that she learned here tonight."

"No!" Julia shouted, climbing on a chair herself despite Galerio's efforts to stop her. "I am not here as a spy, but just as a Reader protecting a friend. Capero agreed—"

Capero drowned her words with a loud guffaw. "Is that likely?" he demanded. "Allow the like of her to spy on my good customers?"

There were, of course, no other Readers there. A woman shouted, "Kill her! Show Aradia what we think of her spying on us!" Julia recognized Octavia, who ran the largest brothel in Zendi. Tinius, Octavia—as well as all the rich merchants crowded in here tonight? Galerio had been set up all right—but to get at Julia! To discredit the Readers, who had disrupted their cheating and confidence games ever since Lenardo and Aradia had brought hundreds of them to the city.

Until this moment, Julia hadn't been afraid. Now, alone, she faced dozens of people who hated her—some of them with Adept powers! //Help!// she sent out to any nearby Reader. //Capero's establishment! They want to kill me!//

Galerio kicked over the dice table, Mosca and Antonius adding their efforts.

Julia jumped down from her perch, Reading that the three young men would clear a path for her to the door, Reading Wicket draw a knife, pretending to join the attackers but actually elbowing and tripping people trying to close off their escape route.

Galerio, Mosca, and Antonius also had knives drawn, but they faced swords, clubs.

Knives flickered through the air!

Mosca went down with a yelp as a knife lodged in his shoulder, then a horrifying gasp when a man ran his sword through him.

Antonius tackled a woman in their way, knocked her against a man trying to skewer Julia with his sword, and fell, head crushed by another man's club.

Galerio plunged ahead, using his small Adept skill to stay the hands of those who would slash or strike. They could see Wicket now, bumbling about as if very drunk and very angry, actually clearing a space near the door.

Still broadcasting her call for help, Julia followed in Galerio's wake, Reading behind them.

Capero held a spear!

"Galerio!" Julia shouted, grasping his arm to pull him down as the weapon flew at them.

He came around instead of down—and the spear dipped in its flight, Capero's Adept power keeping it aimed at Julia! It was about to impale her.

Galerio flung himself at the spear, trying to grasp it out of the air.

Julia Read his utter exhaustion. The last of his small Adept power was not enough.

The spear pierced his heart, and he fell across her, dead.

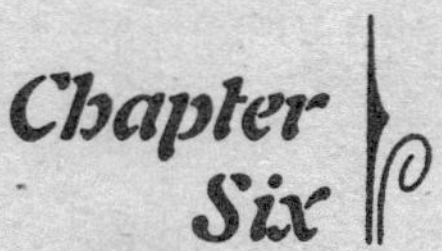

Chapter Six

Julia cowered on the floor, soaked in Galerio's blood, too terrified and grief-stricken to do anything but Read.

Antonius and Mosca were dead.

Galerio was dead.

Wicket was trying to reach her, pretending to be a patron wanting to kill her.

Capero pulled Galerio's body away and hauled Julia to her feet. "You're not hurt—yet." He had to hold her up, for shock had taken all the strength from her limbs. Her mind seemed to have gone numb.

Capero turned to his patrons. "What shall we do with this one? Let's make her an example—let Lenardo and Aradia know what we do to people who try to control us!"

//Julia! Get down!//

The powerful voice in her mind broke through her numbness; she squirmed free of Capero's grip and dropped to the floor—

As an arrow pierced the gambler's heart!

Heads turned.

Some of Capero's men started toward the door, where a shadowy figure fired three more arrows in rapid succession before people began to close on him. He dropped bow and quiver, kicked his closest assailant in the groin, slung a knife into the throat of a man poised to gut him with a spear, and moved through the gap he had thus created.

Pyrrhus.

The conflict between frightened people trying to get

out of his way and angry people trying to get at him created a passage that he walked through, unscathed.

When he reached Wicket, his friend took a position at Pyrrhus' back, knife at the ready.

They worked their way toward Julia amid a breathless hush.

Octavia pulled a long, wicked blade from her sleeve. Julia fought her lethargy, remembering neither man could Read, but was drawing breath to warn them when the woman moved.

Wicket met her descending arm with an upward blow so hard the whole room heard the crack of breaking bone. He caught the knife that fell from her limp fingers as she fainted from the pain. Now he had a knife in either hand, and no patron was foolish enough to challenge.

Capero's men, however, moved in—seven of them forming a phalanx against Julia's two rescuers.

As they moved to separate Julia from Pyrrhus and Wicket, weapons flew again. A bull-like man heaved a spear with both physical strength and Adept power, enough to pierce both men—except that they turned sideways and bent away, and it sailed harmlessly between them.

When they swung back, they were side by side.

Almost faster than Julia could Read, Wicket's knives were buried to the hilt in two of their opponents, while Pyrrhus flung two knives as well, grasped a spear convulsively thrown his way by one of their death throes, and drove it through a third.

Two on two now, Wicket and Pyrrhus glanced at one another, crouched, and let their assailants spring. Both were armed with knives, and both were dead by their own weapons in scant seconds.

Pyrrhus did not look at the men he had killed, but he studied Wicket's victims one by one. Every weapon had pierced a vital organ; all were dead. "Congratulations," said Pyrrhus dryly. "You've finally learned to fight."

Julia Read Wicket's start of conscience, but all he said was "Had a good teacher, didn't I?"

The two men stepped over the bodies, and while Wicket knelt to examine Julia, Pyrrhus asked the staring people left alive, "Anyone else care to challenge our right to take this child home?" He smiled in that bone-chilling way that Julia suddenly understood, and everyone backed up a step.

Recognizing that they did not want to be caught here, people started for the door—too late.

Readers and Adepts were entering at both the front door and the back, city guards, healers, watchers.

Only then did Julia realize that barely minutes had passed since she had sent out her call for help. The response had come as fast as humanly possible—but if Pyrrhus and Wicket had not been on the scene already, she would have been dead.

As dead as Galerio.

Aradia never found the right opening that evening to tell Master Clement about her strange dreams. Hours later, last night's terror seemed foolish, nothing but a pregnant woman's overreaction.

She was just saying goodnight to the Master Reader when Julia's call for help came. Master Clement allowed her to Read it through him, then broadcast it to all the Readers in Zendi with his own great mental power.

At the same time, he grasped Aradia's arm, holding her from dashing out into the night. "It's too far!" he exclaimed, continuing to Read for her the scene unfolding in Capero's gambling establishment.

"No!" Aradia gasped, trying to kill Capero where he stood.

Once, it would have taken no effort to stop the man's heart at that distance.

Tonight, she might as well have no Adept powers at all.

She returned to Reading, clinging to Master Clement

lest he leave her to her own weak ability. Terror rose as they Read Julia, helpless.

Readers and Adepts left what they were doing to run to her aid, but they could not reach Julia, nor could the minor Adepts come within range to use their limited powers, before Capero or his patrons killed her.

Then came the sudden eruption of Pyrrhus onto the scene, and a virtual massacre as Wicket turned out to be already there, and the two destroyed Capero and every one of his henchmen brave enough to challenge them.

By the time the rescuers arrived, there was no need for rescue.

The two efficient killers gently eased Julia out of the establishment, away from the corpses of her friends. //Let them bring her home,// Master Clement instructed the healer who wanted to examine Julia. //She's not harmed physically. She needs to get away from that place.//

He broke contact, focusing now on Aradia. "Come," he said, leading her back into the parlor. "Julia is unharmed, just badly frightened. Let her fear teach her, Aradia."

"What?" said Aradia, letting him guide her to a couch where she sat down and put her feet up.

"I had thought the girl had outgrown taking foolish risks. What was she doing there? Did you know?"

"No! I didn't know she was out of the house. What were my guards doing? And where was her sense, to go to such a place? She is in my care. Lenardo will never forgive me!"

"Be calm," said Master Clement. "We'll find out what happened. But I don't think Julia will be ready to talk about it until tomorrow. Thank the gods for Pyrrhus and Wicket!"

"*That's* why Pyrrhus left us earlier!" said Aradia. "Do you think he knew what Julia was up to?"

"I doubt it. I think he suspected Wicket was heading for trouble—and the only way he could find out where he went was to follow him."

Aradia nodded at the grim reminder of their other problem: Pyrrhus. She had never known anyone who would not succumb to Master Clement's gentle strength before. If he could not persuade Pyrrhus to stay and learn to use what powers he had left, she didn't understand why the Master Reader thought *she* could.

Unless he had suspected. . . .

Aradia's servant barely managed to get into the parlor before Pyrrhus and Wicket, who did not give him time to announce them. By this time Pyrrhus was carrying Julia. Oblivious to the bloodstains, he laid her down on a couch and turned to Aradia and Master Clement. "You Read—?"

"Yes," said Aradia. "Thank you—both of you."

She Read anxiously along with Master Clement. Julia was pale, sweating, trembling. She was conscious, staring up at the ceiling, but Aradia doubted she knew where she was. "I must put her into healing sleep for the night," she said. "*That* much I can do," she added grimly, remembering her earlier helplessness.

"Your powers will return," said Pyrrhus, "after your child is born."

She realized only after guilt had stabbed her that for the first time he had spoken without bitterness.

When Julia was safely sleeping, Aradia called servants to put her to bed. The minor Adepts on her staff would clean away the bloodstains without waking her, and in the morning Aradia would deal with this new problem.

"She seemed so reliable!" she said to Master Clement. "I worried about Galerio's influence, but I never dreamed Julia could get into this kind of trouble. Gambling! What was she doing—helping her friends cheat?"

"Uh, Lady Aradia," Wicket said hesitantly. "Capero had cheated Julia's friends, and she was trying to help Galerio set it straight."

"What?!" demanded Pyrrhus. "You didn't just follow Julia—you knew what she was doing? Wicket, were you part of their scheme?" His sharpness was back, as if the one slip into humanity had never happened.

Wicket cringed slightly. "Well, they were green kids, and Capero was playing the old sucker game on 'em, t'force 'em to work for him. I was just tryin' to help 'em out." His bright brown eyes went to Aradia, begging for understanding, but all she understood at that moment was that he had almost gotten Julia killed—and that he was wearing a tunic she recognized as Lenardo's. Thief as well as fool! "Had no idea it was a trap for Julia. How could I?" he pleaded.

It took all Aradia's self-control not to strike out at the man.

Master Clement said, "I think you had better tell us the whole story—the truth, if you please. A Master Reader *can* Read through the nonsense you're shielding with, but it's late and we're all tired. Let's not make it a contest of wills."

Wicket's shield of Adept power went up, and Master Clement glanced at Aradia, who nodded.

Pyrrhus ordered coldly, "Do as he says, Wicket. I already know what a fool you are. Tell us your latest folly."

Wicket slumped onto one of the couches, all defenses down. Through Master Clement, Aradia Read that he told the unvarnished truth about catching the boys stealing at the horse market, and becoming involved in the plot to trick Capero. When he told how Julia had turned the horses, his shields went up again, but when they dropped as he skipped to this evening, neither she nor Master Clement said anything.

"And only then did any of us know it wasn't Galerio he wanted, but Julia," Wicket finished up. He sat, head in his hands, a picture of abject misery in the blood-spattered yellow tunic. "I only meant to help those kids. And now three of 'em are dead!"

"Aradia," said Master Clement, "much as I disapprove of Julia's attempts to right a wrong with another wrong, what chance would you have given this plan's success had you heard of it this morning?"

"I would have put a stop to it!" Aradia said.

"That is not what I asked. Given Julia's skills, and Wicket's, would you have expected them to succeed?"

"This morning? Yes. This morning I had no idea such hatred toward or Readers and Adepts existed in Zendi. I would have expected even citizens patronizing establishments like Capero's to defend Julia—or at least not attack her! I would never have thought Capero would try such a scheme. How can such resentment exist without our knowing about it?"

"I do not think," Master Clement said softly, "that it does exist."

"Then what happened? Why did all those people turn on Julia?"

"Did you notice their feelings afterward?" the Master Reader pursued. "The prevailing emotion among Capero's patrons was . . . bewilderment."

"You mean someone used them?" Pyrrhus asked. "They were *caused* to feel anger and hatred? Clement, you're talking about a breach of the Reader's Code so vile—"

"Unthinkable," the old man agreed. "But then, we all know that even Readers are capable of doing the unthinkable."

"Were," corrected Pyrrhus. "Or," sudden feral hope, "Portia's cohorts?"

"All dead," said Master Clement. "And Lenardo and I have restructured the Council of Masters so that there can never be an inner circle like Portia's again. It is no longer possible to hide from the majority of Masters what the central few are doing—and the central few change yearly."

"Then who could have done such a thing? It would take several Master Readers to control as large a group of people as that. How could they not be Read?"

"The same way whatever Adepts are causing whirlwinds and hailstorms are not being Read," said Aradia. "They have to be Readers, too—or have Readers working with them. And our best Readers can find no trace of their existence!"

"They are misusing their powers," Master Clement said, frustration clear in his voice. "We *know* that weakens them! And even Lenardo cannot project thoughts or feelings at just one person; such thoughts would be Read by any Reader nearby."

"There would have to be a number of Readers working together, to control so many people at once," added Aradia. "I cannot believe our Readers would not detect them."

Master Clement nodded grimly. "We are dealing with something that is theoretically impossible."

"No," said Pyrrhus. "We are dealing with somebody crafty enough to make it *look* impossible—someone who wants to terrify you."

"Well, he's certainly doing a good job!" observed Wicket.

Pyrrhus gave an icy smile. "*I* could do it" he said.

"Eh?" Wicket asked.

"'I *didn't* do it," he added, "but I know how it was done." This time the smile was smugly self-satisfied.

"Well," said Wicket, "are you waiting for applause, or are you going to tell us?"

"Please tell us," Aradia added.

"It would take at least a Magister Reader, although we're probably dealing with a Master," said Pyrrhus. "A single person could do it, using one of the techniques taught at Gaeta. Implanting a command, with something to key a later action."

"Of course!" said Master Clement, relief clear in his voice. But he did not spoil Pyrrhus' explanation.

Seeing that neither Aradia nor Wicket understood, Pyrrhus continued; "Sometimes a person with mental illness is violent, toward others or himself. It may take months or years for Readers to cure him—and in the meantime the person would have to be locked up to protect himself or others, were it not for implanted commands. Usually it is simply 'Whenever you hear a key word, stop what you are doing and become completely calm.' And then some uncommon word is given as the key, and the person can return to his family between treatments. If he becomes violent or self-destructive, anyone can stop him by shouting the key word."

"Ingenious," said Aradia. "By the way, a Lord Adept can also implant commands in people's minds; we are not necessarily dealing with a Reader. But either way, we could not Read anyone driving that roomful of people, because nobody was driving them at the time they became violent."

She nodded, working it out. "I see how it was done. Ahead of time, each one had the command implanted to go to Capero's this evening, and try to kill Julia when she was revealed as a Reader. The ones who were confused and afraid," she added, "were people who just happened to go to Capero's tonight, not part of the plan—but they were outnumbered."

"It's not quite that simple," said Master Clement. "An implanted command that goes strongly against a person's feelings and beliefs doesn't work very well. Sometimes not at all. Sometimes it sends the person into shock because what he believes opposes the command he must obey."

"Ah, but the people at Capero's tonight were gamblers, brothel owners, merchants who resent Readers keeping their measurements and accounts honest," said Aradia.

She smiled at Pyrrhus. "That's twice in one evening you have served me well—first rescuing Julia, and now assuring us that we are not dealing with some supernatural force. I will reward you with gold, of course—in fact, I would like to reward you with a house, if you will stay in Zendi and work for me."

"Work for you?"

"First, help me find this renegade Reader or Adept who is attacking our people. It may be someone with both powers, but if so he will have one strongly, one only weakly."

"Why is that?" Pyrrhus asked.

"The two powers are the same," said Master Clement, "and yet they are in conflict. Usually a person becomes proficient in the talent which manifests earlier, and develops the other weakly or not at all. Using Adept powers depletes the body, which reduces Reading ability. That is why, at my age, I see no reason to attempt to waken my Adept powers."

Pyrrhus' lip curled into a sneer as he asked, "You really think you have Adept powers?"

"Oh, there is no doubt of the potential," the Master Reader replied. "Except for the most minor talents, anyone who has one power has both. Aradia has just succeeded in awakening Adept powers in Decius, one of our young Magister candidates."

Wicket was staring, wide-eyed. "But that means—"

Aradia could not help smiling at him. "Yes, Wicket, that's what it means."

Wicket jumped up, and thumped Pyrrhus so hard on the back he almost knocked the man over. "Pyrrhus—that's how you do it! How I did it tonight, after Julia told me what it was!"

Regaining his balance, Pyrrhus stared haughtily at his friend, who was practically dancing with joy. "Do what?"

"Always hit your mark. Never miss. Pyrrhus—you're an Adept! Just like me!"

Pyrrhus shook his head in mock sorrow. "Wicket, I always feared that you would go mad one day."

"Wicket is right, Pyrrhus," said Aradia. "Both Master Clement and I Read what happened at Capero's. You used Adept power to control your weapons, and so did Wicket."

For the first time, Aradia saw Pyrrhus at a loss for words. He stared first at her, then at Master Clement, then Wicket, went to the couch Wicket had vacated, and sat down as if he didn't trust his legs to hold him. "It's not possible," he said finally.

"Of course it's possible—in fact, it is a natural compensation for losing your ability to Read," Aradia said.

"Compensation?" He nearly choked on the word. "For Reading? How can you Read at all and say that?"

"That's not how I meant it, Pyrrhus," she replied gently. "I meant that the body and mind compensate when any sense is taken away, the others becoming sharper. Certainly no blind nonReader would feel that more acute hearing makes up for lack of sight, but it is still nature's way of attempting to do so. When you lost the ability to Read, you naturally began to develop the other half of your power."

"Then why didn't I know it?" Pyrrhus asked.

"Because you continued to think of yourself as a Reader," said Master Clement. He smiled. "Look at you. You still eat like a Reader, don't you?"

"Why not?" Pyrrhus shrugged.

"Because," said Aradia, "a Reader's diet doesn't give an Adept adequate nutrition. That's why you're too thin, and why you've never had enough power to manifest anything that could not supposedly be accomplished with a strong arm and a good eye. And of course you didn't know you were an Adept. What you believe determines what you can do."

Master Clement added, "If you had known you have Adept powers, and been trained to use them efficiently, you would not have been injured in the marketplace."

"True," said Aradia. "When you saw the vat of oil about to spill on the child, you would have directed the flow another way, protecting both the child and yourself. You'll soon learn to accomplish what you want with the least expenditure of energy. Even Lords Adept do so, since we prefer not to spend half our lives in recovery sleep." A new thought occurred to her. "Pyrrhus, you were a Master Reader in all but final testing and ceremony."

"That's right," Master Clement agreed.

Aradia continued, "If you stop mourning the powers you have lost, and practice the powers you have gained, you have the potential to be a Lord Adept."

"A Lord Adept!" Wicket whispered reverently. Then he sat down beside Pyrrhus, putting a hand on his shoulder. "Think what we could do with that kind of power, Pyrrhus!"

Pyrrhus turned his head to look at Wicket, and closed his eyes for a moment in a frown, shaking his head just slightly. "Like you. You said, just like you."

"Yeah!" Wicket said brightly. "Julia told me the way I make money or dice fall right the way I want—that's Adept power. Never knew till yesterday. But tonight I used it in the fight—just feeling the same as when I want somebody's money pouch to fall in my hand—and my knife went right where I told it to. Good a fighter as you are now!"

Pyrrhus stared at his friend for a long moment. Then, helplessly, he smiled. The smile became a chuckle, and finally he threw his head back and laughed.

Julia woke to a touch on her forehead, between the eyes, and looked up to find Aradia sitting on her bed. "How are you feeling?" her stepmother asked.

Before she could unstick her tongue from the roof of her mouth to answer, memory flooded back. She had been tricked. The people she had thought loved her hated her.

And—because of her foolishness—Galerio was dead.

"You can Read for yourself," she replied sullenly.

"Julia," said Aradia, "you know you did wrong, but you paid a terrible price for your mistake. I need add no further punishment. I was also wrong. It was convenient for me to treat you as if you were grown up. But you are still a child in so many ways, and I should have allowed for that. For the moment you are relieved of all your duties except your lessons. Later, with Master Clement's help, and your father's as soon as he gets home, we will determine a work load appropriate for your years and experience.

"Now get up and get dressed. No lessons today, but I'm here if you want to talk, or you may go talk with Master Clement if you'd rather."

"Why should I get up?" asked Julia. "My people hate me. Galerio is dead. Father and Wulfston have gone away, and will probably never come home. Why didn't you just let me die?"

"Julia!" Aradia said sharply. "You have the right to grieve—and at the funeral today you will speak for your friends. But you must go on with your life, learn from your mistakes."

Then her stepmother became gentler, sitting on the edge of the bed and taking Julia's hand. "Child, your foolishness in getting involved with gamblers—even if Capero had not discovered your scheme, it would still have resulted in punishment for you when Master Clement or I found out about it. When, not if.

"But it should not have resulted in death, Julia. The hatred you Read last night is *not* the attitude of Zendi's citizens. It's not your fault that your friends died."

"They were trying to protect me," Julia said wretchedly.

"Yes, they died honorably, and will be remembered so. But *think*, Julia. Stupid people don't reach Capero's level of success. He could not possibly have thought he could get away with harming you—if he had been thinking for himself. We have an enemy, probably within our borders. There may be Adepts and Readers working together against us. No one has ever succeeded in defeating our Alliance with Adept force, so someone is trying a different form of attack."

Julia stared at her. "You mean somebody *made* Capero try to kill me? A Reader?"

"Or an Adept," replied Aradia. "I'll explain it all later, when you're feeling better. We're going to need every Reader alert, for we have a subtle enemy this time, Julia. At the moment we have no clues as to who he is, or where he is—and that leaves us vulnerable."

When Aradia left, Julia got up and put on the gray mourning clothes laid out for her. She was late eating breakfast, and Cook was subdued as she dished out food. Julia ate only until she had quelled the worst of her appetite. Leaving half of what she had been served, she returned to her room until it was time to leave for the funeral.

Every time she thought of Galerio, pain lanced through her chest, and she wanted to sob in agony. Because she could not stand to think about him, she sought something else to occupy her mind—and remembered Portia's scrolls.

Lying down on her bed, she began to Read where she had left off the night before, about Portia's frustrated efforts as the young Master of Masters to give Readers a greater say in the government of the Aventine Empire.

Before the funeral, Aradia and Master Clement met with Pyrrhus and Wicket. The Master of Masters had no good news. Only one person they were certain had been influenced had survived the battle at Capero's: Octavia. She remembered absolutely nothing of the evening. The Readers determined that her memory loss was quite real.

"All our Master and Magister Readers are on alert. Perhaps now they will notice any strange Reading activity in Zendi. What I find difficult to understand is that even now, after the fact, no one remembers anything unusual. How could thirty or forty people have had commands implanted, without one Reader in this entire city noticing?"

When no one spoke, Pyrrhus shrugged. "Sorry, I can't help you on that score."

"Don't," said Wicket.

Pyrrhus glared at him, but Wicket stood his ground. "You have no reason to be angry at Lady Aradia and Master Clement. They're trying to help us—even me, when I helped get Julia into trouble."

"You also helped get her out," said Aradia. "And we need your further help. Pyrrhus, we do not give charity. You have proved your value, and once you have learned to use Adept power efficiently you will be an ally to be reckoned with."

"You want to use me."

"As Portia tried to use you? No. We don't force people to do what we want. But we need someone to keep order in the city. Our Readers tend to be . . .

naive. Adepts have to learn to work with nature, and that includes human nature. We could ban gambling, prostitution, wine, gladiatorial contests. Do either of you know what would result?"

Wicket replied at once, "Unregulated gambling, unchecked prostitutes spreading disease, theft, drug dealing, cockfighting, dogfighting, and maybe even slave-fighting."

"There is no slavery anymore, Wicket," said Master Clement.

"Might as well be," Wicket replied, "if people have to go to the likes of Capero for their pleasures. Gambling debts where no one regulates losses can enslave someone just as effectively as Aventine law—and white lotus is even worse."

Aradia smiled. "Pyrrhus, you do not place enough value on your companion's wisdom."

"Don't tell him that," replied Pyrrhus. "Wicket attempting to be wise is a phenomenon I prefer to be spared."

"If you accept my offer, I'm afraid you won't be spared it," Aradia said, "for Wicket already understands the first rule of Adept power: it is futile to work against nature. People must have recreation, and certain types of recreation will continue, whether regulated or not. What people *will do*, whether we permit it or not, we permit. What we cannot permit is the step too far—dissemination of enslaving drugs, gambling debts destroying a life's work, influencing people in power through their recreational follies."

"Or," added Wicket, "forcing children or animals to fight to the death for onlookers' amusement."

Pyrrhus studied him. "You . . . ?"

"Yeah," Wicket replied, "when I was fourteen. I managed to win. I still don't know how, except I was desperate. Ran away the next day. Ran for a long time after that, 'fraid I'd be caught and made t'do it again."

"We do not want any children to experience such fear," said Aradia. "Pyrrhus, you see why I want you and Wicket together as Zendi's peace officers?"

"Yes," Pyrrhus replied. Then he smiled at Wicket, a sincere smile immediately echoed by the other man. "I never said we didn't work well together."

"Very good. Take as long as you need to learn the city, and then draw up a plan. We will give you all the Readers and minor Adepts you need to implement it. Master Clement, can you recommend a Reader to work with them now?"

"Decius," he repelied at once. "Let him be useful while he gains control of his Adept powers. At the moment he is unable to work on his studies for the rank of Magister because he is depleting himself with Adept tricks. He can certainly Read well enough to help Pyrrhus and Wicket—and learn along with them how to use his Adept talent. It will take less of your time, too, Aradia, if you work with the three at once. For now, I suggest that Julia concentrate on her Reading."

"Efficient as ever, Clement," said Pyrrhus. Aradia noted that he had still not forgiven his old teacher, but there was at least less bitterness in his tone than when she had first met him.

"As we will expect you to be," the Master of Masters replied. "You're the one who determined how we are being attacked. Now tell us how to locate and identify our attackers."

Somehow, Julia got through the funeral for Galerio, Mosca, Antonius, and the people killed at Capero's. It was held in the forum, and virtually the entire city was there.

News of the attack had spread throughout Zendi. Julia Read bewilderment in the crowd, and both love and sympathy for her as she stepped forward to speak for Galerio, Mosca, and Antonius. Buoyed up by the acceptance she had feared was gone, she was able to get through her speech, although she choked on her words.

Dilys and Piccolo, Blanche, Diana, and Georgio were all there, lost without Galerio. Out of the whole crowd, theirs was the only resentment Julia felt—and she could not blame them.

After the funeral pyre blazed into white heat, reducing the bodies to ashes in minutes through Adept power, everyone filed silently from the forum. Julia started toward the five young people, but they turned away and lost themselves in the crowd. Julia was left standing alone.

With a sigh, she turned and walked through the subdued people in the streets, until she reached home. There she went to her room, and buried herself again in Portia's scrolls.

Amazing how similar Portia's circumstances in Tiberium then were to Julia's in Zendi now! She had a title, a position, great Reading ability for her age, and great responsibility, yet she was frustrated because the political structure of her community would not allow her to make things better.

And, just as a mysterious enemy was attacking Zendi, Portia's Aventine Empire was shrinking year by year through attacks of the Savage Adepts no one truly understood, and everyone feared. Her Readers were used, conscripted into the army to guide it—and they died in battle, often as not, first target of Adepts who knew they would have the Aventines at their mercy if they could blind, deafen, and silence them by destroying their Readers.

But all Portia's efforts to get the Senate to change the law, to allow Readers a say in the government of the Empire—to have even *one* senator to represent them—fell on deaf ears. NonReaders feared Readers, Portia slowly came to recognize, especially nonReaders who had acquired some power of their own through money or political influence.

When she put the scrolls away for the night, Julia felt confused. She hated Portia. Portia had tried to kill her father, had destroyed Pyrrhus' Reading, had manipulated Readers and nonReaders alike. But the Portia of those scrolls was a different person—someone Julia sympathized with.

She would read more tomorrow, as Master Clement had asked her, to find the connection. How had the devoted, benevolent Portia of the scrolls she had read today become the power-mad villain Julia had known?

In the early-morning hours, Julia was once again awakened by Aradia's screams. This time she did not get up, Reading it was just another nightmare, and that Devasin went immediately to waken and comfort her mistress. Again Aradia could not shake off the dream after she woke, insisting, "She's trying to kill me! She's stealing my powers!"

If only Lenardo were here.

But Julia's father was gone. Wulfston was gone.

Torio was gone. Melissa was gone.

Zanos and Astra had gone with Wulfston to rescue Lenardo.

Lilith and her son Ivorn remained in their own lands to the north, fighting off a series of border infractions that pounded against the Savage Empire now just as the Savages had pounded against the Aventine Empire in Portia's day.

Who was left to protect Zendi? Julia, young, her responsibilities now taken from her. Master Clement, old, his powers possibly waning. Decius, also young, but much as Torio had been when he had first joined their battle to create the Savage Empire. But Decius was crippled in body if not in mind, and unused to the new powers he was acquiring.

And that was it, out of the entire group who had toppled an empire and built a union of allies on its ashes.

No wonder Aradia had nightmares!

And no wonder she pounced on the opportunity Pyrrhus and Wicket presented to gain new allies. But they knew so little of those two. Wicket admitted to an unsavory past, even if he gave few details. Pyrrhus, though, was more mysterious, even if they knew all about him.

Or did they?

Swordsmanship was taught in the Academy—but where had he learned to fight with a knife, or to shoot, or to use all those other weapons in his portable armory? Julia was fairly certain she knew *when* he had learned: between the time he escaped from Portia after she had crippled his mind, and the rapport which ended the Aventine Empire and killed Portia.

Pyrrhus must have set about to learn every form of weaponry he could, not only to protect himself once bereft of the ability to Read an attacker, but also obviously to take his revenge on Portia if the opportunity presented itself.

The opportunity had been mental, not physical—a far more satisfying revenge. Yet Pyrrhus had seemed far from satisfied when he appeared in Zendi.

Why had Pyrrhus and Wicket come to Zendi in the first place? Aradia had found out that they were successful and had a good reputation as bodyguards in Tiberium. Why leave?

Determined to find out, she let herself drift back to sleep.

Aradia's nightmares continued, but she was learning to live with them. She wished Lilith could come earlier than she had promised, but she could not ask when there were constant border skirmishes against Lilith's lands.

There were also continuing Adept attacks, but none near Zendi now that the Readers were watching for anything unusual. Some of the events might be natural phenomena—when whirlwinds came out of thunderstorms, who was to say that they were not produced by nature? If an irrigation dam broke in Wulfston's lands and flooded acres of farmland, that again could have happened naturally. The only odd thing about the events occurring now was that there were so many of them.

Cattle stampeded. The wall of a stone quarry collapsed, killing three workers. High winds of the first winter storm destroyed a bridge in the mountains south of Tiberium, cutting off the main trade route through the center of the Empire for almost a month. Even with Adept aid, it took that long to rebuild the vast expanse and reinforce it against such winds in the future.

People started talking about the "hard-luck year," and in Zendi gossip attributed it to Lenardo's being kidnapped. On one hand, Aradia was always pleased to see how beloved her husband was, for he had won these people as a stranger and a Reader in the days when the first was to be distrusted and the second executed upon discovery. She had deliberately put him in a hopeless situation, and Lenardo, not knowing any better, had turned the decaying city into a shining example of hope and enterprise. That was when she had fallen hopelessly in love with him.

On the other hand, it was difficult not to be annoyed that they did not place the same faith in Aradia that they did in her husband. And as her powers waned there was less and less she could do personally to show them she could care for them as well as Lenardo did.

As weeks passed with one problem after another, and no clues as to where the attacks came from, Aradia even began to lose faith in Master Clement. He was as frustrated as she was, none of his Readers picking up the slightest hint of upcoming attacks. They just happened, out of the blue—and once in a while a nearby Reader would be able to tell which minor Adept had suddenly shifted the wind or knocked the main prop out from under a half-constructed building.

Pyrrhus' theory was the only reasonable explanation: the people who were used had commands implanted, keyed to some expected occurrence. When it happened, they acted, and immediately forgot. Even Master Clement could not discover who had implanted the commands, for consciously the recipients did not know that the commands had been implanted, or even that they had performed the acts.

The Master Reader explained to Aradia, "I can sometimes uncover the command—but not who put it there. Whoever it was, he or she was unknown to the victim. To learn more, I fear we have no choice but to subject one of those victims to having his mind delved into by a circle of Masters."

They were in Aradia's study. She and Master Clement had arrived first, then Wicket and Decius. They were still waiting for Pyrrhus.

At Master Clement's suggestion, Wicket shuddered. "Sounds horrible!" He picked up a stylus from Aradia's desk, and twirled it between his nimble fingers.

"It is," said Master Clement. "The technique is normally used only on sick minds, to uncover suppressed memories necessary to the healing process. It is painful for both the patient and the healers. I do not want to do it, Wicket, but it may become necessary to ask for a volunteer from among those we know to have been used."

"Volunteer to have his mind peeled like an onion?" Wicket asked.

Master Clement winced. "An unfortunately apt comparison. If we must do it, the best healers from Gaeta will work with me, to minimize the patient's trauma."

"I don't want to know when you do it" Wicket muttered. He balanced the stylus on end on the desk and let go, holding it upright with Adept power.

"You mean you don't want Pyrrhus to know," Master Clement said gently.

"It's what they did to him, isn't it?" Wicket concentrated on the stylus—a neat demonstration of sustained use of tiny increments of power, showing the tremendous progress he had made in the past few weeks. He should not waste such effort, of course, but Aradia understood that he needed that concentration in order to bear the subject under discussion.

"I assume so," Master Clement answered his question. "A similar process to isolate the area—" The old man cut off his speculation at the other's look of sheer revulsion. "Wicket, you understand that *I* did not harm your friend. What he blames me for is not being aware that it was happening, and therefore not preventing it. I accept that blame. I had the ability to Read what Portia was doing . . . if it had ever occurred to me that it was so evil that it overrode her right to Privacy."

Wicket shook his head. "All me life, in Tiberium, the Readers were supposed to be good, and the savages, the Adepts, were supposed to be the monsters." He gave a sad snort of laughter. "Come to find out, Readers can be just as cruel—more so, usin' people's minds like dice t' play their games."

The stylus broke with a loud snap, and the pieces fell to the surface of the desk in a perfect circle. Wicket left them there, and looked over at Master Clement as if challenging him to deny the charge.

"Some *people* can be cruel," Master Clement replied. "We can only try to heal the damage they do, as best we can."

The door opened, not Pyrrhus but one of Aradia's servants with a small casket. "A message from Lord Wulfston's lands, my lady." She accepted it, and set it aside as the man left. The casket was decorated with the black wolf's head, her brother's symbol, and she knew it contained letters and accounts sent to her monthly while Wulfston was away. Odd—she had received reports only a few days ago. Perhaps there was news.

"Aradia," said Master Clement, "I will not Read its contents, but there is a letter to you from Lord Wulfston in that chest."

She gasped, and pulled the casket in front of her with trembling hands, wishing she had a Magister Reader's ability to Read the pages. But she would never be that good a Reader, and besides, she wanted his letter in her hands.

The lock required an Adept to open it. The central mechanism was completely enclosed, the tumblers not intended to be reached with a key. She had to Read or know how it was made to open it, but of course she had known the complexities of her brother's lock code since the day it had been developed for him.

With shaking fingers, she pressed the outer studs in order, and began concentrating on the tumblers. But in her eagerness she slipped like a child, the mechanism gave a loud click, and the studs sprang out again, leaving the casket firmly locked. She was tempted just to split it open and be done with it.

At Aradia's grimace of annoyance, Wicket said, "Please allow me, my lady," reaching for the casket. "There's few locks I can't jiggle open," he added, pressing the outer studs and tilting the casket slightly sideways.

"I don't think you—" Aradia began, and then heard the first tumbler click. How could he—?

Decius was Reading the inner mechanism, about to tell Wicket the order of the tumblers.

//No—don't!// Aradia warned him

"Don't what?" asked Wicket, not looking up.

Decius' mouth opened in amazement, but he contained his surprise, as did Master Clement, who after a moment smiled at Aradia over Wicket's head.

//Don't break it,// Aradia improvised.

Wicket laughed. "You can't break one of these things. The worst that can happen is you don't get it open." He became blank to the three Reading him, the rest of the tumblers clicked in sequence, and Wicket lifted the lid and set the casket on the desk in front of Aradia. She waited until the shield of Adept use relaxed, and she could perceive Wicket's presence again.

//Thank you,// she told him.

"You're—" He was looking at her. He realized she had not spoken, and his shields went up reflexively. Then, "Oh, no." He shook his head. "Oh, no—not me. That's not fair. It isn't *fair*! You can't do that to me—I won't let you!"

"What are you doing to him?" snarled Pyrrhus from the doorway.

"Nothing!" Wicket gasped, turning to face his friend. "It's nothing, Pyrrhus."

"Nothing done *to* him," Aradia agreed.

Pyrrhus looked over the tableau, Aradia behind the desk with the open casket in front of her, Wicket standing before her, the two Readers sitting off to the side. He tilted his head with a puzzled expression. "Then—what have you done, Wicket?" An enigmatic smile. "Finally learned to Read?"

Wicket's mental shields were no defense against Pyrrhus; the ex-Reader knew he had hit home by the way the color drained from Wicket's face. "No! I—I *won't*! I mean—" Realizing that he was not helping the situation, he stuttered to a halt, shoulders slumping in defeat. He looked away, refusing to meet Pyrrhus' eyes.

"Wicket," said Pyrrhus, "you've known that this was inevitable from the day we learned that the two powers go together. Now stop acting like an idiot."

The other man looked up, incredulous. "You . . . you don't mind?"

"I mind that I *can't*. But why in the world should I mind that you *can*? Who knows? As a Reader you may even prove useful!"

Aradia hardly heard them, didn't hear whatever they said next, as Master Clement and Decius drew them into a discussion to give her the privacy to read her letter.

The date was nearly three months ago. Wulfston had not yet found Lenardo. His ship had been damaged in an Adept conflict, and had had to be repaired, forcing him to follow Sukuru all the way to Africa. He was sending this letter from a place called Freedom Island, off the coast, and would write again at the first opportunity.

//Julia,// she called mentally to the girl, and let her Read the letter through her eyes, sharing relief at news at last, disappointment at how scant it was. She tried to tell herself it was better than nothing, to keep Julia's spirits up if not her own.

At first she thought the ball of pain just below her heart was her disappointed reaction. Then it spread, increasing in intensity, stabbing through her swollen belly, driving coherent thought from her mind as she gasped aloud.

The four men turned to look at her. Master Clement would have Read her, but she didn't feel it because her own Adept powers manifested automatically at pain.

But it didn't stop!

For the first time in her adult life, Aradia's healing powers were not enough to stop her own pain!

A moan escaped her as the agony cut like a knife. "My baby!" she gasped. "Lenardo's child—oh—don't let me lose her!"

Chapter Seven

Gratefully, Julia Read the letter from Wulfston with Aradia, sharing her disappointment at how old the news was, and that it contained no information as to Lenardo's whereabouts. If she could get her hands on it, though. . . .

Before she could suggest it, pain stabbed Aradia. Julia gasped, but refused to break the rapport. Aradia stopped Reading as she attempted to invoke Adept healing, and Julia stopped feeling her pain.

She shifted her Reading to join Master Clement's mind. He tried to reassure her even as he focused on Aradia. Still Reading, Julia left her room and ran to the study. Her stepmother gasped in pain despite all the Readers could do. The double focus on the scene in the study and her own movement was no longer strange to Julia; she neither lost contact nor stumbled.

She burst in just as Pyrrhus was saying, "Tell me what's wrong with her! Damn you, Clement—you know I can't use this new healing power unless you tell me where to focus!"

Julia caught Decius' shock at the way Pyrrhus dared address the Master of Masters, and the young Reader's own unsuccessful attempt to ease Aradia's pain.

The four men had laid Aradia on one of the lounges, and were gathered around her, perplexed.

"Direct healing heat into this area," Master Clement said to Pyrrhus. Then, "Aradia, the baby is unharmed, and the pain is not a contraction. You are *not* miscarrying! Do you hear me?"

Sweating, teeth clenched, Aradia managed to nod. She struggled to breathe.

"It's a muscle spasm," said Master Clement, "below your diaphragm. It's pressing on a nerve, causing the pain. Can you Read with me?"

Julia felt Aradia try to open to Reading, but she could not sustain it. All her life's training made her instinctively brace her Adept powers against pain. Feeling helpless, Julia knelt beside Aradia and took her hand.

"We'll ease the spasm," said Master Clement, Reading for Decius exactly where it was. To Pyrrhus he gave the name of the muscle that had contracted and refused to release. Julia watched and Read as the two concentrated. Healing warmth focused in the recalcitrant muscle until, finally, it relaxed, and Aradia began to breathe normally again.

Trembling, Aradia looked up at Master Clement. "Thank you. But what caused that? It's not normal."

"Aradia," said Master Clement, "it was painful, but it did no lasting harm. Any Reader my age has consulted on enough pregnancies to know that each is unique. There is no such thing as a 'normal' pregnancy in every detail."

"I couldn't control the pain!" Aradia said fearfully.

"It's all right," Julia tried to reassure her. "You'll get all your powers back after the baby is born."

"My mother didn't," Aradia said grimly, and Julia felt a shock. It was the first time Aradia had ever mentioned her mother.

"Your mother did not have both Adepts and Readers to help her through her pregnancy, and her recovery afterward," said Master Clement. "Worry won't help you or your child. I will contact Lilith. You need her here now, and we may have need of her powers."

"The border—" Aradia protested.

"Lilith's people are completely loyal, and she reports that her son Ivorn is making rapid progress. She has an excellent system of Readers and Adepts to protect her lands in her absence. Aradia, none of the attacks against Lilith's border have succeeded—you've heard the reports. It is just possible that they are intended to keep her from coming here."

"Divide and conquer," suggested Pyrrhus.

Aradia tried to sit up, but Julia put her hands on her shoulders. "Stay there and rest."

"Not when I'm being attacked!"

"No one said you were being attacked," said Julia. "Did you Read something?" She looked up to include Master Clement in the question.

"No, Aradia," said Master Clement. "I did not mean to imply that your pain came from Adept attack. However, your pregnancy is no secret. Neither is the absence of Lenardo and Wulfston. Torio and Melissa have been gone for some time. We are vulnerable; we must prepare for attack."

"Better," said Aradia grimly, "to be prepared and not be attacked, than to be attacked when unprepared. I will—"

"You will sleep now," said Master Clement.

"Sleep! There's no time—"

"Aradia!" Master Clement said in warning tones. "You must rest. Put yourself into healing sleep, or Pyrrhus will do it for you."

"Pyrrhus? He's only—"

"My Adept powers are stronger than yours at this moment," Pyrrhus interrupted her. "Do you wish to put it to the test?" he challenged. "This time *I* will win."

Julia saw the struggle in Aradia's eyes, but then she said, "Very well. But first—"

"First you rest," said Master Clement. "Decius will stay with you until Master Selina and Vestor arrive. From now on you will be attended by both a Reader and an Adept healer at all times, Aradia, until your daughter is safely born."

"That's not necessary," Aradia said.

"Humor me," replied the Master of Masters. "Remember, when Lenardo returns, I will have to answer to him for your safety and that of his child."

He knew the one argument that would always persuade Aradia. *Or me*, Julia admitted to herself.

But she was greatly concerned about Aradia. Her nightmares still occurred, although since Master Clement was trying to help her it was not every night. But she still woke screaming, with the conviction that her child was stealing her powers and trying to kill her.

Aradia's mother went mad and tried to murder her own child.

Julia forced the thought away. It was easy enough to do in daytime, with Master Clement nearby. But at night, as she Read Devasin soothing Aradia back to sleep after one of her dreams, Julia could not help wondering if Aradia would also go mad. What if Lenardo returned to find his wife powerless and crazed? And the child she carried—if Aradia had inherited her mother's madness, would her daughter also inherit it?

Born of Lenardo's own blood, that child would displace his adopted daughter as heir to the empire they had all worked so hard to create. That Julia had fought and nearly died for.

Aradia lapsed into healing sleep. Decius sat down on the other lounge, to wait for his replacements. Julia went to the desk for Wulfston's letter, and Master Clement started for the door.

"One moment, Master Reader," said Pyrrhus. "Don't forget to take *him* with you." He gestured at Wicket, who stared back at him in confusion.

"Why?" asked Master Clement.

"Take him to the Academy and assign him some tutors. Train him as fast as you can. *I* want him to Read for *me*."

Master Clement looked from Pyrrhus' determined face to Wicket's, which evolved from bewilderment to pleased anticipation. "Oh, yes!" he said. "We've always made a good team, Pyrrhus an' me. If he wants me to Read for him, I'll learn—I promise! I'll be the best pupil you've ever had!"

To her intense disappointment, Julia got nothing from Wulfston's letter to tell her where Sukuru might have taken Lenardo. She did learn, as she held it and Read the impressions of her uncle's feelings as he wrote it, that what he had described as an "Adept conflict" had been an all-out battle, in which he had come out the loser.

Wulfston must have relived the battle in his mind as he decided how to phrase the description for his sister, for Julia found the memory sharp and clear as she clutched the worn paper. In the midst of the battle Julia realized, as Wulfston must have, that his opponents could as easily have sunk his ship as disabled it. They didn't want to kill him. But they didn't want him to rescue Lenardo without going all the way to Africa.

Divide and conquer.

Surely the kidnapping of her father could not have anything to do with the attacks on the Savage Empire?

//Julia.//

//Yes, Master Clement?//

//Please come to the Academy. I have a task for you.//

Well, at last she was to be trusted with responsibility again. Ever since Galerio's death she had been assigned lessons and occasional Reading jobs, but no continuing responsibilities. For a time it had been a good thing. She had suffered from debilitating fatigue; many afternoons, trying to read the scrolls Master Clement had given her, she had found her thoughts turning instead to Galerio, and wept until she fell asleep, waking with difficulty hours later.

But now the bouts of exhaustion came less often. She wasn't sure how much responsibility she could deal with, but she was ready to try.

It was late winter. Julia met the Healer/Adept team in the corridor, red-cheeked from the brisk winds. By the time she had wrapped herself in a woolen cloak, Decius joined her. "That wasn't a very long strategy session," she commented.

"It is difficult to plan strategy against unknown factors."

"Pyrrhus and Wicket seem to do so quite successfully," she commented.

Decius gave a snort of laughter. "Some strategy! They've got the lowlife in this city scared to death of them. You know, I've been watching Adepts work for years, but when those two go into action it's like—like an explosion. As if they don't care who gets hurt, any more than an earthquake or a whirlwind."

"They never hurt anyone trying to get out of their way," said Julia. "And those trying to get *in* it deserve what they get." She thought vengefully of Capero, and felt Decius pick it up before she realized she should have shielded the thought. He was getting too good!

"Julia, Capero was *used.* He was a shrewd gambler who would take fools for everything he could get, but he was not a cold-blooded killer."

"Galerio is just as dead," she replied. Then, to change the subject, "Hasn't anyone told you that using Adept power is supposed to dull your Reading?"

"I haven't done much today," he replied. "And . . . maybe it's my age, when my powers are growing rapidly anyway, but it seems that after a day when I *have* used my Adept powers a great deal, after a good meal and a night's sleep my Reading is even sharper in the morning."

Julia walked quickly against the cold, and noticed that Decius kept up easily despite his wooden leg. Now that he could keep the stump healed, he had no more pain and was not afraid to put pressure on it.

If Decius can learn to use Adept powers, why can't I? Julia wondered for the thousandth time. But no one seemed to have the answer to why some people found it easy to access both elements of power, while others, no matter how proficient in one, found it impossible to develop the other.

Sometimes, of course, that was fortunate. Suppose their old enemy, Drakonius, had learned to Read for himself instead of merely forcing Readers to work for him. Or Portia. The thought of Portia with Adept powers added further chill to the cold day, and Julia was happy to see the doors of the Academy looming ahead, promising warmth and a fresh task to take her mind off morbid thoughts.

To Julia's surprise, the assignment Master Clement

had for her was training Wicket. "But . . . I'm not a teacher," she protested.

"The more you teach, the more you learn," said Master Clement. "Pyrrhus is right—Wicket's Reading will add greatly to their efficiency as peace officers. They are a natural team and already well practiced. Pyrrhus would be the ideal person to train Wicket, of course, but deprived of his own Reading powers he cannot. My tutors are all Academy-trained. Wicket needs a teacher with flexibility, and experience out on the streets where he works."

For the first time in weeks, Julia felt her mood lighten. "You'll let me teach him guttersnipe Reading?"

"Guttersnipe Reading?" To Julia's delight, she provoked a laugh from her teacher. "I can see I have found the right tutor. Yes, Wicket's not going to test for the upper ranks, Julia. He needs practical experience. So long as you drill the Readers' Code into him, teach him what you think will help him most. You have experience at guiding Adepts, much more than my best teachers. *That* is what Wicket needs most of all.

"Now," he continued, "go find your pupil, while I contact Lilith. I wish she could Read, but the best I can hope for is that whoever is Reading for her today has strong persuasive powers. Aradia needs Lilith here, Julia—and not merely as her friend, or as a Lady Adept to strengthen our circle. She needs the example before her eyes of a woman who has borne a child and regained her powers completely."

Julia felt warm pleasure at the way her teacher was treating her as a full member of their circle again. "Did Aradia tell you about her mother?" she asked.

"That is privileged, Julia. There are times when I must act as healer with Aradia now, not merely friend. Have I not assigned you a task? Why are you dawdling here when we both have work to do?"

So Julia went to find Wicket, who was in an empty classroom, staring at the rules of the Readers' Code on the wall. He was closed to Reading; Julia had to find him by visualizing, for, with casual trust in her abilities, Master Clement had not said where he had left Wicket.

There was something wrong. Wicket looked nervous and upset, glancing around furtively.

"Just open to Reading," said Julia as she entered the room. "Then nobody can sneak up on you."

He gave her a forced grin. "Hello again. What're you doing here?"

"Master Clement assigned me to tutor you. Have you memorized the Readers' Code?"

"That?" He gestured toward the wall.

"Yes, that. All Reading is taught within the Readers' Code, so before you begin you have to learn it." He paled and dropped his eyes from hers. "What's wrong?" Julia asked. "Does something in it conflict with your personal beliefs?"

Wicket stared at his hands, shielded strongly. Finally he mumbled, "I . . . dunno." Having gotten that out, he said more clearly, "Dunno what it says. I . . . can't read."

"Well, if you'd stop bracing to use—" Julia began, and then suddenly realized what he meant. "You mean you can't read words? Or write?"

He nodded glumly. "Never could learn more'n t' write me name. Pyrrhus tried to teach me—but everything gets all jumbled up. It . . . it lost us our chance in Tiberium, an' now if it ruins us here, too—"

"What happened in Tiberum?" Julia asked.

"We done—did—really good at our bodyguard service, an' then the city councilors decided to hire us. We did several jobs for 'em, always as equal partners.

"Only . . . there were contracts to sign. One time we had to accept one and get right to work if the terms were all right. When Pyrrhus had to read it to me, the councilors—well, they wanted t' change the terms. I knew them high-an'-mighties never liked me from the first, 'cause I come outa the gutter. But I can talk good enough if I have to, and Pyrrhus insisted we worked together or not at all.

"But when they found out I'm . . . illiterate, they told Pyrrhus he could have that job or any future ones alone, and he could hire me if he wanted to—but they wouldn't make any more contracts with *me.*"

"And what did Pyrrhus say to that?" Julia asked.

Wicket gave a quavering smile. "I didn't know he even knew some of the words he used. If he hadn't got so angry, we mighta worked it out. I wouldn't of minded working for him—it's Pyrrhus insisted we were partners."

"Wasn't he drawing on your experience?" Julia asked.

"Yeah, I guess. Street experience. But I shoulda known better than t' think, even with Pyrrhus' help, I could have what amounts to a government post—when I can't even learn to read. I'm just stupid, that's all."

"Wicket, I've known you long enough to know you're not stupid," said Julia. "Open to Reading and look at the Code."

"Eh?"

"Just do it."

He shrugged, and complied. Julia closed her eyes and Read through Wicket's. As he had said, it was a jumble of letters, not the words she knew. Even as he stared at them, they shifted into new combinations. "No wonder you couldn't learn," said Julia. "Now close your eyes."

She opened her eyes, and let Wicket Read what she saw and read. He gasped. "It makes sense! I got as far as learning the sounds of the letters—this way they make words!"

He opened his eyes and turned to stare at her. "How did you do that?"

"You can always Read through a stronger Reader," she replied. "I don't know much about your problem with words, but I'll bet Master Clement does. I do know that some people have trouble learning to read. If you're a farmer or a cobbler, who cares? But if you're a city official—"

Wicket sighed. "I shoulda told Lady Aradia. Pyrrhus has been covering up for me, reading all the directives we get. But you're right: how could I read an urgent written message if he wasn't available?"

"As long as someone else was," said Julia, "you'd be all right. Perhaps you can learn to visualize."

"To what?"

"Let's find out if you're doing it already. Read the next room for me, Wicket."

Julia Read only through him, and perceived the usual sense that there were several people there, without identifying them. //Withdraw,// she instructed. //Do not invade their privacy.//

"Uh . . . you didn't say that out loud," Wicket observed.

//No—you try it.//

//Why can't we Read the next room?//

//Because we haven't asked those people's permission to practice on them. I will in a moment. But people are easy. You've been Reading objects like locking mechanisms and dice without knowing it—and that's really *hard.* Try the room behind *that* wall.//

It was Master Clement's outer office. His assistant was not there at the moment, so the room was empty of people. At first all Wicket Read was shapes of furniture. //Try to see what color the walls are,// Julia suggested.

Hazily, the room "appeared" in her mind. The furnishings were only vague shapes, but the soft blue of the walls was definite. She smiled. "You *can* visualize already. That's a high-level skill, Wicket. If you can hone it, then you won't need anyone to read your messages for you. They won't get all jumbled up if you Read them."

He grinned. "This is fun. What next?"

She put him through every test she could think of, stopping him each time he would have stepped beyond the confines of the Code. They got permission to practice Reading the class in the next room, and when their lesson was over two of the children were happy to play Reading games with them, each designed to teach or strengthen a Reading skill.

Julia spent several hours with him each day, and Wicket made rapid progress. He was unusually good at details and close work, but had a very limited range. That did not disturb him—until Pyrrhus complained.

When Pyrrhus demanded a different teacher for

Wicket, Master Clement called Julia and Wicket to meet with them.

"Julia has done an excellent job," Master Clement insisted. "Pyrrhus, surely you recall enough from training Readers yourself to recognize how well Wicket is doing."

"Yes—at what she's teaching him. Wicket can tell me every item in my pocket, but he can hardly Read into the next street! We need *range* for our work, Clement. Get Wicket a tutor who can Read beyond the city walls."

"*I* can Read beyond the city walls!" Julia protested.

"Then why can't Wicket?" Pyrrhus demanded.

"I told you," Wicket protested. "I'm never gonna be a Master Reader! Why can't you accept that?"

"I'm afraid you do have to accept it, Pyrrhus," said Master Clement. "Had Wicket's Reading manifested in childhood, he might have accomplished a bit more than he can now, but not much more. He's very good at fine discernment, but he does not have the power for great range. I would not even consider trying to teach him to leave his body. It would be too dangerous. Wicket is a Dark Moon Reader, Pyrrhus—not because I say so, but because that is the limit of his talent."

Pyrrhus rose from his chair, fists clenched, and paced away from the other three. "I'd hoped. . . ."

Master Clement said, very gently, "You hoped your friend would have all the powers you have lost. I'm sorry. We've taught him all we can. Remember that he has *both* Reading and Adept talents. Your job now is to work out how best to combine the powers you have between the two of you."

"Combine!" exclaimed Julia. "That's it, Pyrrhus!"

He turned, and stared at her blankly. "What's it?"

"You want Wicket to Read beyond the city walls. He can't with his own powers—but he can with yours!"

Pyrrhus frowned at her, his dark eyes wary.

Master Clement said, "Julia, I had not thought of that. Sit down, Pyrrhus. At least try the experiment."

"What experiment?" Pyrrhus asked suspiciously, but he sat.

"That is the disadvantage of growing up in the Academy," said Master Clement. "We teach the same techniques to one generation after another, and do not think beyond them. Wicket knows what experiment. He and Julia are not bound by what has always been done."

Pyrrhus turned a challenging look on Wicket, who said, "A weak Reader can Read through a stronger Reader. *You* can Read beyond the city walls, Pyrrhus."

"What good does that do me if I don't know what I've . . . oh." The incipient anger drained from his face. "Yes!" he said in an intense whisper. "Let's try it!"

Pyrrhus opened to Reading. He was helpless to focus his powers precisely, but he directed them toward the lands south of the city. Julia was reminded of Reading with her father, for Pyrrhus' range was that of a Master Reader, taking them far beyond the grounds of the summer fair and horse market, to farms and woodlands gray under a lowering sky. Winter was lingering beyond its time this year as if to underscore their other frustrations.

"It's cold," said Wicket. "There's some woodcutters out, but nobody else. There's a village, people gathered around their fires, pots of soup cooking—I can smell it! And bread baking. They're tired of the cold weather, but happy to have warm homes and enough to eat.

"Then, maybe two miles farther south, there's a big farm with a huge new house. Man and his wife in the main room, talkin' about—"

//Privacy, Wicket!// Pyrrhus warned automatically, and for the first time Julia truly believed that he had once taught in an Academy.

Wicket laughed. "You sound just like Julia. All right, there's some deer in the woods—cold an' awful hungry. Frightened."

"I'll have Aradia tell the foresters," said Julia. "The farmers should put out hay for them, or our hunters won't find enough game next year."

"And I'll have the Dark Moon Readers check the game in that section more carefully," said Master Clement. "There may be other hungry animals."

"It's starting to snow!" Wicket said suddenly. "Oh—it's beautiful! Big flakes, stickin' on the trees. Are we far enough north to get real snow? I've never seen it except in the mountains. I mean more than a few flakes, that is."

"No, we don't get much here, either," Julia said, adding wistfully, "I'd like to have enough to play in, just once."

"Where is the snow?" asked Pyrrhus.

"Huh?" responded Wicket.

"How many miles? What direction?" But Pyrrhus' snarl of impatience didn't have its usual bite.

"Um. . . ."

Master Clement pulled a map from the scroll rack and unrolled it. How often they had done this during Adept battles, Readers showing Adepts where to center their powers.

"Here!" said Wicket, drawing a circle with his finger in an area several miles south of the city, near the main road to Tiberium.

"Julia, you'd like some snow to play in?" Pyrrhus asked her.

"Yes!" she said with a delighted grin that he echoed back at her.

Suddenly their panorama of the lands south of the city was cut off as Pyrrhus braced Adept powers.

Wicket blinked, startled until he realized what had happened.

//Read with me,// Master Clement invited, and again they saw the woods and farmlands—and felt the wind shift, blowing the storm northward.

"Wicket, keep Pyrrhus informed—" Master Clement began.

But Pyrrhus raised a hand, saying, "No, just tell me if I lose it."

He did lose it once, but after that he began to open to Reading every few minutes, letting Wicket rather than Master Clement be the one to keep him on target.

Well before the snow reached Zendi, the Watchers reported its unnatural movement. //It's all right,// Master Clement assured them. //Spread the word—*we* are controlling this storm. It's an experiment, not an attack.//

The light from the windows dimmed as black snow clouds concentrated over the city. The first flakes began to fall, then a steady stream of pure white beauty, for the wind died now, leaving the clouds to empty their burden on Zendi.

"Let's go outside!" Julia said.

Wicket jumped up, eager as a child himself, and Pyrrhus smiled indulgently at him and got up as well.

Taking her cloak off the peg by the door, Julia noticed how Pyrrhus moved, stretching his body, testing his balance. He looked much healthier and stronger than the man Aradia had healed of burns last autumn. Before, he had been all bone and tendon. Now he carried a layer of muscle, laid on by the Adept regimen he was following. Adepts never put on fat; Pyrrhus had simply filled out to his natural physique.

"I'm not tired," he said to Master Clement, half surprise, half satisfaction in his words. "I'm learning not to expend more energy than necessary."

"*I* coulda taught you *that*," Wicket said in mock scorn, and Julia realized that she had never seen the minor Adept exhaust himself, nor noticed his Reading impaired by the use of Adept strength.

"*You*," Pyrrhus told him, "practice laziness, not efficiency."

By this time they were all wrapped up in woolen cloaks, ready to venture into the snow.

The Academy faced on one of the little parks dotting Zendi. It was rapidly filling with fluffy whiteness. Julia could not resist running out into it, glad she was wearing woolen stockings under her boots as she felt the cold attempt to penetrate.

The snow was ankle-deep already and falling fast. Wicket scooped up a handful, tossed it into the air, caught it, then in one motion turned and flung it at Pyrrhus, hitting him dead center in the chest. "That's for calling me lazy!"

For one moment Pyrrhus stood, startled. Then a

wicked grin flashed to his face, and he gathered his own handful of packed snow to hurl at his friend—only to have it bounce off an invisible shield a handspan from Wicket's cloak.

"Oh, is *that* the game we're playing?" Pyrrhus asked dangerously. Although his eyes never left Wicket, suddenly the branches of the tree over the minor Adept's head shook rapidly, and Wicket was doused with snow.

"Wasting your powers, Pyrrhus," Wicket taunted. Scooping up a double handful of snow, he ran toward his friend as if he were about to tackle him. As Pyrrhus ducked the charge, though, his feet slid out from under him.

Wicket tripped on nothing, and twisted in midair to avoid landing atop Pyrrhus. "Slippery, innit?" he asked conversationally as he sat up, shaking the snow from his cloak onto his friend.

Master Clement stood in the Academy doorway, watching in amusement. //Julia, wasn't there something about bringing this snow here for *you* to play in?//

She giggled—a mistake. Pyrrhus and Wicket turned to her, climbing to their feet. "That's right," said Wicket. "You were the one wanted snow."

"So," added Pyrrhus, "come and play!"

"Unfair!" she gasped through her laughter as they stalked her. "I'm not an Adept!"

"Don't need to be," said Wicket, grabbing her hand and pulling her with him up through the terraced garden, now empty and dead after the long winter. At the top, he turned to the smooth side of the little hill, spread his cloak on the ground, sat on it—and slid down the bank.

That looked like fun—and it *was*, Julia quickly discovered. So did the Readers from the Academy, released from their work by Master Clement's command, for in Zendi's normally temperate climate it might be many years before they would again see a snowfall so perfect for their games.

The park filled with laughing children and adolescents, and Wicket was not the only nominal adult to indulge the sensation of flying down the hill. The young Magisters had their turns, to the children's squeals of delight.

Only when they were all thoroughly wet from the snow soaking through their woolen garments did the party break up—although the snow still fell. Preparing to leave, Pyrrhus asked Master Clement, "Shouldn't we send this storm away now? The Lady Lilith is on the road. I am sure she did not anticipate snow this late in the season."

"The weather watchers will take care of it," the old Reader replied. "People are enjoying it too much to stop it. At this time of year, even without control it would be gone by tomorrow night. Lilith won't be here for two more days."

Dressed in borrowed dry clothes, Julia walked home, Reading pleasant tiredness on every side. The snow had been an excuse for everyone to drop work and go outside. She passed snow sculptures, and splattered designs on walls that showed that Pyrrhus and Wicket's had not been the only mock battle of the day. A holiday spirit hung over the city as the scent of hot spiced cider permeated the air.

Julia ate her supper eagerly that night, telling Aradia what they had done. Her stepmother smiled indulgently, but seemed distracted. Perhaps it was that she was in no condition to go out and have fun in the snow; all it had meant to Aradia was being stuck indoors.

After supper, Julia went to her room. Her schedule for today had called for her to read more of Portia's records before supper. After the freedom of the afternoon, she didn't really feel like working. She especially didn't want to touch the scrolls and Read Portia's frustrations. She had forgotten her own for a few hours; why relive someone else's?

So she took a leisurely bath, and read a book from Aradia's library, a retelling of the legend of the Ghost King. But as she sat on the lounge in her room, cold air seeped in through the window, even though it was shuttered outside and curtained inside. The candles seemed dim, too. Julia shivered, wondering if she had caught cold from the afternoon's activities.

No, she wasn't feverish, her glands were not swollen, her throat didn't hurt. She could Read that there was absolutely nothing wrong with her health. So why did she feel half frightened? What of? Maybe she was just tired.

But she wasn't sleepy. She didn't like this book, she decided, stretching. Her eyes fell on the pile of scrolls. Maybe she should read and Read one tonight. It had become a habit, after all.

She picked up the next one in sequence—and found Portia discovering a way to influence political decisions. A senator who had risen from poverty had allowed himself to be bribed for a surprisingly small sum by merchants wanting him to vote their way on an issue on which he had no personal opinion. The Academy treasury was not large, but Portia could afford that much. The next time an issue of importance to Readers came up, Portia approached him, delicately.

It worked! His vote swung two others, and the issue came out in favor of the Readers.

There were other senators amenable to bribes . . . but they were far too expensive for even the Master of Masters to afford. Unless, that is, the Academy could find a way to enrich its coffers.

Portia remembered a merchant who had dropped hints to her that knowing the plans of one of his competitors could be worth a considerable sum. At the time, she had scathingly ejected him from her office. But if she was to be better prepared the next time she needed money. . . .

She struck a deal with the merchant, and made sure she Read some of his most private and personal secrets. Only as insurance, she insisted to herself, should he ever threaten to expose her. Never would she breach the Readers' Code to reveal such secrets.

She put out of her mind the fact that she had broken it to obtain them in the first place.

Her brother died, and her nephew became Emperor.

In Portia's opinion, the boy was as close to an idiot as the royal family had ever produced. He drank, he gambled, he ignored his pretty but fatuous wife and chased after any other attractive woman who crossed his path.

Portia began to study how to throw attractive women in his way. Not prostitutes. Mostly discreet young wives of men who would be powerful, men who knew how to pretend they didn't know should they find out just how their wives were helping their careers along. It was surprisingly easy to play on the greed and vanity of young women raised solely to be entertaining and decorative, to make them think their actions were clever, even loyal to their husbands. And of course the Emperor's attentions were flattering.

But the Emperor must not become a laughingstock. Liaisons with women who would keep them secret kept his attention from women who might be less discreet. Portia was actually preserving the dignity of the royal family.

Julia Read that Portia knew in her heart that she wanted the Emperor to retain the respect of the Senate and the populace so that his decrees would not be questioned. Those decrees were often to the great advantage of Readers . . . or at least of the Master of Masters among Readers.

At last Portia found an entree into military planning sessions, bribing and pressuring the Emperor's strategists into urging the Emperor to try battle plans she devised, putting Readers to more efficient use than ever before.

The Aventine army began to win! They drove the savages back steadily for the first time in generations, reclaiming lands thought lost forever.

The Emperor became a hero to the people. Portia was a heroine to the strategists, who no longer had to be bribed and pressured to seek her advice. Triumphantly, she recognized that the Readers' Code might be meant for other Readers, but not for the Master of Masters. Her powers, her wisdom, had set her above the others—and she had acted well. The Aventine Empire was better off for her manipulations.

For once, she lost her resentment of having been born female, unable to rule, and then being torn from her family when her Reading manifested, and forced into a life of sworn poverty and public service. Using the Reading power that had ruined her life, she triumphed over adversity.

If she could not be Empress in her own right, she could rule Tiberium through the Emperor—and the fool would never know that he was merely her tool!

She took to having her Reader's garments made of silk rather than linen, and began to use the accumulated wealth of her Academy to provide luxuries, not only for herself, but for the girls and women in her care. She *deserved* the finest foods, the softest bed, the richest clothing, the most precious gems. If the world truly understood what she had done for her country, it would agree.

Years passed, and Portia extended her power. There was too much to do alone. She found a few select Master Readers who understood how she helped both the Readers' system and the Aventine Empire. Occasionally someone discovered what they were doing, but such Readers could either be drawn into the circle or exiled in one way or another. Young upstarts often found themselves on the Path of the Dark Moon, but a circle of Master Readers made certain they would be quite happy there.

The scroll ended. Julia put it aside and lay back, wondering what had gone wrong. Portia was so successful, so strong, so intelligent. She worked with human nature, just as Adepts did. As far as Julia could see, Portia was far better qualified than her foolish nephew to rule the Aventine Empire.

Just as Julia was far better qualified than the child Aradia carried to be Lenardo's heir.

Practically on cue, Aradia's screams erupted through the cold silence of the night. Julia Read her sobbing in Devasin's arms again, and felt contempt. *If you could see Aradia now, Father, you would see that she is no fit wife for you—and any child of hers not fit to be your heir!*

* * *

Aradia woke feeling cold, even though blankets were piled over her and the fire was burning. She sat up, conscious of her awkward body, and felt cold air move in behind her to chill her spine.

Her breath clouded in the air of her bedroom.

Wrapping the blankets around her, she thrust her feet into felt slippers and went over to the fire. It heated only a tiny area, and she felt the chill air on her back even as she sat down facing the fire and held out her hands to it.

How could it be so cold? Especially inside? The calendar said it was nearly spring!

Ordinarily, this time of year brought sunny days interspersed with cold rain, occasionally sleet or a few flakes of snow. She had never known such bone-penetrating cold to come so late.

Devasin came in with an armload of warm clothing, saying, "I've never felt it so cold! You'd think it was the middle of winter instead of nearly spring."

"I'm sure the weather watchers are working on it," said Aradia.

"I certainly hope so!" Devasin replied with a shiver. "All the fountains are frozen, and so are the water pipes. Every fire talent in town is out thawing them."

Devasin helped Aradia dress in wool over silk, woolen stockings, two undertunics, a robe over her usual outer woolen dress. Still she was chilly as she went to breakfast despite Devasin's offer to bring it to her room. "Walking is good for me," she insisted. "Besides, I must get ready for Lilith."

Tomorrow. Tomorrow her friend would be here, a powerful Lady Adept, able to ward off—

Ward off *what*?

If only their enemy would show himself!

Herself?

At the thought, Aradia tried to Read the child in her womb. But with no more powerful Reader to help her, all she could tell was that her daughter seemed healthy, and was sleeping. *No wonder, after tormenting me all night.*

No—that was a dream. It all came from feeling so weak, with her powers diminished. When Lilith arrived she would feel safer, and perhaps the dreams would stop altogether.

At breakfast she carefully hid such thoughts from Master Selina, allowing the Reader to check her physical condition. "It won't be much longer," the woman said, delivering the platitude in a gentle voice that gave it genuine reassurance. But there was still a month to wait for Lenardo's daughter to enter the world. With each passing day, Aradia's hope weakened that he would be home to greet her.

After breakfast Master Clement contacted Aradia from the Academy, not subjecting himself to a walk outdoors in the bitter cold which held the city paralyzed.

//Our weather controllers are trying to dissipate the cold. It came in last night, out of nowhere. Yesterday's snow is frozen, making the streets nearly impassible. But the strange thing is, the snowstorm we so casually evoked left here at dusk and traveled up the North Road, to empty into the passes in the hills north of here. Our weather controllers could not stop it. Unless she is willing to expend a good deal of Adept strength, Lilith will not be able to get through until the cold lets up and the snow melts.//

Aradia tried to hide her pang of disappointment, excessive response to the news that Lilith would arrive a day or two later than expected.

But Master Clement said, //I will be glad to have her here, too, Aradia. We need a fully functioning Lord Adept. Pyrrhus will be that soon, but right now he is still learning to control his powers, and he lacks experience.//

Pyrrhus didn't lack energy, however. Before Master Clement had finished reporting what had happened in the night, the ex-Reader was charging up to the villa, melting a path for himself through the frozen snow, Wicket trailing in his wake.

Although well wrapped up against the cold, both men were also using Adept powers to keep themselves warm, a technique Aradia could no longer sustain. As both were braced to use Adept powers, they could only be Read visually—and the impression Aradia got was that Pyrrhus' angry eyes were melting the snow as he looked at it.

//I had hoped after yesterday,// Master Clement commented sadly, //that Pyrrhus was losing his furious response to every small setback.//

They soon learned, however, that Pyrrhus was not overreacting. The moment he and Wicket were ushered into Aradia's study, he asked, "Is Master Clement in contact with you?"

"Yes," Wicket responded before Aradia could reply.

Pyrrhus glanced at his friend, almost apologetically. But his mind was on a new problem. "Good. I've been working with the weather controllers since dawn—and we *cannot* break this cold wave with all our combined strength!"

"Then we will have to gather more Adepts," said Aradia. "Form a stronger circle."

Pyrrhus nodded. "Yes. The weather talents can direct the strength of other Adepts, correct?"

"That's right," agreed Aradia.

"Our problem, then, is to *define* what must be done. Clement, have you Read how far this cold extends? All Wicket can tell is that it goes beyond the city to the north as far as I can Read."

Wicket said, "He says then it has to be intended to delay Lilith, as they suspected."

Pyrrhus' fists clenched and his jaw set. "They *used* me!" he exclaimed furiously. "Whoever did this used *me* to bring that snow in. Why waste *their* energy if they could find someone foolish enough to do it for them? Just for children's games and trying out my powers!"

"You couldn't know," Wicket echoed Master Clement, putting his hand on Pyrrhus' shoulder.

Pyrrhus shook him off and began pacing. "I *should* have known! If I could Read—"

"*I* didn't Read anything," said Wicket. "Julia didn't.

Even Master Clement didn't. Come on, Pyrrhus—you never Read better'n the Master of Masters!"

For a moment Aradia expected an explosion, but Wicket was the one person Pyrrhus took such raw truths from. He stopped in his tracks, and acknowledged the statement with a snort of self-derisive laughter.

Aradia said, "Then perhaps Master Clement can Read the extent of the cold for us."

//I will leave my body," the Master Reader said. //Surely no weather front can extend beyond my range in that state.//

Aradia was glad of her small Reading ability, for it allowed her to Read with Master Clement after he had left his body, and his mind touched hers and Wicket's again. She was seated at her desk, aware of the murmur of Wicket's voice as he tried to describe his first experience of what it was like to leave the confines of the body, to float, pure mind, untouched by heat or cold, hunger or thirst, pain or pleasure.

Even vicariously, the only way Aradia or Wicket would ever know the experience, it was beautiful beyond belief. She felt Wicket force his thoughts away from the fact that Pyrrhus had once known this state, and never could again.

Master Clement focused on the North Road, keeping his disciplined mind on the extent of the devastating cold. Although he could not feel the lack of warmth, he could Read it, and the farther north they traveled, the colder it became.

There was no physical effect from the cold on pure mind. The landscape, coated with snow and frost, was a sparkling fantasy in white, blue, gray, and the occasional black of tree trunks. Where the sun shone through the scattered clouds, had they been there in person they would have been blinded by the brightness of its reflection on the snow.

But beneath that snow, a herd of cattle lay frozen.

Birds, fluffed into little powder puffs in their attempt to survive, stood erect although quite dead, frozen to the branches they had taken shelter in.

And still the cold grew more intense.

Travelers caught by the unexpected storm had built a lean-to and a fire. The fire was out, their dog a lump of icy brown fur frozen in position to guard them, their horse slumped lifeless against the side of their wagon. Man, woman, and child lay stiff in one another's arms.

My people, Aradia mourned.

Inexorably, the cold grew worse as Master Clement's mind followed the road northward. They were coming close now to the border between Lilith's lands and those Aradia and Lenardo ruled. Aradia's heart began to pound as she "saw" blue shapes against the snow. Lilith's pavilions.

There was no smoke from campfires. Everything was still as death.

But a fully functioning Lady Adept surely could not freeze to death!

At Aradia's panicked thought, Master Clement focused quickly on locating Lilith. She was inside one of the pavilions—alive! She lay on a pallet, fully clothed, a blue woolen cloak covering her. She appeared to be asleep, perhaps healing sleep, which would automatically keep her body warm and living. Except . . . it was not healing sleep they Read. It was something Aradia had never Read before—and neither had Master Clement!

Unconscious, her face utterly serene, her dark hair framing her pale features as smoothly as ever, Lilith was a powerful source of Adept energy.

And the terrible, life-draining, soul-freezing cold was emanating from here—

—created by the Adept energies of the Lady Lilith.

Chapter Eight

//What's wrong with her?// Wicket asked.

"Wicket, what have you found?" Pyrrhus demanded.

"Lady Lilith. Master Clement's Reading her."

"Why can't you talk to her through her Readers?"

"They're unconscious. Let me concentrate! I'll tell you as soon as I know anything."

//Her energy is draining away!// Aradia recognized.

Master Clement said. //She must be stopped!//

//If only someone could wake her,// Aradia fumed.

//Everyone is asleep. Some are dead. Aradia, could Lilith drain away to death?// Master Clement asked.

//A Lady Adept should not to be able to. Oh, Clement, what can we do against a Lord Adept powerful enough to use Lilith this way?//

//Surely not only one,// the Master Reader reassured. //It has to be a circle, and they have gone to great pains to prevent us from completing our own. Once we have Lilith here, we can combat them. We have done it before.//

Master Clement searched for Readers among Lilith's entourage. He recognized two, both frozen to death. Adepts he knew by healing sleep, their bodies warm despite the hideous cold. There were five, but no way to contact them. Besides . . . //Aradia?//

//I agree—it's not merely healing sleep to survive. It's restorative sleep, as if they've used their powers to the limit. In that cold, with a continued drain on their energies, they may never wake.//

Wicket continued reporting to Pyrrhus, his soft voice tense with fear of things he didn't understand.

//We must waken Lilith,// said Master Clement, and turned his attention to the nearest Watcher's post. There were two men in it, a Dark Moon Reader and a minor Adept.

The Adept was not certain he had the strength to keep them both warm—alive—on a five-mile walk, but the moment he learned it was to waken Lady Lilith from a life-draining trance, he said, "We'll wake her—or die trying!"

It took them nearly two hours to reach the blue pavilions. Once they found Lilith, all that was necessary was a finger touched to her forehead.

She woke, frowned, and asked, "Who are you? Where are my people?" She tried to sit up, and fell back in exhaustion, putting a hand to her head. "Why am I so weak?"

"Master Clement sent us to wake you," the Reader explained. "The cold. . . ."

Even as he spoke, the cold was beginning to dissipate, the spell broken with Lilith's waking.

But what had the spell *been*?

Awkwardly, they communicated with Lilith through the Reader, then sent a message along the Watchers' route for more of Lilith's people to protect her, and others to care for the dead. //The attacks in Zendi stopped,// Master Clement noted, //as soon as our Readers began watching for them, our Adepts ready to counter.//

Lilith had no choice except recovery sleep, but with the cold gone it would restore instead of draining her. Once she was safe, they broke the rapport.

Losing touch with Master Clement's powerful mind—and the incredible experience of being beyond one's body—was always disorienting.

Aradia glanced at Wicket, who started as if a support had gone out from under him. Although they were seated, Pyrrhus put a hand under his elbow as if he had stumbled. "Your body feels cumbersome when you return."

"*I* wasn't out of my body," Wicket said.

"If I know Clement," Pyrrhus told him, "he made you feel as if you were."

"Yeah," Wicket whispered with a soft smile.

Not allowing Wicket time to spoil his experience by remembering that Pyrrhus could not share it, the ex-Reader turned to Aradia. "And you, Lady Aradia?"

She smiled. "I've experienced it before, with both Master Clement and my husband." She took a deep breath, stretching, and then frowned. "But it's never been so long. I didn't think to ask Master Clement if it was safe for him to leave his body for that long." She couldn't help remembering the time they had almost lost him forever.

//It was,// the Master Reader's mental voice told her. //I am back and quite well. The city will warm quickly now. We must do as you instructed Lilith: gather as many Readers and Adepts as possible. We know what can be done with large numbers in cooperation.//

They all knew: topple a nation.

It was three days before Lilith arrived in Zendi. The dark circles about her eyes testified that although she had perforce succumbed to recovery sleep, she had had little ordinary rest.

Aradia welcomed her, but without the relief she had anticipated in having Lilith's strength to rely on. That evening they met with their circle—so few people to combat . . . what?

Julia sat in her room, Portia's scrolls on her lap, feeling left out. Aradia no longer needed her, a Reader. Now she had Lilith, an Adept.

But then Aradia had never wanted Julia. She wanted her own daughter, Lenardo's daughter. When Lenardo returned, Aradia would turn him against Julia. Aradia's child would be his heir, to rule lands Julia had risked death to conquer.

Portia was right. People were stupid, selfish, and easily led—even by poor leaders. Merely being the eldest son of the Emperor made an Emperor. Portia's grandnephew followed his father on the throne in Tiberium, less lecherous, but no less foolish.

The previous Emperor had died in the battle for

Zendi, when the tide of victory had turned. Under the power of Drakonius, the walls of the Empire were driven back and back once more, and Portia's advice was given less and less credence. More was demanded of Readers, while they were accorded less respect. Portia began again to rely on bribery and extortion.

She discovered an Adept secretly living within the Empire. Vortius the Gambler. There was little wonder that he was successful at his profession, and it was not difficult to persuade him to work for her rather than risk exposure. Especially when she could throw lucrative deals his way, make him feel that they were partners.

When age touched Portia, Vortius' healing powers kept her body from deteriorating. It gave him a hold over her, and she wove her threads of power throughout Tiberium to be sure she could squeeze him from many directions, should it become necessary. She dared not be dependent. She could not need anyone. Other people were simply to be used.

She yearned for Adept powers of her own. If she had been born with those powers instead of Reading, she would have made herself Empress by now! But the only effective powers she could command were money and influence, and she sought voraciously after both.

And then one day she discovered—

//Julia!//

Master Clement's mental voice was angry. Julia dropped the scroll.

//Oh—I'm late,// she realized. //I'm coming, Master.//

//Bring those scrolls with you. Why did you take them from my office without permission?//

//What? But you told me to Read Portia's scrolls.//

//I gave you a selection—I did not tell you to immerse yourself in Portia! I am sorry I ever gave you that assignment.// But his anger was gone; he accepted that she had misunderstood, and now he blamed himself.

Closing her mind to Reading, Julia smiled. She had fooled the Master of Masters. She knew he had not meant her to Read beyond the first set of scrolls, but once introduced to Portia's inner feelings, Julia had felt compelled to know everything about her.

She had learned much. Now she could protect herself from Aradia, from Aradia's child, and if necessary from Lenardo as well. She tied up the small bundle of scrolls, and went to join Zendi's inner circle.

What a feeble group they were. Master Clement, growing old, so trusting that she could fool him without even trying. Aradia, pregnant and half mad. Lilith, once proud and strong, now frightened of the force that had used her own powers against her. Decius, crippled in body by Drakonius and in mind by Master Clement's naive teaching. Wicket, half clown, half simpleton, unable to stand without someone to lean upon—and Pyrrhus, Wicket's crutch. Julia understood Pyrrhus least of all. When he first came to Zendi he had seemed strong, using his powers to fight and kill. Now he was no better than the rest—weaker, for he actually allowed himself to be *used* by Readers, by Wicket of all people.

Julia hid her contempt, handing the scrolls meekly to Master Clement as she took her place with a sweet smile.

Lilith began, unable to conceal her fear. "Why didn't you warn me?" she demanded. "You left me helpless!"

"We did not *know*," Master Clement explained. "How could we anticipate a Lady Adept's being used that way? We told you everything that had happened here."

"It is forming a pattern only now," added Pyrrhus. "Our attacker uses Adepts who cannot Read. First people with small powers, like the weather controllers. Lords Adept have strong shields against such influence."

"The attacker is learning to get around them," said Master Clement. "It must be implanted commands again, for surely no one can control an Adept exercising power."

Lilith studied them. "You are saying that at some time when I was not using my powers . . . someone put in my mind a command such as 'When you make camp near your border, you will fall asleep and cause cold weather'?"

Aradia nodded. "I fear that that is what happened."

"But I live surrounded by Readers!"

"Either it was done by an Adept, unReadable while using his powers," said Master Clement, "or else by a Reader out of his body. Then he could not be Read unless he touched another Reader's mind."

"I feel better," Aradia said. "This is all within our own scope of power—simply unthinkable to us to use Adepts so. For a time I felt as if we were dealing with the Ghost King!"

"But who's doing it, and where's he hiding?" asked Wicket. "Every Reader's been alert for weeks, and we still haven't a clue."

"Perhaps," Master Clement said softly, "Aradia just gave us one."

"I did? What?"

"The unthinkable. Aradia, may I have permission to Read your library?" asked the Master Reader.

"Of course. What do you expect to find there that isn't in the Academy library?"

"Let me pursue it first," he replied. "I am hoping to prove my suspicions wrong."

"What if they prove right?" asked Pyrrhus, the hard edge back in his voice.

"Then," replied Master Clement, "we will rely on what has always been our best skill: dealing with new situations in new ways."

Wicket looked at Pyrrhus with a grin. "I guess we fit right in then, don't we?"

Julia remained silent, disdainful of the pitiful camaraderie. Whistling against the darkness.

"Since I am not an Adept," Master Clement continued, "I would like a Lord Adept with me until we resolve this situation. Aradia, you also need protection. Lilith, stay with her. Pyrrhus— "

"I'm not a Lord Adept."

"We don't have tests, as Readers do," said Aradia. "You will prove yourself in action soon, Pyrrhus. I have no doubt of it. Master Clement will be safe with you. Wicket—"

"I know. Pyrrhus doesn't need me when he has Master Clement, so I'll keep up our regular duties."

A few days later, Julia found Pyrrhus alone in Master Clement's outer office. He still went fully armed, she noticed, although Adepts did not normally wear even a sword.

"I'm afraid it's Master Juna for you again," Pyrrhus told her. "Clement is treating a child they brought in an hour ago, suffering from hallucinations. None of the other Masters could help him."

It was the third day in a row that some emergency had kept Master Clement from his appointments with Julia, and it seemed recently that most lessons they did begin were interrupted. Master Juna would be ready for Julia in a few minutes. So she sat down and asked, "Pyrrhus, why did you first become partners with Wicket?"

"What?"

"After you saved his life, why did you team up with him? He couldn't even read—I mean, he was illiterate."

"Wicket's a survivor," Pyrrhus replied, as if that were sufficient explanation.

When he did not elaborate, Julia asked, "What do you mean?"

He studied her face, an odd look in his eyes. Then, with a smile that was more a grimace, he said, "Let me tell you something about revenge, Julia. It gives you a reason to stay alive, to stay healthy, to gain skills. But if that is all you live for, once you achieve it there is nothing left.

"After the fall of Tiberium—after Portia's death—*I* had nothing left. I wasn't a Reader anymore. I had no plans, and only one skill that did not depend on Reading." The smile became self-deprecating. "I had learned a hundred ways to kill someone with my hands, and then helped kill my target with my mind.

"When it was over, I had no idea what to do with myself, until I rescued Wicket. When you save someone's life, you take responsibility for him. Did you know that?"

"It's an Adept law," Julia replied.

"Yes," Pyrrhus murmured. "It doesn't have to be

taught, like the Readers' Code. It just happens. So there I was, suddenly responsible for Wicket." He grinned sardonically. "Until you gave him the confidence of his powers, Julia, that was a heavy responsibility. Wicket tends to attract trouble. Like it or not, I had something to live for again. Eventually we developed some plans together, and you know the rest."

"Why do you stay partners with him now, though?" she asked. "He's got a good job, and money. He doesn't need you to take care of him anymore. And you're a Lord Adept."

His eyes narrowed. "Why do you stay with *your* friends?"

Julia shrugged. "Maybe I won't, after I outgrow them." Just then, Master Juna called her to her lesson, so she left with the feel of Pyrrhus' eyes trying to pierce through to her meaning. But she was safe with Pyrrhus; he couldn't Read.

Aradia hated her clumsiness, her constant fatigue, in the last days of her pregnancy. Lilith spent hours just sitting with her, talking of her own pregnancy, and of Ivorn as a baby, happy memories of a doting mother.

Aradia clung to hope. Although her powers were severely diminished, she was still able to Read—especially through a stronger Reader—and perform minor Adept functions. Her mother, she had been told, had lost everything.

No. She would not think about her mother, her madness. Aradia was not mad. Master Clement reassured her that strange dreams were nothing to fear.

Devasin came to tell Aradia and Lilith that Master Clement and Pyrrhus were there to see them. It was spring now; they met in the courtyard amid soft warm breezes and the fragrance of first blossoms.

"Aradia," said Pyrrhus, "I had a very strange conversation with Julia today. It seemed almost as if she were trying to drive a wedge between Wicket and me."

Aradia frowned. "I don't understand. She's been so . . . good, so caring, since Galerio died. As if with

Lenardo and Wulfston missing, and then losing her friend, she had learned the value of close ties."

Master Clement said, "I wonder if she is developing an unflattering snobbishness. Possibly because her association with minor Adepts got her into such a frightening situation."

"I will talk to her," said Aradia. "Now, have you turned up anything in your research, Master Clement?"

"I am not certain. We both have copies of Torio's and Melissa's reports of events in Madura."

Aradia smiled. "We all had the same thought. Lilith and I have studied them—but the cold we experienced could not be the cold white fire they told of. That was a life-devouring energy from the planes of existence, and uncontrolled it threatened to consume all life in Madura."

"The cold created through me," Lilith took it up, "simply disappeared the moment I stopped generating it. It could not have been the same thing."

"No," said Master Clement. "And yet somehow what happened to Torio and Melissa seems to hold a clue, if I could only see it."

"Torio and Melissa?" Pyrrhus asked.

"Four of our friends, Torio, Melissa, Zanos, and Astra, traveled north to Madura to look for Zanos' family," Aradia explained. "They found the land in possession of a sorcerer who tapped a source of destructive power." She went on to tell how the sorcerer Maldek had allowed Melissa to die forcing that power back onto its own plane, and Torio had gone to rescue her from the plane of the dead.

"Melissa stayed in Madura," she finished, "to . . . contain Maldek, as it were. We don't know where Torio went; he was a Reader, but his Adept powers wakened in Madura."

"What happened to Zanos and Astra?" Pyrrhus asked.

"They went with Wulfston, to rescue Lenardo," Aradia replied.

"So . . . everyone who might help you is spread all over the world," Pyrrhus mused. "Divide and conquer."

Aradia stared at him. "Pyrrhus, surely events in

Madura and Africa could not all be part of one gigantic plan."

"You are carrying the heir to the Savage Empire," he replied. "Your husband is gone, your brother is gone, your best friend's powers are used against you, a Reader/Adept mysteriously disappears, other Readers and Adepts who have worked with you before are flung to the four winds. Coincidence?"

"When you put it that way . . ." Aradia admitted.

Pyrrhus smiled kindly. "There are times," he said, "when paranoia is a survival trait."

"You are the target, Aradia—or your child," said Lilith. "We must protect you."

"Lilith is right," said Master Clement. "Can you provide me with a room here, Aradia?"

"Of course."

"Pyrrhus, call Wicket. You two work best as a team—I don't want you separated anymore. Julia will take her lessons here, with me. Until the child is born, let us offer Aradia the best protection we can."

That night, Aradia dreamed again of her daughter, the young woman with the beautiful face, until she opened eyes filled with hatred.

This time she said, "Mother, I am taking your powers, just as you stole your own mother's, for I am ready to be born, rightful ruler of the Savage Empire.

"You cannot fight me. Without your powers, you are nothing. You are going to die, Aradia—*die*!"

Aradia woke to Devasin's touch on her forehead, and in moments Lilith was there. It was light in the room—the sun was up.

The two women soothed Aradia. "She said I was going to die," Aradia sobbed, hating her weakness but unable to control it.

"Hush," said Lilith. "It was only a dream. You're not going to die. Your friends are here to protect you."

Devasin and Lilith helped Aradia get up and dressed, but she was still shaking. "Here," said Devasin, "just lie back on the lounge now. I'll open the curtains to the courtyard, so you can enjoy the fresh air while I get your breakfast."

But before Devasin reached the door, Julia was there with a tray. "I brought your breakfast, Aradia. Didn't you Read me telling you?"

"Read—?" Aradia tried, panic stabbing as she opened to Reading and met . . . nothing! "Julia—let me Read through you, please."

"Of course."

There was still nothing. "I can't Read. She *is* taking my powers."

"Who is?" asked Julia.

"My baby!" Aradia answered furiously. "She said she would take away my powers and kill me—just as I did to my mother!"

"Oh, my lady, no!" exclaimed Devasin. "You did no such thing, and you mustn't think it of your poor little baby."

Shuddering, Aradia forced herself under control. "I'm sorry," she said. "I must not let dreams affect me that way."

"Eat your breakfast," Lilith said gently. "It won't be long now—only a few more days."

But the food had no appeal. Aradia managed only to drink her tea. Then she sat with her feet up, looking out at the courtyard, and tried the test she had been putting off.

A tree branch swayed gently in the spring breeze. It should take only a modest Adept effort to make it swing farther on each stroke. She applied the effort. The branch continued to move exactly as it had before.

Aradia looked toward the candelabra, and willed fire. A child's trick.

Nothing happened.

Lilith saw where she was looking. "Aradia. . . ."

"It's gone, Lilith. I'm helpless."

Lilith took her hand. "It's temporary. All your energies are going into producing a healthy child. Try to sleep some more. Then maybe you'll be able to eat."

"No—just give me some more tea."

Lilith poured her another mug from the pot Julia had brought, reheating it with Adept power. *Yesterday I could have done that for myself,* Aradia thought morosely.

Master Clement came a little later, to reassure her that her baby was fine. Of course the *baby* was fine! It was Aradia who was weakening, dying.

The Master Reader frowned. "Aradia, you mustn't think that way."

"Oh, no," she whispered, hot tears stinging her eyelids. "I cannot even shield my thoughts anymore."

"Oh, child," he began, "if you can just think of. . . ." He broke off, eyes unfocused for a moment, and she knew he was Reading something. Then he looked at her, and his ancient face crinkled into a grin. "Aradia! Lenardo is home!"

"Home?" she cried, grasping his arm to sit up. "Where is he?"

"No, no—he's not in Zendi. But he and Wulfston have landed safely at Southport, taken on supplies, and started up the coast toward Dragon's Mouth. They'll be here within two days!"

"Lenardo—safe! I've worried so about you. And Wulfston—oh, little brother, I've missed you, too. Please, Master Clement, send them my message."

"Already done," he assured her. "Now, with that good news, surely you can eat something. I will have Julia bring you a fresh tray—if she can stop dancing for joy long enough to carry it."

Julia sparkled with happiness. "Father will be here soon—and by tomorrow he'll be in range for Reading!" Then, "Oh—I'm sorry, Aradia." Somehow, her apology didn't sound sincere. Perhaps she was just too happy to be sorry for anything.

So was Aradia. She just smiled at Julia, and found that food suddenly tasted delicious.

After she ate, she felt sleepy. In the courtyard, Master Clement, Julia, Decius, Pyrrhus, and Wicket were talking. "Go join them, Lilith," she said. "I'm falling asleep, and certainly the group of you can protect me from twenty paces away!"

To warm thoughts of Lenardo's being home for the birth of his daughter, Aradia drifted off to sleep.

And dreamed.

She saw herself, on this very couch. Out in the courtyard, her friends shared stories of Lenardo and Wulfston with Pyrrhus and Wicket. Wicket leaned back after a time, staring over at Pyrrhus, but he didn't say anything.

The dream turned to the disorienting sensation of looking down at her own distorted body. Did she really look that terrible, lips and eyelids puffed, jaw slack?

She was dead!

In the dead woman's womb, the child squirmed. It was dying—and its pain communicated to the Readers in the courtyard.

Everyone dashed to Aradia's room. "She's dead!" exclaimed Master Clement. "But the child is alive. Lilith?"

"I'm trying—her heart won't beat. What are we to do?"

"Save the baby!" said Julia.

"Keep the child alive, Lilith," said Master Clement. "Pyrrhus, give me your sharpest knife."

He slit her clothing, then her flesh, lifting the living child from the dead mother. The babe gasped and wailed like a normal child—and then suddenly opened hate-filled eyes and stared at the Master Reader. "I have won, Clement," she said in the voice of a woman grown. "Now I have both powers—and as Lenardo's daughter I will rule at last! How fitting that I rule the Savage Empire!"

Aradia woke, feeling death in her veins. There was poison in her blood! But it came from her womb, where harbored that thing of evil, seeking its revenge.

She might die, but she would take that creature with her.

Fighting for every movement, Aradia rolled off the lounge onto her knees, crawled to the chest which held her clothes, and dragged herself to her feet.

Outside, Aradia could hear the murmur of conversation, but she did not let her attention wander. No

Reader must know what she was doing until it was done.

Hanging on the wall over the chest were spears, swords, and knives. Aradia chose a large, sharp blade. She could barely lift her arms to take it from its scabbard. Finally, though, she fumbled it into position. It must impale the child. If only she could Read how it lay . . .

In the courtyard, Wicket's voice rose above the others. "Pyrrhus, *what* are you using Adept power for?"

"Adept power? I'm not—" And then a shout, "Blessed *gods*!" and it was as if someone grasped Aradia's arms, pulling them up and away as she tried to plunge the knife into her womb.

"No!" she wailed, struggling. "I must kill her! She'll kill us all!"

But Pyrrhus and Wicket were on either side of her, prying the knife from her hands.

"She's been poisoned!" exclaimed Master Clement. "Lilith! Pyrrhus! Decius!"

Healing fire flowed through Aradia's body, purging her blood. Pyrrhus and Wicket caught her as she collapsed, and laid her on her bed. She fought to remain conscious.

"The baby?" Lilith asked anxiously.

"Unharmed," said Master Clement. "Someone protected the child while the poison worked on Aradia. Thank the gods you saw her, Pyrrhus!"

"If Wicket hadn't said I—" Pyrrhus went pale, and put his hands over his face. "*I* was protecting the child!" He lowered his hands, eyes burning. "Someone *used* me. Clement—"

"Portia," Aradia and Master Clement said with the same voice.

"In Aradia's baby?" exclaimed Lilith.

"Yes!" said Aradia. "Kill her, Lilith! Use your powers—kill her now!"

"No, Lilith!" Master Clement ordered.

"Why?" Pyrrhus' voice grated with fury as he stepped forward.

"Pyrrhus, please," begged Aradia. "Kill her!"

"No!" Master Clement said again.

Wicket threw an arm across Pyrrhus' chest to pull him back, as if his physical strength could affect Adept power.

"Portia is *not* in the child!" the Master Reader continued. "Wicket—Read with me. Tell Pyrrhus Aradia is wrong!"

"She's there!" Aradia insisted, tears of weakness sliding down her cheeks. "She's killing me—can't you see? Does she control you all?"

"It's just a baby," said Wicket. "Pyrrhus, it's an innocent little girl. *Please* trust Master Clement. Don't harm a child!"

"They're lying!" said Aradia. "She's fooled them."

"No!" said Master Clement. "I know Portia. She is here . . . but she is not in Aradia's baby." Suddenly he demanded, "Who poisoned Aradia?" Glancing at the abandoned tray on the chest, he said, "The tea—there is poison in—"

He whirled, scarlet cloak flaring, and Aradia saw Julia behind him.

Lenardo's daughter had not joined the circle around Aradia's bed. She looked up at the Master of Masters in round-eyed innocence—but there was something about those eyes.

"Oh, blessed gods!" the girl cried. "She used me, too. She made me poison Aradia!" But there was not a single note of sincerity in the performance.

"That's not Julia!" Wicket said in a horrified whisper.

"Why would Portia poison Aradia?" Pyrrhus flung off Wicket's arm and stalked Julia, who did not back off. "Why *did* you? I can see you, Portia, even if I can't Read." He smiled—the smile Aradia had not seen since he had first come to Zendi, colder than the freeze Portia had brought upon their lands.

Julia's young face responded with an equally cold smile, her eyes empty of warmth and humanity. "Go ahead, Pyrrhus—kill the daughter of the Lord of the Land. Lenardo is on his way home now. When he arrives, you can explain why you killed me!"

Pyrrhus raised his hands, clenching them into fists—but the gesture was one of frustration, not threat. "No," he said. "Not because of what might happen to me, but because of Julia. You almost made me harm one child—but I will not. You will never use me again, Portia!"

He put his hands on her shoulders, staring into those cold, dead eyes. "Julia! Julia—fight her! Master Clement, help Julia."

"He is," said Wicket. "So are you, Pyrrhus—Julia's there! She's afraid. Come on, Julia—you can do it! Fight her off! Portia's got no right to take over your life! Fight her—"

Cowering in a shadowed corner of her own mind, Julia huddled in terror as Portia controlled her body. She could hear Pyrrhus and Wicket, but could not respond.

I don't deserve to live. I got Galerio killed! I tried to kill Aradia and her baby!

//No, Julia—you were used,// Master Clement told her. //Portia played on your strengths and weaknesses, turned your courage against you. Don't let her do it now, Julia. Fight her—drive her out.//

I can't. I'm evil. I don't deserve to live.

//Die, Julia!// said Portia, pushing at Julia's presence.

//Julia!// It was Wicket. //Don't let that evil woman have your body—remember what she did to people. To Pyrrhus. She'll hurt more people if you let her live!//

I can't fight her—I don't have the strength.

//Use my strength,// said Master Clement.

//And mine,// said Wicket.

//Mine, too,// added Decius.

Julia rallied, focusing on Portia's evil. She must not live again! But despite the support from the Readers, she didn't know *how* to fight.

Evil laughter mocked her. //You are weak, Julia, lost! Let go now—before I must kill even your consciousness!//

Portia's poisonous mind pushed blackness at her from all sides. She struggled desperately, but each attempt to push back the void allowed it in from another direction. She was being squeezed into nothingness!

A ray of warmth pierced the void. Like a spring sunbeam, it offered life and hope. She followed, feeling now that it was . . . love. Master Clement, Lilith, Decius, even Pyrrhus and Wicket were pouring love for her into that void, and buoyed by it she struggled, resisted until she finally felt—

//Father? *Father?*///

Her mind leaped eagerly, training on that communion of family, strong and whole and determined.

Before the combined power, Portia fled. Julia's knees gave way, and Pyrrhus caught her. She opened her eyes. "Where is Father?" she asked.

"On his way," replied Master Clement. He smiled at her. "Julia, Lenardo is too far away to Read us, even with his great powers. What you felt was not your father's love. It was your mother's."

Tears leaped to Julia's eyes. She pushed away Pyrrhus' support, and went to kneel beside the bed, taking Aradia's hand. "I tried to kill you, and yet you. . . ."

Aradia managed a weak smile. "It wasn't you, Julia, any more than it was me trying to kill my baby. As soon as I understood what Portia had done, how could I help lending what strength I have?"

"Sleep now, Aradia," said Lilith.

"Yes," Aradia agreed, drifting off.

Julia stayed where she was, Reading turmoil among the other Readers.

Pyrrhus said, "Portia won't give up that easily. Now that she has escaped from the plane of lost souls. . . ."

Master Clement said, "We must find her, prevent her from taking over someone else."

"I don't think you'll have to look very far," said Wicket.

"What?" asked Master Clement. Then, "She might. . . ."

Pyrrhus stared at Aradia. "Wicket," he demanded, "Read the baby!"

Julia raised her head with a start. "That's why she made you protect the baby until she thought she had me! She would have had power right away, because I'm almost grown up. In a baby she would have to wait for her powers to manifest."

"But an infant has no will to fight her," said Master Clement.

They Read the baby again, finding nothing but a normal, healthy child almost ready to be born. She slept peacefully in her private ocean, emblem of innocence.

//Too obvious,// observed Master Clement.

The hand Julia held tightened almost imperceptibly, and she perceived a thrill of wicked glee.

Leaping up, she said, "Portia's in Aradia! She knew we'd Read the baby, so when Aradia went to sleep she entered her mind."

"She's been in all our minds," said Pyrrhus.

"While we slept," said Lilith. "That is when she implanted her commands—and caused Aradia's dreams."

"Lady Lilith," said Pyrrhus, "I'm afraid she has learned to manipulate Adepts who cannot Read at any time, hiding from Readers behind our shields."

"That is why our Readers could not discover her," said Master Clement.

"Protect Aradia physically," Pyrrhus advised Lilith. "I do not think she can manipulate you while you are using your powers."

"If she seeks to return permanently, the child is her only refuge now that we know her intentions," said Master Clement. "Julia, Decius, Wicket—defend the baby. Pyrrhus, lend them strength. Portia must act now, before Lenardo adds his strength to ours. She is desperate—and very dangerous."

"As dangerous as the Ghost King," said Lilith. "We always thought those stories were pure legend."

"The Ghost King was defeated. We will defeat Portia as well," said Master Clement as he lay down on the lounge by the window. He would have to fight Portia beyond the body, as she was beyond it.

Julia, Decius, Wicket, and Pyrrhus sat on the floor, joining hands. The three who could Read consciously "borrowed" and guided Pyrrhus' power, forming a mental barrier against Portia.

Even so, Portia's strength of will almost overpowered them before Master Clement's mind touched theirs. Portia retreated.

Evil laughter taunted them. //Clement, you have grown old and dull-witted! Why should I take this child? You would simply kill her—and I would move on, take someone else, or remain out of body. But perhaps I *should* take her over, merely to force you to kill Lenardo and Aradia's child!//

Her presence made another feint at the babe in Aradia's womb, but this time it did not test their strength.

//I do not underestimate you, Portia,// said Master Clement. //How could I, when you managed to follow Torio through the planes of existence?//

//That fool! Oh, he took pains that I should not follow him to the plane of the dead and thence back to this world—but he never thought that I would backtrack along the path he followed on his way *to* the plane where we met!//

//However you did it,// replied Master Clement, //you must go back now to the plane of the dead—and this time I will see that you pass beyond the portal.//

//Oh, no. I like it here. I can control people, kill my enemies, enter anyone's body I please to enjoy the pleasures of the flesh, and escape onto the planes of existence when I encounter opposition. And no one can stop me—not you alone, Clement, and not any pitiful circle you can muster, no matter what powers they claim!//

Master Clement ignored her boasting. //Portia, I will guide you .// His mental presence urged Portia's.

Julia, never having experienced anything like this, had no idea what Master Clement was trying to do, and neither did Wicket, who was trying to explain to Pyrrhus what they Read.

"He's trying to force her to another plane," Pyrrhus interpreted. "One Master Reader can't do that alone, especially not to another Master Reader!"

Decius was holding Julia's left hand. At Pyrrhus' comment his hand suddenly went limp in hers, and she realized that he had left his body to try to help Master Clement.

"Decius—you fool!" hissed Pyrrhus. Then with the power of his mental "voice": //Decius—you haven't the experience to help. Portia will use you against Master Clement!//

"She is," Wicket said tightly, trying to describe how Portia had seized upon Decius' intrusion, putting the young Reader's presence between herself and the old Master.

//Decius—go back!// ordered Master Clement.

Decius broke free of Portia's manipulation and joined his strength to Master Clement's. //There is no one else to help you.//

Portia cut Decius off from Master Clement, surrounding him with darkness. He fought valiantly, but he was no match for the woman who had been Master of Masters.

Master Clement projected through the cloud of darkness, providing Decius with a focus, but as the young Reader struggled—

//Master Clement—Portia's getting away!// Julia warned. But he could not abandon Decius!

"Pyrrhus, *no!*" Wicket's voice shouted in Julia's right ear, his hand jerking convulsively as in the "world" they were Reading another presence blocked Portia's way.

The fury radiant from Pyrrhus wavered for a moment, overshadowed by a rush of ecstatic pleasure—away from his nerve-burned body, he could *Read*!

But his need for revenge quickly overshadowed all else. More menacingly cold than Julia had ever Read him, Pyrrhus advanced on Portia. From the opposite direction, Master Clement closed in.

Decius was free now, observing, for the darkness disappeared when Portia's attention shifted to Pyrrhus. Instead of retreating, she moved toward him, her presence growing stronger as she approached. Heartless laughter underscored her words. //So you would kill me again, Pyrrhus? Fool! You have killed only yourself!//

Wicket's start of fear for his friend stabbed through Julia.

Portia, though, seemed to grow and flourish as she absorbed Pyrrhus' rage, Wicket's fear.

Despite their bodiless state, Julia felt that same menace Pyrrhus projected when he stalked someone—but again Portia only drew upon the anger, the frustration.

Suddenly Julia recalled something Pyrrhus had told her. //Pyrrhus—remember what you told me about revenge?//

//It's sweet!// asserted Portia. //Go on, Pyrrhus—take your revenge! It's all you have left, now.// Her power flared as she absorbed his fury.

//Pyrrhus—// Master Clement began.

//I see it,// Pyrrhus replied, his mental voice soft with amazement. Julia could feel him Read what Portia was doing. His will to revenge faded. //I had my revenge, and it was *not* sweet. Such feelings are pleasant only to a creature such as Portia has become. She gains strength from fear, or hate, or anger.

//We don't fear her.//

Julia felt Wicket struggle to control his fear, felt Portia weaken slightly as the negative feelings faded.

//But you hate me!// Portia snapped.

//Oh, I did,// Pyrrhus agreed. //It is amazing how much energy I wasted hating you, Portia. While you fed on that energy! That, and the fear and pain you generated with the storms and accidents and cold—oh, yes, you gained strength, but it fades quickly, doesn't it? To gain permanent power in our world again, you must have a body. But we won't allow that, now that we know you. You are nothing but a poor dead woman who won't accept that she's dead.//

//I'm not dead!//

//Portia,// Master Clement told her gently, //your time is over. Now you must rest. Come—let us escort you to the plane of the dead. It is your rightful place—you will find healing there for all your suffering.//

//No!//

But together, Master Clement and Pyrrhus surrounded Portia, radiating pity.

Portia shrank from that feeling, but the two Master Readers held her inexorably within it.

Julia Read an unspoken question from Pyrrhus. //I know the way,// said Master Clement. //I escorted Portia there once before.//

//And I will escape, as I did before!// Portia asserted.

//No, not this time,// said Master Clement.

Portia replied only with a defiant moment of wicked glee.

Julia's curiosity surged in frustration. Master Clement and Pyrrhus were about to move to another plane, where she could not Read them—it infuriated her to be too young to leave her body. It wasn't fair!

Determined to Read everything she could before they moved beyond her perceptions, Julia focused her power on Portia, Master Clement, and Pyrrhus.

The universe shifted with a sickening jolt!

Chaos whirled about her.

She wanted to scream, but she had no voice, no body.

Sheer terror gripped her as she was whipped endlessly through formless darkness.

She staggered, and was caught by strong hands. She was in her body, on a plain, Decius beside her—standing on two healthy legs. It was his hands that steadied her.

There were other people on the plain, walking toward a gateway through which Julia saw a welcoming warm light, much like the warmth of love that had guided her from the darkness where Portia had tried to trap her. She wanted to go toward it.

"Julia!" Decius whispered sharply. "You shouldn't be here! *I* shouldn't be here," he added in wonder.

"Shhh!" she said, her fear completely gone.

Just ahead of them, Master Clement and Pyrrhus walked with a woman between them, their arms linked through hers. It must be Portia, but not the shriveled crone Julia had known. This woman stood tall and strong, and her hair was unsilvered.

But she struggled, twisting in their grasp, and Julia recognized her face—a face marked with frustration and determination. Portia when, with all good intentions, she had first turned from the Reader's Code, thinking the ends would justify her means.

"Look behind you, fools!" Portia spat. "Take me into death, and you take *them* as well!"

Even together, the two men could not hold her from forcing them to turn around.

"Julia! Decius!" exclaimed Master Clement. Julia could Read his dismay, and realized that Portia had used the insatiable curiosity of young Readers to bring hostages with her to the plane of the dead.

"Julia, let them take me and you are dead," said Portia. "I will take you back to your world, give you my power—together we will rule!"

"You influenced me through your scrolls, Portia," Julia said. "They made me accept you then—but they also made me know you. Now I see what your life made you. I will never become like you."

"You'll never have the chance. Clement is about to abandon you. Neither Decius nor Pyrrhus can take you home. If you would live, you must help me to live again!"

Julia stared at Master Clement. "Is it true?"

"I must take Portia through the portal," he replied. "Otherwise, she will not go."

"But what about *us*? Do we have to die too?"

"Yes!" Portia hissed. "Pyrrhus is dead already—he can never return to his body. You will die unless Clement takes you home."

"No!" said Decius, taking Julia's hand. "I've moved from one plane to another before. I'll get us home."

Portia laughed. "You'll be lost on the planes of existence!"

Master Clement, for all his experience, had become lost when he brought Portia here before. How could Decius find the way?

Portia drew strength from Julia's fear—and Decius'.

Pyrrhus said, "Portia is right. Take them home, Master Clement. I will take Portia through the portal."

"No," said Master Clement. "I must complete the

task I failed before. You will take Julia and Decius home, Master Pyrrhus."

Julia Read Pyrrhus' shock. "I can't be a Master Reader," he said. "I wouldn't be able to Read once I returned. If I could return."

"Then be a Lord Adept," Master Clement replied. "My work in that world is finished. You have much to do yet, Lord Pyrrhus." He turned away as if the matter were settled, and spoke to Decius.

"Decius, learn to use both your powers well. You may be both a Master Reader and a Lord Adept one day."

"Yes, Master," Decius said uncertainly.

"And Julia," her teacher told her, "your powers are great for one so young—I underestimated you, child. It never occurred to me that you could leave your body, let alone follow us here."

"You see, Julia?" said Portia. "Clement did not appreciate your powers—and now you will die for it!"

Despite herself, fear swelled in Julia. Portia fed upon it, and broke free of Master Clement's grasp. "I am your only hope, child," she said, reaching for Julia's hand. "Let me take you safely home, teach you to *use* your powers, not deny them!"

Julia shrank from the grasping hand. "I'm afraid of being lost—but I'm much more afraid of becoming like you!"

Master Clement recaptured Portia. "You won't be lost, Julia," he told her. "Pyrrhus will take you home. You will study, and gain control of your powers. Your father will aid you to use them wisely, as will your mother—and you must help them with your little sister."

"Yes, Master," Julia said helplessly.

They turned and moved toward the beckoning light once more, only Portia struggling futilely. The rest were drawn to it—Julia wondered why she should *want* to go back when the promise of joy and peace lay ahead, through the portal.

The first rays of light touched them.

Portia screamed and writhed as if she were burned!

Both Master Clement and Pyrrhus had to exert their full strength to hold her. She was burning. They could Read her pain, see flames engulf her struggling form.

Portia's agony was transmitted to the two men holding her, but they would not let her go, let her escape.

Master Clement moved ahead, pulling Portia with him, reaching across her to disengage Pyrrhus' hands as he moved farther into the brightness.

The old Master was almost blotted out by the brilliance. Julia squinted against it, seeing Portia still writhing, trying to seize the advantage when Pyrrhus let her go—but she could not escape Master Clement's grip.

And then, to Julia's amazement, the woman's struggles ceased.

The flames were washed away by the brilliance of the pure light—and Julia understood that they had been Portia's last defense. As they faded, the brilliant light increased. Julia could not be sure of what she saw in that blinding light, but it seemed to be Portia as she had been when she first became Master of Masters—young, bright, honest, and determined to use her powers for good. She stared into the light, and it seemed to Julia that a warm smile made her unutterably beautiful.

And then the two forms disappeared in the blinding light.

Instinctively, Julia and Decius stared to follow—but Pyrrhus grasped their arms. "It is not your time," he said. "You must go back now."

With gentle firmness, he turned them away from the beckoning light. "Read with me."

They did—and all light was gone!

Again the sickening twist, chaos, darkness, whirling winds.

The illusion of a physical body gone, Julia struggled to stay in rapport with Pyrrhus and Decius as they plummeted and twisted through the planes of existence.

Pyrrhus in control of his Reading was a clear, strong force—no question that he was a Master Reader. He brought them to a halt in a starry void, peaceful and beautiful. But they were not on the ground looking up at stars; they were disembodied minds floating, with the stars around them in every direction. //Picture our physical world,// Pyrrhus instructed, //the room we left—now!//

There was that odd twisting feeling again—and they were minds floating in nothingness. Even the stars were gone. Julia could not control her thought: //This isn't home!//

It was a vacuum that sucked at her as if it would draw her mind out into millions of separate bits, out of contact.

//Julia!//

Pyrrhus was there, and Decius. //It's the plane of privacy,// said Decius—although in the naked clarity of thought here she perceived that he merely *hoped* that was "where" they were.

//Again,// directed Pyrrhus. //Aradia's room, our bodies in the circle.//

But Julia had forgotten what it was like to have a physical body. She shared Decius' and Pyrrhus' attempts to reach out for their bodies, but they were as unsuccessful as she was. Panic ruined her concentration. She began to fear they would never get home, but Pyrrhus' strong, gentle intelligence insisted, //We will get there. You will return, even if I cannot. Read for—ah!//

Julia felt it, too—the sweet, silly, frightened but brave presence that was Wicket's unmistakable mental aura. Clumsy but determined, he sent out a wordless call to Pyrrhus. They followed it.

For one moment Julia hung above the scene, looking down at herself, Decius, Pyrrhus, Wicket, still holding hands, Wicket's mind desperately searching for theirs.

//You're back!// his mind shouted in glee, and with a jolt, Julia found herself, stiff and sore, in her own body on the floor of Aradia's bedroom. Wicket looked over at her in relief, glanced at Decius as he opened his eyes—but across from Julia Pyrrhus' body remained slumped, unconscious.

//Pyrrhus?// Wicket questioned.

//Yes—I'm here, Wicket//

//Come back, Pyrrhus, please.// Wicket pleaded. //I

don't mind translating for you—you can always leave your body again if you want to Read. But come back now, please?//

//I can't . . . find the way.//

It was as Portia had said: he could not return to his body.

Julia Read his problem: he could not "feel" his body through the destroyed nerves that should have made the connection between the mental and the physical. Wicket Read with her and choked down panic. //What can we do?//

//I don't know,// she told him, feeling sick now that she once again had a body capable of reacting to her emotions. Master Clement should have known this would happen!

But the old Master had seemed so certain that Pyrrhus could return. Oh, surely Portia could not be right and Master Clement wrong!

Then she remembered. //Master Clement said to be a Lord Adept, Pyrrhus!//

//What? I can't use Adept power without—// As if to demonstrate, he attempted to brace for Adept power—and they all felt the shock as he fell back into his body. With a gasp, he opened his eyes. Then he blinked, and laughed. "Not graceful, but effective. Thank you, Julia."

"Yes, thank you," said Wicket. "I don't think any of us were ready for anther ghost hanging around!"

He turned back to Pyrrhus, who was stretching with a wince. Then his Adept powers automatically began to ease his cramped muscles, and the headache from his abrupt transition to the physical. Decius also exerted Adept strength to relieve his discomfort, but all Julia could do was stretch, with a grunt as her mistreated body protested her leaving it in that position on the cold floor.

Lilith had come over when Pyrrhus first spoke. Now she put a hand on Julia's shoulder, and healing warmth eased away her misery. "What happened?" the Lady Adept asked.

"Portia is where she belongs," said Julia. "Master Clement. . . ."

Lilith's eyes darted to the still form on the lounge by the window. "Oh, no," she whispered, paling.

"Lilith," said Julia, "he took Portia, knowing he would have to go with her. But—it's beautiful. I can't tell you. . . ."

They were all climbing to their feet now, Wicket sniffing as a tear escaped his control. "Poor old man," he said.

"No," said Pyrrhus. "If you had known him longer, Wicket, you would not grieve. If any man ever fulfilled his life, it was Master Clement."

Lilith nodded. "Pyrrhus is right. We all miss him, but if we grieve it will be for our loss of his strength and wisdom, not for the unfulfilled potential that causes our grief over most deaths."

And Julia felt no grief at all—only a deep determination to pattern her own life after that of the Master of Masters.

Aradia wakened to a cramping pain. After a few moments she realized that she was in labor, and that her body had been coping with such pains for some time. At least to the extent of suppressing pain, her Adept powers were back!

She Read, and found her child in position for delivery, but it would be hours yet. It was not quite dawn. She should try to get some more sleep before—

Suddenly she remembered—when? Yesterday afternoon. Portia possessing Julia, threatening to possess her unborn child.

//Julia! Julia—wake up!//

But it was Wicket who answered her call. //Aradia! You'll wake up every Reader in the city. Julia's all right. Everybody's all right, except—//

Wicket was too upset to verbalize it, but even with her weakened powers, Aradia caught the knowledge. //Master Clement . . . is dead.//

//He took Portia to the plane of the dead, Pyrrhus says. Aradia, should I wake Lady Lilith for you?// Then: //Hey! You're Reading!//

//I'm all right,// Aradia said, realizing that although she would miss Master Clement deeply, she did not feel the shocking grief she had when they had thought him dead before.

//You are all right,// a familiar "voice" suddenly spoke in her mind, //but you are also in labor, Aradia.//

//*Lenardo!* Oh, Lenardo—where are you?//

//On the fastest horse from Wulfston's stable—except for the one he's riding.//

//We'll be there by this evening, Big Sister,// came another familiar "voice" although she had never Read it before.

//Wulfston! You've learned to Read!//

//And that's not all the news—but we'll tell you when we get there. If my new niece arrives before we do, tell her hello for me.//

//Father!// Julia suddenly joined the conversation. Aradia let her ask questions, discover Wulfston in the rapport, while she coped with another contraction.

But Julia was too alert. //Father,// she said, //we have so much to tell you—adventures, new friends. But right now, my little sister is trying to get born. So I'm going to go be with Mother till you get here!//

A few hours later, Lilith laid her newborn daughter in Aradia's arms. With Adept help, the birth had been easy, and she smiled as she touched the baby's incredibly soft skin, felt the tiny fingers curl around hers.

And then—the baby opened her eyes.

Violet eyes, like Aradia's own, like her father's—and nothing in them but newborn innocence. Her heart seemed to overflow with love at the sight.

By evening Aradia's husband and her brother were there to greet the new arrival and present her with an unexpected bonus: Wulfston had found a wife in Africa! Aradia liked Tadisha at once, although she was too tired to do much more than rest in Lenardo's arms and listen, half asleep, to their adventures—all, indeed, brought on by Portia's desire to separate them as she tried to take over the Savage Empire. It was she who had inspired the witch-queen Z'Nelia to the deeds that had sent Sukuru to seek Wulfston, and to kidnap Lenardo to force Wulfston to come to Africa.

"But all Portia did in the long run," Julia said, "was to bring us even closer together."

The next day, after a night of healing sleep, Aradia was able to attend Master Clement's funeral. Not only was the entire city there, but people had flocked in from many miles distant to pay their respects. Even Zendi's huge forum could not hold them all, and so they trooped out of the city, to the area where the summer fair was held.

Hundreds of people came forward to speak for the beloved old Master—but like Aradia, everyone who had known him well felt peace and joy, not sorrow, at his passing. Even her own father might have achieved much more had he lived longer; no one felt that Master Clement had left anything undone.

Readers from all over the Savage Empire were there in spirit if they could not come in person, creating such a massive group-mind that Aradia suspected even nonReaders could feel their presence.

Afterward, they shared a feast with family and friends, old and new. Lenardo and Aradia, Julia, Wulfston and Tadisha, Lilith, Decius, Pyrrhus and Wicket, all gathered around the table in the dining hall in Lenardo and Aradia's villa for the traditional celebration of life.

Wulfston's entourage had caught up with the three who had ridden on ahead, bringing with it another unexpected addition to the family: a rather vague young man named Norgu, who was some sort of relative to Wulfston. Aradia determined to get the story straight as soon as possible, remembering something about a battle by a volcano on another plane of existence from the stories she had listened to so sleepily last night.

Norgu appeared to be a victim of that Adept/Reader battle, healed in body now but badly scarred in mind. But if anyone could help him find himself, she was certain Wulfston could. In the meantime she welcomed the boy to the family, and gave him a place at the table.

There were people missing—not only Master Clement, but Astra, too, was dead. Zanos had stayed in Africa. She wondered if Torio would ever come back, or Melissa.

But if their circle had lost some members, it had gained others, and this was a time for celebration. "Lord Pyrrhus," Aradia announced, "I promised you property here in Zendi. And Wicket. . . . Lenardo, we must think of some appropriate title for people who may not be either Lords Adept or Master Readers, but who join both powers. Meanwhile, Wicket, you also will have your reward, for both of you risked more than your lives to protect our daughters."

After the toast had been drunk to Pyrrhus and Wicket, Lenardo rose as Devasin brought their infant daughter in. "Aradia and I have thought long about what we should name our child," he said. "Today we decided. In honor of the renewal and growth of our circle, we vow again our dedication to peace and cooperation throughout the Savage Empire. And in remembrance of that sacred pledge, we name our daughter Arlana."

And the toast rang out: "To Arlana, daughter to Lenardo and Aradia, sister to Julia, and sacred pledge to the unity of our Savage Empire!"

The adventures of Wulfston and Lenardo in Africa are told in *Wulfston's Odyssey*. Torio's adventures in Madura are in *Sorcerers of the Frozen Isles*. Both are available as Signet paperbacks.

About the Author

Jean Lorrah is the creator of the *Savage Empire* series, in which *Empress Unborn* is the seventh book. The other six are *Savage Empire, Dragon Lord of the Savage Empire, Captives of the Savage Empire, Flight to the Savage Empire, Sorcerers of the Frozen Isles,* and *Wulfston's Odyssey. Flight* and *Odyssey* are coauthored with Winston A. Howlett. She is coauthor with Jacqueline Lichtenberg of *First Channel, Channel's Destiny,* and *Zelerod's Doom* in Jacqueline's Sime/Gen series, and has written a solo novel in that series, *Ambrov Keon.* She is also author of two professional *Star Trek* novels, *The Vulcan Academy Murders* and *The IDIC Epidemic.*

Jean has a Ph.D. in Medieval British Literature, and is professor of English at Murray State University in Kentucky. Her first professional publications were nonfiction; her fiction appeared in fanzines for years before her first professional novel was published in 1980. She maintains a close relationship with sf fandom, appearing at conventions and engaging in as much fannish activity as time will allow. On occasion, she has the opportunity to combine her two loves of teaching and writing by teaching creative writing.